PRAISE FOR THE MATERIAL WITNESS MYSTERIES

"Diane Vallere has stitched up an engaging new series."—Sofie Kelly, *New York Times* bestselling author of the Magical Cats Mysteries

"Vallere has fashioned a terrific mystery, rich with detail and texture. Polyester Monroe is a sassy protagonist who will win your hearts with her seamless style and breezy wit...promises readers hours of deftly-woven whodunit enjoyment." —Daryl Wood Gerber, Agatha Award-winning author

"There's a new material girl in town...[A] resourceful and gutsy sleuth."—Krista Davis, *New York Times* bestselling author of the Domestic Diva Mysteries

"Vallere weaves a tapestry of finely knit characters, luxurious fabrics, and...murder."—Janet Bolin, national bestselling author of the Threadville Mysteries

"With delightfully engaging characters and riveting mystery, it is a series I am looking to see more of!"—*Open Book Society*

"Vallere stitches an intrepid heroine together a nicely layered plot that fits well with the fabric imagery. The secret of the velvet makes for a clever surprise. Fans of Jenn McKinlay's Hat Shop novels may also enjoy this small-town cozy." —*Booklist*

"This entertaining series that began with *Suede to Rest*, continues with yet another fantastic read. In fact, this one may be even better." —*Suspense Magazine*

"Vallere has a good cast of characters as well as a good mystery, but there's always something more." —*Kittling Books*

"I realized just how much I have come to love these characters when I started the book. It was absolutely fabulous to be spending time with them again." —*Carstairs Considers*

"This is a well-written whodunit that quickly became a page-turner …. The pacing reached its high point when Poly's nosiness propelled others to take action and we discover the truth of her sighting. Overall, this was a delightfully entertaining tale." —*Dru's Book Musings*

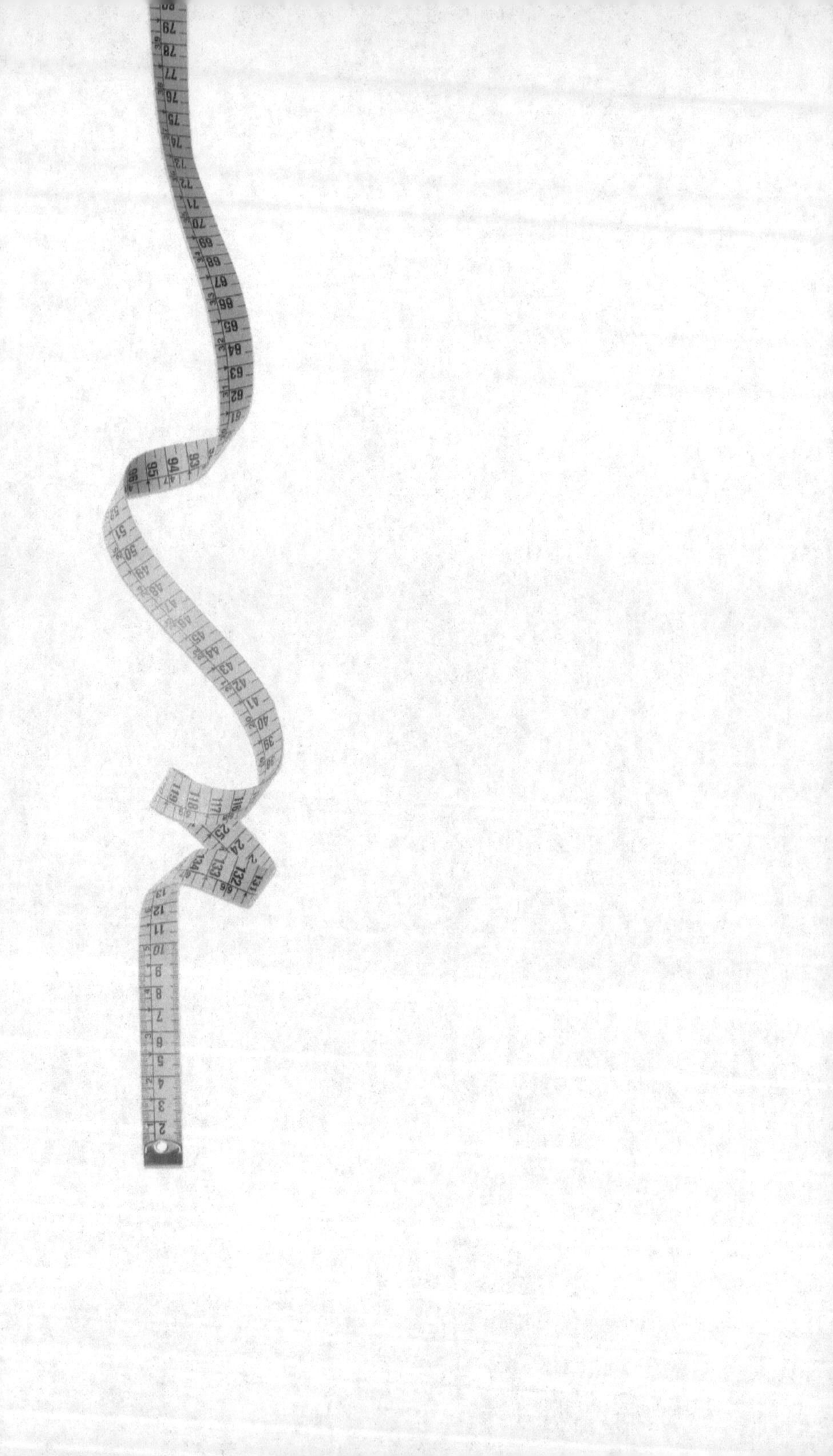

CONTESTING *the* WOOL

CONTESTING THE WOOL: A Material Witness Mystery

Book 6 in the Material Witness Mystery Series

A Polyester Press Publication

This is a work of fiction. Characters, places, and events are the product of the author's imagination or are used fictitiously. Any resemblance to real people, companies, institutions, organizations, or incidents is entirely coincidental.

Print ISBN: 9781954579361

e-ISBN: 9781954579231

THE MATERIAL WITNESS MYSTERY SERIES

<u>Material Witness Mysteries</u>

Suede to Rest

Crushed Velvet

Silk Stalkings

Tulle Death Do Us Part

Sheer Window

Contesting the Wool

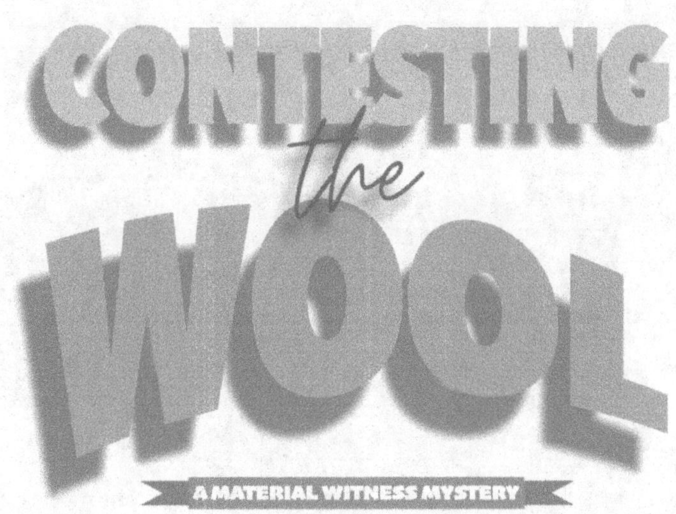

DIANE VALLERE

READING, PENNSYLVANIA

To the staff of Fabric Mart

CONTESTING THE WOOL

1

THE READING OF REGINALD VILLAMERE'S WILL WAS the event of the season, and until last week, I didn't know the man existed. That was the day the official invitation requesting my presence at the private ceremony was delivered to Material Girl, the fabric shop I had inherited. The return address on the envelope was McMichael Investments. Vaughn and I had been dating over the past several months, and I assumed the invitation was a perk of being his girlfriend.

That didn't mean I wasn't going to go.

I hadn't had a chance to ask Vaughn about the invitation, but aside from my curiosity about his willingness to trade on his firm's reputation to get me a seat to San Ladrón's latest roadside attraction, the answers to any questions I had about the agenda were contained within the letter. The reading of the will was scheduled to take place in the conference room of the Villamere, our small town's historic-yet-neglected theater, and Reginald Villamere's legal team would be in attendance to oversee the proceedings. Confidentiality was requested, and I had a feeling "requested" was a misleading choice of words. Phrases like "legal team" suggested there would be signed and notarized documents involved. Vaughn and I had been getting closer of late, but an entrée to the reading was a step beyond my recent offer to provide the fabric to reupholster his new sofa.

I parked my VW Bug in the Villamere parking lot, grabbed my handbag, and dug around on the passenger-side floor for my cane. Last Thanksgiving I'd broken my ankle after an unfortunate tumble down the stairs that led to the shop below my apartment. Klutzy was my middle name, but in that case, there'd been a life-and-death situation that took priority over a calm and orderly descent down the stairs. My broken ankle was a small price to pay. The injury would have healed by now on a person who'd never had an ankle injury before, but I'd been accident-prone my whole life, and sad to say, injury recovery now took more time. The orthopedic team advised me that if I rushed my rehab, I'd be looking at pain for the rest of my life. That didn't sound like a winning gamble, so a cane it was.

A man in an expensive gray flannel suit held the door of the theater open for me. I picked up my pace so as not to inconvenience him, though there was a good chance we were headed to the same place. I thanked him and entered the building, then I stood off to the side of the lobby. I was rooting around in my bag for my letter of invitation when I heard Vaughn call my name.

"Poly?"

It took a moment to spot his location. The Villamere lobby had been renovated sometime in the eighties, expanding the original concession area to include high-top tables and a bar. The theater itself had been built in the thirties, and renovations since then had honored the original concept but not for some time. Carpets were worn where foot traffic was high, faded in spots and stained in others. There were two screens for projecting classic movies and two stages for hosting live performances, though both showed signs of water damage after heavy flooding seeped through an already damaged ceiling.

The theater was not without some upgrades. Some time since the theater's opening, a landing had been added to the floor plan, and now exhibits of movie memorabilia were regularly on display. As many times as I'd come here to enjoy an old movie being projected onto a big silver screen, I'd never once thought about the fact that there was a real live member of the Villamere family who owned the place. Considering I was here for a reading of his will, I guess there wasn't anymore.

I scanned the lobby then looked up a long circular staircase that ran up the center of the building to the second-floor landing. That was when I spotted Vaughn jogging down the stairs toward me. It would take him less time to descend the stairs than it would for me to climb them, so I tucked my invitation back into my handbag and waited patiently for him to reach the bottom step.

"What are you doing here?" he asked.

"Ha, ha," I said. "Did you really think I was going to miss this?"

Vaughn looked embarrassed. "I didn't think you'd crash it."

At this, I stepped back and studied Vaughn's expression. He looked cautiously nervous, and I knew he wasn't kidding. "I'm not crashing it. I got your invitation. I assumed it was a perk of dating you."

Vaughn raised his eyebrows. "A perk?"

"You know what I mean."

"I think you've been spending too much time with my sister."

Instead of debating that possibility, I pulled the invitation out of my handbag and extended the thick, creamy envelope toward him. "Did you not send me this?"

He accepted the envelope and slid the invitation out, then he scanned the text. Unless someone had gone to great lengths to prank me, the invitation was legitimate. Vaughn ran his thumb over the raised logo and return address on his dad's company's letterhead and reread the contents. Eventually, he looked up and held the letter back out to me.

"I didn't send you this."

"But it's legit, right? I didn't misinterpret it?"

"One of our new interns must have made a mistake. I'll talk to them on Monday. As long as you're here, you might as well come in and observe."

Vaughn turned away from me and started up the staircase. I remained rooted in place. He turned back. "Are you coming? Do you need help getting up the stairs?"

"As fun as it sounds to get to sit in on the reading of Villamere's will, if it's going to be a problem for you, I'll go home. I don't want to get anybody in trouble."

Vaughn retraced his steps. "The lawyers are going to have a list of everyone who received an invitation. They won't start the proceedings until all are present. At this point, it'll create more of a problem if you don't come than if you do." He crooked his arm and offered me his elbow. "This place should have put in an elevator by now, but plans always got hung up by the historical preservation people. The conference room is on the second floor. Can you make it?"

"Just try to stop me."

Climbing the stairs took longer than I would have liked, but I made it up the winding staircase and followed Vaughn past the landing to a small hallway. Another man, this one in a brown wool suit with a navy windowpane pattern, stood outside a propped-open door. He had white AirPods in his ears, and he appeared to be embroiled in a heated discussion with the person on the other end of a call. He walked back and forth in the small hallway, gesturing wildly even though the person on the other end of his call couldn't see him.

"There's nothing I can do about it until we locate her," he said. "Until then, my hands are tied."

The good thing about using a cane is that people expect you to move slowly, and I took full advantage of that expectation on my way to the door. The man was on a "forth" leg of his back-and-forth, which gave me a few seconds to study him. Broad shoulders, narrow waist. A full head of thick, steely hair cut into a neat style. Double vented jacket. Fancy watch. Broadcloth shirt. Piercing blue eyes.

Uh-oh. He'd turned around and caught me staring at him.

I smiled, hoping cute and friendly with a cane was a winning—or at least auspicious—combination. The man scanned me, auburn hair to moto boots and back up to my face, and returned to his call.

I entered the conference room. Chairs had been set up in classroom formation facing a long table covered in leather binders and weighty writing instruments. I propped my cane under a vacant seat in the back row and hung the oversized black blazer, the one I'd taken out of my great-uncle's side of the closet, over the back of the chair. He and my great-aunt had left me the fabric store and the apartment above it, including the contents, and the contents included their wardrobes.

Despite the numerous options available at the concession stand on the first floor, a pink bakery box with the Lopez Donuts logo sat on a table at the back of the room. I headed toward the table and helped myself to a cruller. When I turned, I caught Vaughn watching me. He stifled a smile.

The man from the hallway entered the room and cleared his throat. "People, please take your seats. We'll get started at the top of the hour." He glanced at his watch, and most people glanced at their phones.

I checked the clock on the wall. The second hand swept from the five, traced around the bottom quadrant of the clock, and closed in on the twelve just as the minute hand did the same.

Vaughn took his seat at the table at the front of the room, next to the gray-haired man. The man from the parking lot in the expensive wool suit sat at the end of the table and opened a leather folio. As the proceedings started, he took notes. His left hand curled around his marbled pen, leaving behind slashes of ink on a formerly neat document. I wondered whether someone back at the office was going to have to decipher that, or whether workplace standards had changed and he'd do it himself.

I smoothed my black skirt over my black tights and silenced my phone. Now that I knew I was here by accident, it made sense to draw as little attention to myself as possible. I was inquisitive by nature and had more than a passing interest in things from the thirties, so Vaughn's intern's error was appreciated. Even though I would be bound by the confidentiality agreement that was attached to these proceedings, I was curious about who would get what. San Ladrón was a town of secrets, I'd discovered in the short time since I'd inherited the fabric shop and moved into the

Victorian apartment above it, and even though I wouldn't discuss what I learned today with anybody other than Vaughn, I had a feeling the knowledge might come in handy.

Hollywood portrays will readings as exciting events filled with greedy employees and backstabbing relatives. If that was the case here, then people were on their best behavior. In addition to the lawyer who seemed to be in charge, there was a middle-aged white couple in the front row, a cluster of theater employees in burgundy Villamere uniforms in the second, and an older woman with a chic gray bob in an ivory pantsuit on the other end of the back row with me. More of the chairs were vacant than not. The so-called "event of the season" was sparsely populated.

Vaughn closed the door to the conference room and returned to the table. He nodded at the gray-haired man, and the proceedings started.

"I'm Ben Schaffley of Schaffley, Bozer, and Schmidt," he said. "We represent the estate of Reginald Villamere. Mr. Vaughn McMichael is here as a representative of McMichael Investments acting as the executor of the will. In the event someone contests the will, my team will act as an intermediary with Mr. McMichael's office to reach a resolution. It should be noted that the will in question has been on file for over thirty years. Mr. Villamere did not respond to regular requests to update the document. Because of the lapsed time, there exists the possibility that surviving relatives of named inheritors will have to be found and notified."

Murmurs made their way around the room. The world had changed significantly since the will had been written, and who knew what Reginald Villamere had thought at the time.

"The first item on file is the collection of textiles left after the most recent renovation of the Villamere Theater was completed. Any and all materials are hereby bequeathed to the owners of Land of a Thousand Fabrics." The lawyer looked up. "Are Marius or Millie Monroe present?"

My throat hitched. Marius and Millie were not present, but their heir was. I slowly raised my hand. It turned out my invitation wasn't an intern's mistake after all.

2

"I'm Poly Monroe," I said. "Marius and Millie passed away. They left the fabric shop to me."

"You own Land of a Thousand Fabrics?" the lawyer asked.

"Sort of. It was Land of a Thousand Fabrics when they owned it, but I changed the name to Material Girl."

A ripple of judgment traveled through the sparse audience. I wouldn't have minded a chance to explain the reasons behind my decision, but Ben Schaffley's pointed glance at his watch indicated the details were about to be sidelined. He flipped two pages of the will and read ahead, then returned to the page he'd been on and looked up at me. "Do you have documentation of this name change?"

"Yes."

"Is the business in its original location?"

"Yes."

"Can you provide witnesses that it is the same business despite the name change?"

Vaughn leaned forward. "Ms. Monroe is the legal inheritor of everything owned by Millie and Marius Monroe. Her paperwork for the name change of the fabric store was filed with the county clerk's office, and she is recognized as a legacy business in San Ladrón. McMichael Investments backed the loan to fund the reopening of the store. You can review the paperwork at my office when we finish here, but for now I can vouch for the fact that Land of a Thousand Fabrics and Material Girl are the same."

The lawyer accepted Vaughn's answer. "Pending confirmation of business filings, Land of a Thousand Fabrics doing business as Material Girl receives any and all textiles remaining from the renovation of the Villamere Theater." He turned to his colleague. "When was the Villamere Theater renovated?"

The other partner flipped through the binder in front of him, looking for the information.

An older man in a magenta blazer, seated with the ushers, responded. "Nineteen eighty-three," he said. "It was the fiftieth anniversary of the theater. Mr. Villamere wanted to restore the property to its former glory."

The room went silent. Nobody mentioned the current condition of the theater, but anybody who had attended a movie here in the past year couldn't have helped but notice the tattered curtains that hung on either side of the screen, the water-stained ceilings overhead, and the threadbare carpets lining the aisles. On my weekly dates with Vaughn, I'd put on blinders and ignored the theater's run-down condition so I could imagine how luxurious it had been once upon a time. That being said, nostalgia only hides so much.

"And you are?" Ben Schaffley asked the usher.

"Laurence Thibodeaux, theater manager. I've worked at the Villamere since 1971."

"That would make you—"

"Seventy," Laurence said. After a beat, he added, "I started as an usher."

In a world filled with people who either couldn't wait to climb to the next level of the corporate ladder or quietly quit the jobs they held, it was refreshing to know that a man who took pride in his work at the theater existed. I'd seen this man around the building, but I didn't know anything about him.

Seventy looked good on Laurence Thibodeaux. His hair was white, only barely receding, and sprinkled with a few strands of gray. His face was etched with creases that had landed in all the right places, indicating a life filled with laughter. The line of his shoulders under his uniform was solid, and his spine was rigid. He was not intimidated by Ben Schaffley of Schaffley, Bozer, and Schmidt despite the clear display of authority projected from the front table, and I liked him a little bit more because of it. I was also curious about what Reginald Villamere had left to him and the other theater employees. Their presence here indicated something was coming their way.

"Yes. Well. Be that as it may, we're not here for a history lesson. Ms. Monroe, a member of my team will be in touch after we confirm your business standing."

I caught Vaughn's eyes and could tell he was thinking the same thing I was: *lawyers*. Always having to have the last word.

I was more than curious about my new inheritance, but since nothing could be done until Mr. Fancy Pants made a trip to City Hall, I settled in for what was next. The lawyer moved through a couple of uncontested items quickly: an annual stipend directed to the local puppy shelter in perpetuity (the older white couple in the front row), and Mr. Villamere's collection of cars left to the Peterson Automotive Museum in Los Angeles (a gaunt gentleman seated to my right).

Then we learned that Reginald Villamere had had one true love in his life—the theater in which we all sat. He left a ten-thousand-dollar bonus to every employee of the theater who had worked there for more than a decade. Ten thousand dollars was probably a lot to some of them, but I wondered how that number felt to Laurence, who'd given the theater his life.

"And finally, Reginald Villamere left the Villamere theater and his full estate to Josephine Barkley." Schaffley looked up and scanned the room. "Is Ms. Barkley here?"

I looked at the chic woman to my right. She did not move. Her hands clutched a pair of red leather driving gloves. She hadn't responded to any of the items being read from the will, and I wondered how she'd gained entry to the room. Come to think of it, nobody had checked our identification at the door. Vaughn had been wrong—I guess will readings didn't have bouncers.

"Ms. Barkley?" the lawyer repeated. He peered over the top of his glasses, and his eyes lit on each face in the room. When no one responded, he turned to Vaughn. "Did your office invite Ms. Josephine Barkley?"

Vaughn checked his file. "We reached out several times, but she never returned our calls."

"She might want to return your call when she hears this." Ben Schaffley closed his notebook and adjourned the meeting.

There was more than one emotion on display amongst the people who filtered out of the conference room. I had shown up expecting nothing, and there was a very good chance that when all was said and done, nothing was what I was going to get. When I'd inherited the fabric shop, I'd been lucky to find a few of the textiles in good condition, but many had been dry-rotted and had to be discarded to make way for new inventory. The shop had only been closed for ten years, but the fabric coming to me from the Villamere had been in a storage closet somewhere for upwards of forty.

My questions about what would become of the theater were still unanswered, and they would be until one Josephine Barkley was located. There'd been nothing to indicate who she was to Reginald Villamere, leaving behind a mystery in the aftermath of the meeting.

I waited until most of the people had left, then I tucked my cane under my arm and gripped the banister, descending the staircase cautiously and waiting for Vaughn in the lobby. The ushers chirped amongst themselves about what they would each do with their new windfalls. Nobody seemed particularly sad about their benefactor's death.

As I stood off to the side, Laurence, the theater manager, approached me. "Ms. Monroe, it is nice to finally meet you. I knew your aunt and uncle. They were frequent patrons of the theater."

I held out my hand. "It's nice to meet you too, Mr. Thibodeaux."

He clasped my hand. "Please. Call me Laurence."

"Laurence," I repeated. "I'm sorry for your loss."

An unfamiliar expression passed across his face before he composed himself. "Ah. You mean Reginald. He's been all but ignored through these proceedings. Yes, I have lost a lifelong friend, but as they say, no one gets out alive." He offered a smile, and I saw a glimpse of what he might have looked like twenty years earlier.

"Will you be picking up your inheritance yourself? Or would you like me to arrange delivery to your fabric store?"

"It doesn't really happen that fast, does it? I was under the impression that the lawyer needed to check my paperwork before anything would happen."

"Ben Schaffley is working under the restrictions of the law. I'm willing to accept you and Mr. McMichael at your words. Besides," he added conspiratorially, "we could use the space."

"You can't mean..." I studied Laurence's face. He smiled. "There were textiles left over from the renovation?"

"Yes."

"Where are they?"

"Here." His eyes twinkled. "Would you like to see them?"

I bit my lower lip and looked for Vaughn. He was on the opposite side of the lobby by the bar with Ben Schaffley. An old-fashioned glass half full of whiskey sat on a coaster next to the lawyer. It seemed a little early for booze, but who was I to judge? One of the ushers stood behind the bar, filling a second glass with club soda from the soda gun. He added a wedge of lime and a red plastic cocktail stirrer and set the glass in front of Vaughn.

"Ms. Monroe?" Laurence prompted.

I looked back at Laurence. "Lead the way."

3

Laurence led us past the winding staircase to a hallway behind it. I glanced at Vaughn again, and this time he noticed me. I pointed at Laurence's back and Vaughn nodded, then I turned and followed the theater manager. He was a few steps ahead of me but walked at a pace that I could easily match with the assistance of my cane, and with nobody else in the area, it was easy to keep up.

The patrons' portion of the Villamere restricted people to either the lobby or the high-top tables. Occasionally, access to the landing atop the stairs was granted, usually when a collection of Hollywood memorabilia came to San Ladrón for display. Our small California town was about thirty miles east of Los Angeles, which made it easy enough to procure original promotional materials from a studio, collector, or museum and transport them here. Each year there were fewer and fewer theaters showing classic films, though the network of those theaters around the country remained robust. It wasn't unusual for the Villamere to display original costumes and props from a movie that was about to be screened. In my brief time in San Ladrón, I'd been lucky to view items from the closets of Mae West, Myrna Loy, and Greta Garbo up close. I'd even looked at the seams inside Dorothy's pinafore from *The Wizard of Oz*. God bless Adrian, the costume designer responsible for the dress—it looked perfect on the screen, but inside out the construction was a mess.

It was easy enough to keep sight of Laurence in his magenta blazer. He led me into a narrow slip of a hallway less than four feet from side to side. If I tripped, there was no room to fall. That was of little consolation.

The hallway curved with the shape of the building, and around the back Laurence stopped at a door recessed into the wall. He pulled a ring of keys out of his trouser pocket and unlocked the door then pushed it open. Once inside, he switched on the lights and stepped back to give me access. I entered the room and gasped at what I saw.

Row after row of metal shelving lined the walls, each one loaded with bolts of fabric. Each bolt was bagged in heavy plastic and tied off to keep it protected. There were hundreds of them, plastic bundle after plastic bundle lying side by side on the shelves. I scanned the perimeter of the room from the left to the right, where a round trash bin sat behind the door, and a few remnants protruded, end-of-bolt fabric falling away from their cardboard cores. Dust had settled over the exposed fabrics, muting the colors significantly.

I approached the bin and stroked the end of the fabric. Dust motes detached from the surface and filled the air in a puff. I retreated a step and waved my hand back and forth.

"All of this is left over from the renovation?"

"Reggie had big plans for the theater. He had the fabrics produced to his specifications, and he bought them in bulk. He wanted to ensure there were enough excess textiles on hand to complete any maintenance over the years. He was a visionary when it came to this theater. We've returned to this closet over and over to make repairs."

"Why did the renovations stop?" I asked. I didn't want to insult the manager, but I'd have to be a fool not to see that somewhere along the line, the nips and tucks had ceased.

Laurence looked down at the keys in his hands. He didn't say anything, not immediately. Sometimes silence says more than words, and sometimes silence is what people need more than questions or advice.

After a long stretch of quiet, the theater manager looked up at me. "There was an electrical fire at the theater in the early aughts. We lost most of our equipment. During the renovation, priority had been given to the appearance of the theater, and the safety measures were not kept up to date. The damage you've no doubt seen in the theaters was sustained then. Money for the renovation was reallocated to cover an updated alarm and sprinkler system.

"The insurers pressured Reggie to show new releases to supplement box office and concession sales with a new audience, at least until we got ourselves back on our feet. He did not like that. He said the Villamere had survived for all these decades for one reason: to keep the movies of the past alive. Reggie was a wealthy man, and for a time, he used his own money to pay our bills while we recovered from the loss. Eventually the Villamere came back from the tragedy. Even though he had the materials to renovate the place, he chose to leave things as they were. He always thought the theater experience was more authentic that way."

I wasn't going to disagree. The truth was that the Villamere did have an element of authenticity that other theaters did not.

Reginald Villamere's choice to stay true to the original design style added to the romance of the property. There were two chain cinemas nearby, and if superhero movies were your jam, you could get your fill there.

"Did anyone ever complain?"

"About the appearance of the theater? I've heard squabbling from time to time. Nothing significant. Our clientèle is more forgiving when it comes to things like modernization." He turned to look at the fixture next to him. "I think you're among them. You may have renamed your family's fabric store, but from what I've read about you in the papers, you've preserved what your family built."

I should have been flattered that anybody knew anything about my efforts with the fabric store, but it wasn't my business acumen that had led to those articles in the newspaper. They centered around my involvement in a few murder investigations that had been related to the shop. The articles were good for publicity—they let people know the once-closed store was open again—but other factors kept people away. Those who say there's no such thing as bad publicity probably never found a body on their property.

Conversation lapsed as I walked the perimeter of the room. I wouldn't be able to check the condition of the fabrics bagged on the shelves until I cut the plastic open, and it was smarter to leave them bagged until they were back at the shop. There were enough bolts that I'd need something bigger than my VW Bug to transport them, and my first thought was to call my friend Charlie. She ran an automotive store and had access to all sorts of vehicles. The favor would come with a battery of questions that I probably shouldn't discuss, but Charlie had a way of getting around pesky things like that.

"I can't take anything today, but if it's okay with you, I can probably come back later this week."

"Of course. Let me know ahead of time. I'm the only person with a key to these closets, and I won't be able to steal away during operating hours."

I turned toward the exit. Before I left, I pulled an almost finished roll of gray wool from the circular bin. It was a delicate weave, not the fabric one would use for durability in a highly trafficked theater. I turned back to Laurence. "What was the wool for?"

"Staff uniforms." He pulled out his wallet and extracted a photograph. It showed a young man in a gray wool uniform, standing alongside a handsome man and a thin young woman in a floral dress. The photograph had creased and faded over time, but I could make out the Villamere marquee in the background.

"Is that you?"

"It is," he said. "The *San Ladrón Daily Ledger* sent a photographer out to take a picture for the paper. Reggie thought it would make for a better picture if it wasn't just him."

"So that's Reginald Villamere?" I looked closer at the photo.

Laurence didn't respond. He put the picture back into his wallet and tucked his wallet into his pants pocket. "I should be getting out front. We will be opening soon for our first screening of the day."

Once again, the theater manager led the way. This time he walked quickly to handle a problem at the concession stand, leaving me trailing behind him. All morning he had been the consummate professional, showing no signs of having been let down by the reading of the will. Maybe he was exactly what he seemed—an employee who had given most of his life to this building. If that were the case, then he probably wouldn't stop putting out fires now that the owner had died. I briefly wondered what would happen when Josephine Barkley was notified of her inheritance and asked to decide about the future of the theater and the people it employed.

4

Vaughn and I had planned to have lunch together after the will reading, but the legal team of Schaffley, Bozer, and Schmidt demanded his time, leaving my dance card empty. Already it was obvious that, while Vaughn was the executor of the will, the lawyers weren't going anywhere anytime soon—probably to ensure the maximum billable hours against the Villamere estate.

I thought about stopping on my way home for something to eat, but I decided to raid my fridge instead. Material Girl was a short distance from the Villamere, and it took only a few minutes to make the trip. I pulled into the lot behind my shop and found Charlie sitting on the stoop by the rear entrance.

Charlie was the town's resident bad girl, or that was what she wanted people to believe. She'd had a rough upbringing, in and out of foster homes, eventually landing with a mechanic who'd taught her everything she knew. For reasons that would make most people run for the hills, she'd returned to San Ladrón and set up her auto shop here. It was her willingness to face her demons every day that defined her, even more than her dreadlocked hair, leather jackets, and love of Van Halen, though those elements conveyed the bad girl vibe too.

"You're late," she said. She held up a waxy bag. "I got us sandwiches from Earl's. Mine's gone." She tossed the bag at me, and I dropped my cane and caught it.

"Did we have plans to meet today?"

She stood and picked up my cane from the parking lot. "You were at the reading of Reggie Villamere's will. I wasn't. Unlock your door and start talking."

I tossed the sandwich bag back to her and let us in. My two rambunctious cats, Pins and Needles, sat on the opposite side of the door, meowing their little heads off. Charlie tucked my cane under her arm and scratched Pins's gray head while Needles, an orange tabby, swarmed back and forth around her ankles, angling for attention. She switched her attention to him, and Pins hopped up on his back legs and swatted the sandwich bag.

"Nope, that's for Poly." She pulled a can of cat treats out of her motorcycle jacket pocket and shook it. "These are for you."

I strode through the fabric shop and climbed the stairs with Charlie close behind me. The cats charged past us and went straight to the kitchen. Charlie shook a couple of treats into their bowls and removed two bottles of water from my fridge. She set them on the table and dropped into a chair.

"You're getting soft," I said. "You never carried cat treats before I moved here."

"Bribe," she said. "Same as the sandwich. I don't want you to be distracted when you tell me about your day."

"Why are you so interested in my day? You never cared about the goings-on in San Ladrón before."

"This is different." She twisted the cap off the water and swigged. "Reggie Villamere was a cool cat. He didn't play politics like the rest of this sleepy town. He stayed in his lane and did his thing. There was a lot of pressure on him to fold the theater into the historical society like the Waverly House did, but he refused. I talked to him about it once, and he said nothing good comes from following the rules."

"Some rules are there for a reason."

"Sometimes people make rules so they can be in control."

"You don't want people running around unchecked, especially when they work for you. You'd know that if you hired somebody." I bit into my turkey sandwich. Until that moment, I hadn't realized how hungry I was. I took another bite as soon as I swallowed the first, effectively giving Charlie the floor.

"Rules are made to be broken. They limit people's potential. How are you supposed to know what's possible when you're given boundaries?"

Charlie had defied the odds. I wondered if she would have succeeded in the same way if someone had told her she wasn't capable of doing what she'd done.

"What else do you know about Reginald Villamere?" I asked.

"Don't try to distract me. What did he leave you?"

"Textiles." I took another bite. "Leftover material from when he renovated the Villamere."

"That place hasn't been renovated in decades."

"Right. Nineteen eighty-three."

"Is that your business plan? To corner the market on old fabric?"

I wasn't going to argue her point. Charlie was baiting me, and I'd learned to weather that particular storm.

I finished off the first half of my sandwich and sat back in my chair. The cats finished their treats and went to the living room. In the background, I heard tinkling from a small bell I'd suspended from the doorway for them to swat throughout the day. Cat people would understand.

"Villamere didn't leave the fabric to me. He left it to my great-aunt and -uncle."

"Didn't he know they died and left this place to you?"

I shrugged. "His will was thirty years old. He never updated it. When he made it out, they were alive. The lawyer wants me to prove that it's the same business even though I changed the name, so I've got to jump through a few hoops before I can take anything. The theater manager took me to the stockroom to see what I'll get. There's thousands of yards of fabric in there."

"Can you use any of it?"

"I don't know. It's still bagged, which means it might be in undamaged condition. There's wool left over from the staff uniforms, but I don't know how much. If the fabric in the room was used in the renovation, then most of it is probably upholstery material, stuff for the curtains or seat cushions. That's not what people want from me. I'd do better to sell the lot of it to a furniture company or someone who does restorations."

"You're not going to do that," Charlie said, finishing off my pickle. "One of the town's wealthiest residents wanted that fabric to come to this store. You like the romance of the story too much. That fabric is a part of San Ladrón's history. You love history. You don't have it in you to take the money and run."

Later that night, while I was lying in bed, listening to Pins and Needles swatting the bell hanging in the living room, I wondered if Charlie was right. About the money, about the rules, and about Reginald Villamere's intentions.

———

THE NEXT MORNING, I waited until a respectable hour to call Vaughn at his office. "This isn't a social call," I said when he answered. "I'm a client, remember?"

"Sure. Let me make a note to bill you accordingly," he joked.

I chuckled. "What do I need to show the lawyers to make my inheritance official?"

"Nothing. I took care if it yesterday."

"Already?"

"You're a client, remember?"

"Sure. I'll make a note to bump your invoice to the top of the pile."

It was Vaughn's turn to chuckle. "Seriously, it's been resolved. After the meeting, Schaffley, Bozer, and Schmidt came back to my office. I showed them the paperwork I had on file."

"That's it? No trips to City Hall?"

"You sound sad."

"I like City Hall," I said, pretending to pout. "It's always filled with people in suits."

"Work my job for a week and see how much you like people in suits."

"You wear suits."

"That's different. People expect their financial advisers to look respectable."

"Speaking of which, the theater manager gave me a sneak peek at the fabric Villamere left me. There's a lot of superfine wool. Like a lot a lot. If you want a custom suit, it's on me."

"But you don't sew."

It was true. I had a degree in fashion design, and after

graduating, I'd landed a job in a seedy pageant dress shop in downtown Los Angeles. My job had involved sketching dress concepts that a multicultural workroom of sewers interpreted into patterns and produced for sale. My boss at the time, Giovanni, was a cheapskate who bought flammable fabric at a discount and altered my designs to maximize his income. It was an all-around unsatisfying job save for the camaraderie, but like a lot of things in life, distance from Giovanni had given me an appreciation for his unique approach to profit margins.

"That's true. I don't sew, but I know people who do. You'll be the envy of your financial circle. You'll be more popular than E. F. Hutton. They'll call you the Wolf of Bonita Ave. Gordon Gekko will ask for your tailor—"

"I would love a custom suit, Poly. Thank you."

We chitchatted a bit more, mostly Vaughn complaining about the legal team that had commandeered his conference room yesterday. He wanted an excuse to get out of the office, so we planned to go to the Villamere together that afternoon. I still didn't have a truck to transport my textiles, but surely a couple of bolts would fit into Vaughn's trunk. I might not be able to sew, but I'd grown up in the fabric store, and I'd developed a lifelong love of fabric. More than anything, I was curious about the condition of the material.

I showered and dressed in a black turtleneck sweater, black trousers, and black moto boots. Shortly after entering the working world, I'd learned that black was functional in terms of hiding grease stains from sewing machines and dirt from sitting on the floor while repairing them. After my favorite silk scarf got chewed up in the serger, I established my own rule— all black, all the time. Charlie was wrong. Rules had their place.

Vaughn had already eaten breakfast, so I prepared a slice of avocado toast and brewed a cup of black tea, fed the cats, and was waiting in front of my building when his small silver BMW pulled up. We were back at the Villamere seven minutes later.

"I wish all of the inheritors were as easy as you," Vaughn said as we walked side by side to the front door.

"Do me a favor and don't write that on the boy's bathroom stall."

"You've been spending too much time with Charlie. Her fifteen-year-old-boy sense of humor is rubbing off on you."

"You're the one who just called me easy."

"Point taken. But so far, you're the only person who has any interest in claiming your inheritance. I can't get Josephine Barkley to return my calls."

I held my cane but attempted to walk without it, like riding a bike with training wheels. We reached the front door, and Vaughn held it open for me.

"Does she know why you want to talk to her?" I asked.

"I've done everything but tell her what she inherited. That's not something you leave on a voice mail, but even with the confidentiality agreements in place, word gets around."

"What about the lawyers? Won't Schaffley, Bozer, or Schmidt make calls too?"

"Not within their purview. Reginald Villamere named me the executor of his will."

"Weren't you a child when that will was written?"

"It's a little like your situation. He named my dad the executor, but Dad has one foot in retirement, so these responsibilities fall to me."

Despite a contentious first meeting, Vaughn and I had a lot in common. I'd inherited my family's fabric store. He was poised to take over his dad's venture capital firm. We were both tethered to San Ladrón, a fact that might have eaten away at more nomadic types, but it turned out small-town life had its own share of ups and downs. Living in San Ladrón had not been boring.

Laurence Thibodeaux was at the concession stand with a team of ushers. He waved at us. We stood off to the side and waited for him to finish his meeting. A few seconds later he left his group and approached us.

"Ms. Monroe, Mr. McMichael. I didn't expect to see you so soon."

"Hi, Laurence. Please call me Poly."

He put his hands over his heart and pleaded dramatically, "Please allow me this one indulgence. It's not every day a theater manager gets to welcome Ms. Monroe to his theater."

"Ms. Monroe it is."

Laurence turned to Vaughn. "Mr. McMichael, I'd like to extend you the same courtesy as well if you'll allow me."

"Done."

Laurence pulled his key ring out of his pocket. "I assume you're not here to take in a matinee."

"I was hoping to spend some time looking at the textiles. I can't take all of it just yet, but I would like to take a couple bolts of the gray wool if you don't mind."

"An interesting choice." He scanned Vaughn. "Perhaps something for the gentleman?"

"We'll see if he can stand still while he's measured."

As we made our way to the back hallway, Laurence's phone rang. He pulled it out and checked the screen. "Oh, dear." He looked up. "There's a problem with the projector in theater one. We're short staffed today. Some of the employees spent their evening celebrating the results of the will reading."

Laurence looked disappointed by this. A vision of ushers dancing on tables in their burgundy uniforms popped into my mind. I did my best to hide my response, as, it seemed, did Vaughn.

Laurence opened his keyring and removed the key to the storage room. He handed it to Vaughn. "It seems more official to hand you the key. I would appreciate if you returned it before you leave. Ms. Monroe knows the way."

Vaughn's hand closed around the key. Laurence headed to the front of the theater, and Vaughn and I went around the corner. I led the way until we reached the door to the storage room, then I stood back so Vaughn could unlock it. He turned the key, pushed the door to the inside, and stepped into the room. He stopped suddenly, and I ran into the back of his suit jacket. I stepped to the side and was about to ask what was wrong when I saw the problem.

The body of Ben Schaffley, the gray-haired partner from Schaffley, Bozer, and Schmidt, lay on the floor in the middle of the room with blood pooling on the floor by his head.

5

"Stay back," Vaughn said. "Call for help."

"We have to... to check if he's... he might still be alive," I stammered.

"I'll check. You call for help."

I remained just inside the doorway to the room filled with my recent inheritance and called the sheriff. San Ladrón had a local sheriff's office, which was part of the Los Angeles County Sheriff's Department. The satellite unit had recently expanded to include a secretary, Etta Velasquez, a stout Mexican woman who brooked no unruly behavior, and Sack Jones, a former football player for San Ladrón high school who'd recently graduated from the police academy. The odds were in favor of catching someone at the mobile unit, and calling them directly would save us a little bit of time.

"Clark," answered the sheriff.

"Sheriff Clark, it's Poly Monroe. You need to come to the Villamere theater immediately. Vaughn and I just found the body of a visiting lawyer in one of the storage rooms. He's—" I looked at Vaughn, who was squatting next to the body of Ben

Schaffley. Vaughn's fingers were on the side of Ben's throat. Vaughn shook his head slowly and retracted his arm. "He's dead."

"Stay put. I'm on my way."

Staying put, by my definition, meant moving to the hallway where the body of the lawyer was out of my line of sight. Vaughn, in wordless agreement, followed. There was no seating in the hallway, so we leaned against the curved wall, me resting more than a normal amount of weight on my cane and Vaughn unbuttoning the top button of his dress shirt and loosening his tie.

"We should tell Laurence," I said. "He needs to know the sheriff is on his way."

"Sheriff Clark might prefer that we don't tell anybody."

"All the more reason to tell Laurence before Sheriff Clark has a chance to tell us what he wanted us to do. All he said was to stay put." I stepped away from the wall.

"I'll wait here. Clark should be here momentarily."

Neither of us stated the obvious. Someone had killed the head lawyer handling the Villamere case and left his body in a locked room in the theater. By Laurence's own admission, he was the only person who had access to that room, but it didn't seem possible that the theater manager who had worked here since he was a teen could commit such a crime. Yet experience had taught me that murder wasn't age exclusive. Anybody could do it.

I rounded the corner and passed a couple of patrons eating at the high-top tables. There was a line at the concession stand, and the room bloomed with the scent of freshly popped popcorn spilling from an industrial popper into a bin behind the counter. A family of four were waiting for their tickets to be taken at the entrance. I approached the ticket taker and stepped in front of the family.

"Hey!" the kids said. "She cut in line!"

I ignored them. "Where's Laurence?"

"He's in the projection booth."

"There's a problem with the projector?" the wife asked behind me. I ignored her too.

"How do I get there?" I asked.

"You can't. It's employees only," the usher said.

"Then get him out here," I demanded. "Now."

The usher looked at me, at the family behind me, and again at me. "Somebody has to stay here and take tickets. That's the rule."

I shook my head in disgust and looked out the front doors. A police vehicle with lights strobing pulled into the lot, followed by a white ambulance. They both pulled up close to the main entrance.

"Dad? Why are the cops here?" one of the kids asked.

This time I turned around. "A crime was committed on the property. There's not going to be a matinée."

The man cursed. "Let's get out of here while we still can." He put his hands on the shoulders of the kids and steered them toward the front doors.

Sheriff Clark and a younger officer in uniform burst through the entrance and blocked his way.

"I'm sorry, sir, you can't leave the premises."

The man looked over his shoulder at the usher. "How do I go about getting a refund?"

I felt the energy within the Villamere lobby change with the arrival of the police. I'd hoped to inform Laurence of the events, to allow him to initiate crisis management protocols, but the opportunity was gone.

"Where's the body?" Clark asked me.

I led Clark back to the hallway with the sounds of "There's a body?" and "What happened?" and "If we're stuck here, can we still get some popcorn?" ringing in the background.

When we turned the corner, Vaughn was sitting on the carpet against the hallway wall with his legs jutting out in front of him. He stood quickly.

"Sheriff Clark," he said. "The body is in there." He pointed at the stockroom door.

Clark nodded and entered the room. Vaughn and I remained in the hallway and watched as the sheriff stooped down and checked the lawyer's pulse. He stood and pulled out his cell phone, turned on the camera, and took pictures of the body. He then turned on his video recorder and filmed the interior of the room while he turned in a full circle. He pocketed his phone and came back to the hallway.

"How'd you happen to find him? What is this room?"

Vaughn and I exchanged a glance. He gestured for me to speak.

"This stockroom holds the textiles acquired by the Villamere theater for their renovation. When Reginald Villamere died, he left them to my fabric shop."

"Villamere planned to renovate? I haven't heard anything about that."

"No," I corrected. "It was the renovation in the eighties. This stuff has been sitting around since then."

"Huh." Clark looked over his shoulder into the room. "I guess if anybody can make something out of old fabric, it's you."

"I don't think Mr. Villamere was thinking about my abilities. He left the fabric to my great-aunt and great-uncle, and his will hadn't been updated in thirty years."

Clark turned to Vaughn. "Your office was the executor of the will, right?"

"That's correct."

"Can you identify the victim?"

"Ben Schaffley," Vaughn said.

"Of Schaffley, Bozer, and Schmidt," I added. Considering the circumstances, I didn't know how many more times those three names would be said in close succession, and it felt only right to honor them one last time.

"Lawyer," Clark guessed astutely.

"Managing partner. Ben was the head lawyer overseeing the disbursement of the Villamere estate. His legal team was in town for the reading of the will yesterday. We worked at my office until about one thirty last night and planned to regroup this afternoon."

Clark nodded as Vaughn spoke. I didn't add anything to this part. My contact with Ben Schaffley had been limited to yesterday morning. His behavior had annoyed me multiple times, but I'd never been a fan of corporate-America types. They reminded me too much of my ex-boyfriend.

"How did you know your fabric was in here?" Clark asked me.

There was no way to answer without implicating Laurence in the murder. I'd hoped that word would have reached him by now, but there was no sign of him.

"After the agenda concluded yesterday, I asked the theater manager about what I had inherited. He led me back here and unlocked the door for me."

"It was locked?"

"Yes."

"Did he lock the door when you left?"

"I assume that he did, but I didn't see him do it."

"What about today?"

I glanced at Vaughn. He reached into his pocket and pulled out the key. "Mr. Thibodeaux gave us his key. He had to handle a problem in the projectionist booth."

Clark pulled a small plastic bag out of his pocket and held it open. Vaughn dropped the key inside, and Clark sealed it.

"Can you get me a copy of the will and a list of everybody who attended the reading?" Clark asked Vaughn. "I can get a warrant if needed, but it'll take a couple of days."

"It's a matter of public record," Vaughn said. "I'll bring it by the sheriff's unit later today."

Clark turned back to me. "You mentioned the theater manager. Does he know about this?"

"I didn't tell him," I said truthfully.

"I'd like to talk to him next. Can you take me to the projection booth?"

"I think I remember how to get there."

When I first moved to San Ladrón, I'd wanted to learn as much as I could about the history of my new town. The Villamere had been among my favorite locations thanks to their interest in showing old movies, and on one Saturday morning, I'd signed up for the behind-the-scenes tour. We got to see the screens up close, go backstage, and eventually, sit in the projection booth. It had been a tour highlight.

Vaughn and I waited while Clark closed and sealed the door with a strip of yellow crime scene tape. He used a second piece of tape to cover the keyhole. It wouldn't be difficult to remove it, but removal would leave evidence of the act, and that was probably what Clark was interested in.

I led the two men around the curved wall to a red velvet stanchion. It should have been hooked on either end, a deterrent to people who wanted to enter the employees-only hallway, but it wasn't. One end was unhooked, and the red velvet cord sat on the floor. We passed the stanchion and went down the hall to the main theater. I entered the dark theater with Vaughn and the sheriff close behind me, found the projection booth door a few feet inside, and went through the door. Narrow steps led to the cramped quarters.

"I'll wait here," Vaughn said.

The three of us wouldn't all fit in the projection booth, especially if Laurence were there too. I was about to offer to wait with Vaughn when I heard the sounds of muffled sobs. I shoved my cane at Vaughn and scaled the stairs, only to find Laurence Thibodeaux crying into his monogrammed handkerchief.

6

LAURENCE THIBODEAUX DIDN'T APPEAR TO NOTICE our arrival. Under normal circumstances, the projection booth was just about big enough for one person, or two if they didn't mind a little close contact. But even with the frail theater manager curled up in the corner, the available space was cramped. Sheriff Clark was literally breathing down my neck.

"Mr. Thibodeaux," I said to get his attention. "It's me, Pol —Ms. Monroe." I straddled the seat behind the projector and touched his arm. "Are you okay?"

The older man blew his nose into his handkerchief. He looked at me, his blue eyes watery and bloodshot, and then past me at Sheriff Clark. He didn't seem scared or angry or ready to flee, just sad. He looked back at me. "I shall survive."

I held out my hand, and he took it and, with a little effort, stood. His handkerchief fell to the ground. The room was too cramped for him to bend down to get it, but he didn't seem to realize he'd dropped it. He brushed dust off his trousers and tugged the hem of his blazer to straighten it.

"My office has more room for a conversation," he said. "We can talk there."

Clark responded, "I'm sorry, Mr. Thibodeaux. I think we'd better talk at my office instead."

"What about me?" I asked. "Vaughn and I can meet you there."

"Not necessary," Clark said. "I have your statements. If I need anything else, I'll be in touch." At least he didn't put anybody in handcuffs.

Clark and Laurence left first. Despite multiple protests, Vaughn and I were asked to remain with the rest of the theater employees. Clark told Sack that everyone could leave after providing our names and contact information.

We'd gotten an early start, and it was still mid-morning. "My place or yours?" Vaughn asked. It was a common negotiation between us, but it didn't mean what most people thought.

"We better go to mine. I have to open Material Girl for business."

"Have you given any more thought to hiring some help?"

"Yes and no. Yes, it would give me autonomy during the week. No, because hiring someone costs money and I'm afraid to promise someone I can pay them and then come up short."

"What about an intern?" Vaughn asked. "That's how I learned the financial business after college. I worked at a firm in Virginia before coming back to work for my dad."

"There's probably more of a demand for financial experience than fabric store experience."

"Don't put yourself in a box, Poly. You're a small business. There are tons of people out there who want to know what that's like. San Ladrón is full of small businesses. It's what makes our town special. There was a time when my dad wanted to knock down Bonita Ave and build a big-box store, but the small businesses rallied together and changed his mind."

"Did they? Or did something else deter him?"

"The point is, this town is made of people running businesses unique to their skills and interests. Just think about it. If you want help writing a job description, let me know."

It never ceased to amaze me how often Vaughn's and my worlds overlapped. When we first met, all I saw was "entitled rich boy." I'd come to San Ladrón with a chip on my shoulder the size of an industrial sewing machine, and I was determined to keep a tight grip on my anger at the world. Someone in this town had murdered my great-aunt ten years earlier, and the murder had never been solved. When my great-uncle passed away and left the store to me, it wasn't because he expected me to get answers, but because he suspected the fabric business was in my blood.

He'd been right. I'd started life in the fabric store after being born on a bed of polyester, which explains both my full name and my parents' sense of humor. And decades later, when I inherited the store, I'd learned a lot more than I'd set out to learn—about myself, about the people I'd judged, and about the importance of looking below the surface. That was when I first saw past Vaughn's rich-boy veneer to the honorable person he was.

Cute, too.

Vaughn parked in the lot behind my shop and followed me inside. I switched on the overhead lights, powered up the cash register, and unlocked the retractable gate by the front door. While I was opening the store, Vaughn went into the stockroom and returned with two cups of coffee. He handed me one.

"What now?" I asked.

"I'm no expert, but I would think you sit back and wait for the fabric-hungry public to swarm your store."

"Aren't you supposed to meet with the legal team this afternoon? Are you going to tell them their partner was murdered?"

"We don't know it was murder."

"Vaughn, there was blood under his head."

"He could have fallen. He could have knocked his head on the way down."

"Against what? He was in the middle of the room. There were bins of fabric on either side, but he wasn't near any of them."

"The room was locked."

"We *think* the room was locked. Mr. Thibodeaux handed you a key, so you used it, but what if the room wasn't locked? What if the killer left it open?" I hoisted myself onto the wrap stand and dangled my legs. "When we took Clark through the hallway, the red velvet stanchion was unhooked. That's supposed to keep people from going back to the employee-only areas. Maybe someone went that way and ducked into a theater."

"There weren't any movies showing," Vaughn said.

"Somebody could have gone through the theater and out the emergency exit next to the screen. They would have ended up in the back parking lot. By the time we found the body, they could have been miles away."

"Or they could have gone into the projection booth and been overcome with remorse for what they'd just done. The local sheriff could have found them."

I stared at Vaughn. "You don't really think Laurence Thibodeaux killed that lawyer, do you?"

"He had the key to the stockroom. He had access."

"What's his motive?"

"He could have been angry at the outcome of the will reading."

"Why go for the lawyer and not the executor?"

"Me?"

"You're as much a part of this thing as Ben Schaffley. Why target him?"

"People don't like lawyers."

"Some people don't like venture capitalists either."

Vaughn didn't say anything. I'd meant it as a joke, but sometimes jokes mask the truth, and while Vaughn and I had gotten past our initial differences, a lot of people still thought of him and his dad as the enemy. I knew Vaughn knew I wasn't speaking for myself, but still, I gave him time to think and process before responding.

"No," Vaughn said finally, his voice on the quiet side. "I don't really think Laurence Thibodeaux killed Ben Schaffley. But I do think whoever did kill Schaffley wanted it to look that way."

It was a sobering thought, mostly because I'd been thinking the same thing.

After Vaughn left, I busied myself with fabric store business. It had been a slow couple of weeks, which meant little effort was needed for store recovery and replenishment, but it also meant I needed a plan to bring in business. I pushed thoughts of the murder and the theater out of my mind and concentrated on the matter at hand.

Five minutes later, I was forced to admit that that didn't work.

There was a side angle to the murder that *did* relate to my business, and that was the fabric. Specifically, the leftover fabric that Reginald Villamere had left me in his will. After Clark released the storage room and the will was executed, I'd be able to take what I wanted. Of the inventory I'd seen, I was most curious about the bolts of wool. I'd offered Vaughn a custom suit, but my experience at the dress shop in Los Angeles had taught me not to underestimate a potential customer demographic. One suit was a present. A custom suit business was an income stream.

If I was right and the superfine wool was in good condition, I could do it. A man's business suit takes a minimum of three and a half yards of fabric with a sixty-inch width, plus whatever fabric was used for the jacket lining. I had bolts upon bolts of lining-grade silk in my inventory.

What I needed was a swatch book to make the fabric selection process easy. Women appreciated the feel of fabric— they liked to run their hands over textiles before choosing. Men liked to point.

I used the bulk of my day to bullet point the scope of the project. In addition to swatch books, I'd need a male mannequin to display the finished product. I'd need to identify a spot in the shop for consultations, measurements, and fittings. Something to inspire shoppers to spend their money. I needed a men's club.

By the time seven o'clock rolled around, I'd all but forgotten about the murder. The best distractions can do that. Between infrequent customers, I'd snipped two-inch swatches from each bolt of silk in my inventory and organized them into piles: solid, striped, plaid, and paisley. I took four precut pieces of three-hole-punched gator board out of my stockroom and attached the swatches using fabric glue. In my neatest handwriting, I wrote LINING OPTIONS along the top of each page and added numbers one through four to the corner of each page. From a business standpoint, today was a loss. From an idea standpoint, I was miles ahead of where I'd been that morning.

I was so buried in the project that I forgot to close the front gate at closing time. Tiki Tom, my shop neighbor, knocked on my open front door and called my name.

"Aloha, Poly! Are you closed for the night, or can I come in?"

I looked up from my notes. "I should be closed, but I forgot about the gate. Come on in. Do you need some fabric for a display?"

Tiki Tom was a sixty-year-old hipster who surrounded himself with Polynesian ephemera. His shop was filled with colorful tiki mugs, puffer fish, cushions covered in barkcloth, and portraits of exotic women wearing little more than leis and sarongs. Occasionally I dressed a mannequin in a colorful Hawaiian print that he placed in his window, and he returned the favor by referring people to Material Girl for the fabric needed to fulfill their tiki decorating needs. We'd collaborated on fabric happy hours in the past, with him providing island drinks and me providing fabric and projects. It had been a boon to both of our businesses. I liked to picture backyard luaus taking place all over the town.

Today Tiki Tom was dressed in a turquoise shirt with hula girls printed on it. Usually he ended each day with a tropical drink, but today he was empty handed. "Whatcha working on?" he asked as he approached.

"I'm thinking of starting a special-order men's suit business."

"Isn't that a lot of work?"

"Suits are made by pattern just like other clothes. It's a

matter of having accurate measurements and a skilled sewer. When you go to a store, you're limited by what some company already made, and most companies go with the most common measurements to meet the largest demand. These suits will be one-of-a-kind. The client chooses everything."

My enthusiasm for the project kept me talking, even though Tiki Tom wasn't my target audience. I'd never seen him in anything other than a short-sleeved Hawaiian shirt, even in winter. When it was cold, he just cranked up the heat inside his shop.

He picked up the cards of lining swatches. "Didn't you use some tropical-flowered silk in my windows a couple of months ago? When you made those muumuus?"

"Yes. Why?"

"Could you use that for a lining?"

"I could, but—"

"What about buttons? Can a customer pick whatever they want?"

"Within reason. They need to be the right size for a jacket and sleeves."

Tiki Tom nodded. "But you could, right? You could use those little buttons carved from coconuts?"

"I suppose..."

"How much would one of these suits cost?"

"That would depend on the selections. Why all the questions?"

"My sister's getting married. She wants me to wear a suit. This might be a way to give her what she wants and get something for me too."

I watched Tiki Tom flip through the swatch cards. It had never occurred to me that there were people out there who wanted something unique, but for every venture capitalist like

Vaughn, there was a Tiki Tom who wanted to express himself. It was what Vaughn told me to consider whenever I thought about events: a unique business proposition. I had my first paying customer. Now all I needed was the fabric from the Villamere estate.

7

"WHEN WOULD YOU NEED THE SUIT?" I ASKED.

"Next month. My sister wants to approve it ahead of time." Tiki Tom rolled his eyes. "Some people want to control everything."

I shared a laugh. "I'm still in the planning stages of my idea, but if you're willing to be my guinea pig, I'll give you a twenty percent discount."

"Sounds like a deal."

I walked Tiki Tom to the door and remembered to pull the gate closed after he left. After amending my notes to include novelty fabric swatches and buttons and officially closing for the day, I headed upstairs with the cats swarming around my ankles, fed them, cleaned their litter box, and left to meet Charlie and our mutual friend Genevieve.

Bonita Avenue was a strip made up of shops owned by local residents. To my left was Tiki Tom's store, and to my right was a vintage shop called Flowers in the Attic. Across the street was a sandwich shop, a couple of salons, a restaurant, and a bank. But perhaps most important to all of us was the bar: Duke's Broadside Tavern.

Duke was a retired army veteran who'd been injured in the line of duty and now used a wheelchair. He bought the bar after he'd been discharged, knowing he needed a source of income. It might not have been what most people would do in his situation, but Duke refused to view himself as a victim. He claimed he understood the need for a watering hole more than anything else, and the crowds he drew on a daily basis proved him right.

Last Thanksgiving, there had been some trouble in the apartment over his bar thanks to a shady couple who'd rented the place. I'd had a front row seat to the trouble from my place across the street, and while nobody believed me when I first said something, thinking I was crying wolf, they eventually came around. The end result was a team effort that saved the Broadside and left me with my injured ankle. We were still in the halo glow of that victory, and as a thank-you, Duke let me and my friends eat for free. Charlie was the only one who took him up on it, though when she thought I wasn't looking, she more than made up for it with a generous tip.

The three of us had gotten in the habit of meeting after our workdays to dish about, well, whatever had come up that day, and I was pretty sure my day trumped theirs in terms of interesting events. My conversation with Tiki Tom made me late, and both Genevieve and Charlie were already in our booth with drinks. Charlie had a beer and an empty shot glass. Genevieve had a goblet of red wine sitting next to a large three-ring binder.

"Yo," Charlie said. "Took you long enough."

"Bonjour, Poly!" Genevieve said. She handed me a glass of red wine like hers.

A couple of things had changed from when I first moved to San Ladrón. First was the clientele of Duke's. In those early days, the place had been overrun by a nasty bunch of threatening biker types who thought of it as their territory. Next came the gardeners—they were equally boisterous and equally dirty but took their aggression out on the gardens around town, not the residents. Sometime around then, Duke had developed an interest in Genevieve, and on her suggestion, he had stopped buying boxed wine and added a curated list from local wineries. From the looks of the place—pool tables and dart boards—you wouldn't expect to be able to get an award-winning glass of wine for under ten dollars, but like everything else in San Ladrón, looks could deceive.

I raised my glass to my lips, and Genevieve stopped me. "It needs about five more minutes to bloom," she said.

Charlie swallowed a large gulp of her beer. "Don't do it, Poly. Don't let Frenchy turn you into a puff like her."

"Poly's a woman of the world," Genevieve said. "She can drink beers with you tomorrow."

Charlie and Genevieve were often at each other's throats, but it was all friendly play. Genevieve softened Charlie's edges, and Charlie toughened up Gen. I was the magnet in the middle that pulled them together.

"You won't believe who came into my tea shop today," Genevieve said. She looked at me, at Charlie, and back at me. "The entire legal team handling the Villamere estate. The lawyers, their paralegals, interns, and two office managers. It was like a suit convention. The door opened, and they just stormed in and took the place over. One second, I was calmly brewing a pot of hot water, and the next, boom! In under five minutes, I sold out of my entire new batch of lily bang tea. Ten minutes after that, they wiped out my baked goods. I had to call in an order to Lopez Donuts just so I had something to offer people until lunch time."

"I guess handing out money works up an appetite," Charlie said.

"It made me think about how unprepared I am for business opportunities like that." She tapped the cover of the three-ring binder. "I've started an online business course, and I'm going to find a mentor."

Charlie rolled her eyes. She finished her beer and gestured to the waiter, Ernie, to bring her another. Ernie was one of Duke's newer employees, a touring musician for a local alt-rock band who picked up hours waiting tables between gigs on the road.

"Slow down there, camper," I said. "Are you planning on drinking your dinner?"

"Depends. Maybe the burgers need time to bloom too."

Genevieve rolled her eyes.

Ernie stopped by with Charlie's next beer. "The usual for you guys?" He pulled a towel from over his shoulder and dried off his fingers.

"Sure," Charlie said. "Put it on Poly's tab."

This time I rolled my eyes.

Ernie nodded. "Heard about your morning," he said to me. "Tough break for the Villamere. You think they're going to recover?"

"I don't know. How'd you hear?"

"Clark's new office manager, Etta, came here to pick up lunch for him and Mr. Thibodeaux. Etta said Clark felt bad for arresting him, but right now it looks like an open-and-shut case."

"I wouldn't be so sure," I said.

I felt the stares of Genevieve and Charlie like two beams of heat aimed in my direction.

"You saw something when you were there?" Ernie asked.

"Maybe. I'm still turning it over in my mind," I said.

"Hope you come up with an alternate theory. I'd hate to see the Villamere close." He knocked on the end of the table. "I'll be back with your food when it's ready."

Five minutes had to have passed by now, so I picked up my wine glass to take a sip.

"Polyester Monroe, don't you dare drink that wine," Genevieve said.

Charlie raised her eyebrows. "What she said."

"So," I said. "Want to hear about my day next?"

While we waited for our food, I brought my friends up to speed. I kept my voice low so as not to spread gossip outside of our circle, but hit the salient points: locked room, murdered lawyer, guilty-looking theater manager, inflexible sheriff.

"I can't believe Ben Schaffley is dead," Genevieve said. "He was in my shop this morning."

Charlie, who was slightly more opportunistic than Genevieve, said, "I know. His inspection expires next month. I was going to hit him up for business."

"Now, how would you know that?" I asked.

"It's on the window sticker," Charlie said.

"Right. Which implies you were skulking around his car."

"It's a public service."

"Ladies," Genevieve said. "Focus. Mr. Thibodeaux is in a holding cell at the sheriff's office. Poly, do you think he could have done it?"

"He could have done it, yes. He was at the theater when it happened. He told me he's the only one who has a key to the storage room where I found Ben's body. Clark and I found him sobbing in the projection booth. That indicates guilt. But there's something that doesn't add up to the whole thing. He could have done it, but I can't figure out why he'd want to."

"It's because you see him as a nice old man who gave his life to the theater," Charlie said.

"What do you see?" I asked.

Ernie returned with our food. Charlie and I had burgers, and Genevieve had a Cobb salad. The arugula and spinach looked suspiciously fresh, as did the cherry tomatoes and daikon radish. It was the small plastic container of dressing that gave Genevieve away. She peeled the lid back and poured it onto her salad.

"You brought that with you, didn't you?" I asked.

"I can't keep eating Duke's food for free. It's not right. I told him either I pay for my meals, or I bring my own."

"He agreed to that?"

"Of course not. I had the salad delivered earlier today when Duke left to make his daily deposit at the bank. Ernie hid it in the refrigerator."

"You could make it up to him in other ways," Charlie said with her mouth full. She waggled her eyebrows.

"Like you do with Sheriff Clark?" Genevieve asked with feigned innocence.

Charlie adjusted how she held her burger, leaving only her middle finger on the top of the bun.

"Back to what happened at the Villamere," I said to recapture their attention. "Charlie, you said you don't see Laurence Thibodeaux as a nice old man who gave his life to the Villamere. How do you see him?"

"As an employee who probably expected more from Reggie Villamere's estate."

"That's right!" Genevieve exclaimed. "You were there for the reading of the will. What happened?"

"Poly scored. Villamere left her a bunch of old fabric."

"You were named in the will?" Genevieve asked. "I thought you didn't know Reginald Villamere."

"I don't. I didn't. I thought Vaughn invited me. He thought his intern made a mistake. But the Villamere will was never updated, and forty years ago, Uncle Marius and Aunt Millie ordered the fabric for the renovation for the Villamere at cost. Reginald Villamere wanted them to have whatever was left over to sell in the store."

"So you get the fabric now that you run the store," Genevieve said. "Congratulations."

"Not quite. Mr. Thibodeaux showed me the closet yesterday. There was way more fabric than I could fit in my VW Bug. Mostly heavy decorating fabric and textiles. But there was a shelf of superfine 150 wool that can be used for suits."

"Isn't that a little snobby?" Charlie asked. "Super fine wool? What makes it so super?"

"That's the term. 'Superfine' refers to the process the yarn goes through before it's spun into cloth. 'One fifty' refers to the number of hanks of yarn used in each yard of fabric. Think about the wool used in a man's suit versus a winter coat."

Charlie was in a more contentious mood than usual. "Why does it have to be a man's suit? Why not just call it a suit? Are women's suits somehow inferior?"

"No, but women's suits are often made out of wool blend or crepe."

"How come?"

I shrugged. "Women's clothes are more subject to the whims of fashion. They don't get replaced because they're worn out, they get replaced because they're out of style.

There's an entire marketing machine aimed at selling stuff to women."

"What do you plan to do with this bounty of super fly wool?"

I knew Charlie was poking me. I just didn't know why. I didn't correct her since it was obvious she used the wrong term on purpose. Besides, I was excited about my idea and I was practically bursting at the seams to tell them about it.

"I'm going to offer custom suits. Allow customers to choose their fabric, choose their lining, choose their buttons. Choose their desired lapel shape, single or double vent, one button, two button, three button, or double-breasted. Pleated pants or flat front, cuffs or no cuffs. I'll have patterns made up for every option so the customer can make his selections and leave me with his measurements. Jun Wong still works with me one day a week, but she can work on these from her home studio. I can offer them at a fraction of the cost a department store would charge for a special order because I already own the textiles."

"That's a great idea," Genevieve said and sighed, propping her chin on her fist. "I need something like that."

Charlie didn't say anything.

I kept talking. "I was thinking I could use a corner of the shop to create a men's club atmosphere. Tweed wingback chairs, a bar cart of whiskey and bourbon and rye, maybe line the walls with bookcases filled with leather-bound books. I can't do cigars because the smoke will get into the fabric, but maybe there's something else I can offer?"

"I want one," Charlie announced with finality.

"One what?"

"A custom suit. I'll come by in the morning, and you can take my measurements."

"Why do you want a suit?" Genevieve asked. "You spend your days working on cars."

"You ever heard of Marlene Dietrich?" Charlie said.

"You wore red Converse sneakers to the Midnight in Paris party last year," Genevieve said.

"With a tuxedo," Charlie responded.

I let the two of them chirp at each other while I finished my burger and wine. Charlie was right. There was no reason my suit project had to be limited to men. No single actress in the history of cinema had done more to make menswear enticing for women than Marlene Dietrich. A new idea, equal parts publicity and community, started bubbling in my mind like water starting to boil. Maybe this idea was bigger than my shop. Maybe there was a way to get the Villamere Theater on board with an event of their own. Now I had two reasons to revisit the scene of the crime.

8

It was after eight when I returned home. Pins and Needles were nestled together on the creamy vintage coverlet on my bed. There were two messages on the store answering machine, one from Clark and one from Mike Bozer. It took me a moment to place the name as the center of the Schaffley, Bozer, and Schmidt sandwich. I briefly wondered what the protocol was in the event of a deceased partner. How soon would they change their name?

Curiosity about the events of the day led me to call Clark back first.

"Sheriff's office," answered a low female voice laced with a Mexican accent.

"Etta? This is Poly Monroe. Sheriff Clark left a message to call him back."

"Hold on, I'll get him. He's playing cards with Larry."

She placed me on hold before I had a chance to ask if they'd hired yet another deputy. Crime in San Ladrón had been on the rise lately, but the sheriff's mobile office operated within the parent structure of Los Angeles, and three murders a year was a drop in the bucket compared to what crossed the city docket annually.

"Clark," Sheriff answered.

"It's Poly Monroe."

"Thanks for getting back to me. I tried to reach Vaughn, but he's unavailable. Mr. Thibodeaux is here in my lockup cell, but I've been getting calls about a group of drunk-and-disorderlies at the theater. Can't see it being good for anybody to put them here with him. I talked to the judge, who set a low bail with the caveat of a monitoring ankle bracelet. Mr. Thibodeaux said he's good for the money if somebody signs the paperwork. Vaughn's the executor of the will, so I thought he'd be best."

"Sheriff Clark, are you asking Vaughn McMichael to be responsible for a man you arrested for murder not ten hours ago?"

"Do you think the theater manager murdered the lawyer?" he asked.

"Do you?"

"No, I don't. But I'm going to need some time to prove it."

"I don't believe you."

Clark lowered his voice to barely above a whisper. "I've already found enough holes in this case to know that if I proceed, Mr. Thibodeaux will walk on a technicality. He's been nothing but cooperative. But the longer I stay focused on him, the more time the real murderer has to get away."

"And you couldn't think of anybody else to call?"

"Mr. Thibodeaux had close ties to the theater, but it's best to put some distance between him and anybody who works there. There's a short list of people I trust in San Ladrón."

I didn't comment on Vaughn being unavailable. It was Tuesday night, the night he had dinner with his mom at the

Waverly House. He protected that time with her the same way he protected date night and client meetings—by turning off his phone notifications and leaving his phone in his pocket. It was likely he wouldn't know he'd missed Sheriff Clark's call until later.

All day I'd been thinking about the murder and weighing the pros and cons of getting involved. This wasn't the first time I'd found a body, and it wouldn't be the first time I'd gotten involved. It wouldn't even be the first time the sheriff had called me for help. We weren't partners, not by any stretch, but we were occasionally on friendly terms, and I'd developed an increasing respect for what he had to do with relatively little support to do it.

"I can't speak on Vaughn's behalf, but I have another idea."

"What's that?"

"I'll sign for him."

"Poly—"

"You have a short list of people you trust in San Ladrón. Am I on that list?" I didn't give Clark a chance to answer. "I better be on that list."

"You're not *not* on the list."

"I'll sign your paperwork and pick up Mr. Thibodeaux, but I have a caveat too. I don't think he should go home. If you're right, then his release will tell the killer you're still on the hunt."

"Once you sign his release paperwork, that's between you and him."

I kissed the cats and left, this time on foot. It was a short walk from the back of my fabric shop through the well-lit alley that ran behind the shops on Bonita Avenue to the Sheriff's Mobile Unit, but I didn't go directly there. Across the street from the mobile unit was the historic Waverly

House that Vaughn's mother oversaw. I walked up the side path and entered the lobby. The dining room had closed, but from the sounds of pots and pans clanking, the kitchen staff was cleaning up for the night. Vaughn and his mother were at a table in the dining room with a chic older woman. Their table was lit by a single candle that had burned halfway down.

"Poly! This is a delightful surprise," Adelaide said when she spotted me. "Come. I'd like to introduce you to someone."

I sat in the empty chair across from the woman. "Poly, this is Wallis Wilson, president of the San Ladrón Historical Society. Wallis, this young lady is the owner of Material Girl on Bonita Avenue."

I recognized the woman from the reading of the Villamere will. Wallis held out her hand to shake mine. A heavy gold chain with a single charm dangled from her wrist. It gave me pause for a nanosecond—my great-aunt Millie used to wear a gold charm bracelet, and my memories of her were forever linked to it. I recovered quickly and shook Wallis's hand. The gold charm bobbed back and forth with the movement.

Wallis looked to be in her late fifties. Her gray hair was cut in a neat bob, smoothed down and streaked with darker and lighter tones. Her shirt collar was flipped up, and a floral-printed silk scarf was knotted around her neck. A coordinating cardigan hung from her shoulders. She wore small shiny gold hoop earrings that matched her bracelet.

"Poly, it's nice to meet you. Didn't your shop used to be called Land of a Thousand Fabrics?"

"Yes. It was closed for ten years before my uncle died and left it to me."

"You didn't want to honor what they'd built by leaving the name they chose?" There was an undercurrent of criticism to the question, which I chalked up to her role with the historical society and her interest in preserving the past.

"There were a lot of painful memories attached to the store. I wasn't even sure if I was going to keep it. When I decided to reopen, I wanted a fresh start."

"Fresh starts. The bane of history." It would have been a funny line if delivered with a smile, but Wallis Wilson looked as if she meant it. I glanced at Vaughn, who sat next to Wallis. He took a sip of water to hide his smile.

"Adelaide, you've been a dear to let me crash your dinner with your son. Think about my proposal. And next time, dinner's on me." She stood and set her handbag in the crook of her arm. "Vaughn, take care of your mother. She's a gem. Poly, lovely to meet you."

Adelaide stood, and the two said goodbye. Wallis left. Adelaide dropped back into her seat. She reached past her water goblet for her wine glass and finished it off.

Most days, Adelaide maintained a fresh-as-a-daisy appearance despite her seventy-plus years of age, but today she looked as if the needs of the Waverly house had pushed her over the edge. Strands of gray hair had escaped her trademark chignon and fanned around her face. Her lipstick was faint, and the chain that held her glasses around her neck had broken and been repaired by an open paper clip.

"Poly, as usual your timing is impeccable. I thought Wallis would never leave."

"You mean you didn't want her here?"

"Oh, Wallis is always welcome. The Waverly House is the jewel in the historical society's portfolio, and even before they acquired us in an official capacity, there's been a long history of financial support that flows to us from them. I would not allow just anyone to crash dinner with my son."

"It's not a big deal, Mom. We do this every week."

"Keep your voice down. I wouldn't want her to think she can do it again." Adelaide quickly looked over her shoulder to make sure Wallis hadn't heard. Adelaide Brooks was one of the most respected people in San Ladrón, and her response to Wallis was amusing.

"She mentioned a proposal," I said. "Another event for the Waverly House?"

"Unfortunately, no. Wallis wants to aggressively expand the Historical Society's portfolio, and she thinks I can be of help. My only concern is that the Waverly will suffer while she leverages her influence."

"Would she really do that?"

"I don't doubt she would try. She lives for our town history. Some days I honestly don't know where she gets her energy." Adelaide smoothed her hair into place, took a fortifying breath, and folded her hands on the table. "Enough about my troubles. My son tells me you two had an eventful twenty-four hours."

"You don't know the half of it," I said.

"She does," Vaughn said. "I told her everything."

"She doesn't know that Sheriff Clark has been trying to reach you to sign off on the release of Mr. Thibodeaux."

Vaughn paled. He put his hand on his suit jacket pocket. "My notifications are off."

Adelaide pulled her phone out of her pocket and placed it on the tablecloth. "Mine aren't. I checked my messages when I went to the ladies' room. I planned to call the sheriff back when Wallis left."

"No need," I said. "I'm headed there now."

"Hold on," Vaughn said. "Clark's releasing Mr. Thibodeaux? Does he have another suspect in custody?"

"He said the evidence on Mr. Thibodeaux is shaky at best. He also said his officer is on his way back to the mobile unit with a paddy wagon full of drunk-and-disorderlies from the Villamere. Clark is of the mindset that it would not benefit Mr. Thibodeaux's situation to be left in the same lockup cell as them."

"I don't disagree, but you don't have space at your place. Last year when your ex crashed on your sofa, things were a little awkward. You said Clark called me first? I'll take him to my place."

"Your place is as small as mine."

"Now, children," Adelaide said. "The solution is staring you both right in the face. I'll put him in a room upstairs."

"Mom..." Vaughn said. "I don't like it."

"We're directly across the street from the sheriff's office. I'll offer Sheriff Clark a complimentary breakfast to ensure he stops by daily. I've known Laurence Thibodeaux for more than half my life. He's gentler than those kittens you pulled out of Poly's dumpster."

"Those kittens are cats now, and they have claws," Vaughn said.

I shook my head at his lame attempt to turn my adorable cats into a believable threat.

"Larry does not. The matter is settled. Sign that paperwork while I fix up a room."

Vaughn kissed his mother goodbye, and we left.

It was a few minutes later when we arrived at the sheriff's mobile unit. Etta was at the file cabinet.

"Is Sheriff Clark here?" I asked.

A toilet flushed from just beyond the lock-up cage, and a moment later, Clark came out, still adjusting the fly on his trousers. Upon seeing me, he quickly thrust his hands in his pockets.

"Poly, Vaughn," he said in greeting. "Come into my office." He stood by an open door and let me enter first. I sat in the chair opposite his desk, and he wedged a rubber doorstop under the door with the toe of his boot to keep the door open.

The room was the size of a walk-in closet, which may have been its initial purpose. The walls and floor were wood, as was Clark's desk. A fish was mounted to a plaque on the wall, and next to it was a picture of Clark in a baseball hat, dangling the fish from a fishing line.

A small table that had been pushed under the window held an electric kettle, and next to it was an assortment of mismatched mugs and a wicker basket with selections from Tea Totalers—for visitors—and packets of Swiss Miss Instant Cocoa—Clark's workday beverage of choice.

"I appreciate this. Sack's going to be back from the theater soon. Mr. Thibodeaux is waiting in the cage. I'll get him."

He went to the lockup cell to release his temporary guest, and I stepped outside the office and turned to Etta.

"Sheriff Clark said Sack Jones is on his way back with a bunch of drunks from the theater. This is the second night in a row the employees have been out partying. Is the sheriff looking at them for the crime? I understand they were happy after the reading of the will, but after what happened today, partying seems a little suspicious."

"Who said the employees are partying?"

"Clark said he got a call about a group of drunk-and-disorderlies at the theater. I assumed it was them."

"You assumed wrong. The drunks being detained at the theater are the lawyers."

9

This information caught me by surprise. "The lawyers were partying? After one of their named partners was murdered?" I glanced at Vaughn. "Is that normal lawyerly behavior?"

"I didn't say they were partying," Etta added quickly. "We got a call about them disturbing the peace."

"At the theater?" Vaughn asked.

Etta nodded.

Clark and Laurence rounded the corner and walked toward us. There appeared to be no animosity between the two men. Whatever had transpired during the theater manager's brief stay in the holding cell, it didn't seem to have troubled him much.

"Ms. Monroe, Mr. McMichael," Laurence said. "It's a pleasure to see you both so soon. I'm afraid my vehicle is still at the Villamere, so if I could request one additional favor on top of the one you've just granted, it would be for a ride there."

"It's late," Vaughn said. "Adelaide Brooks arranged for you

to stay in a room at the Waverly House. She's making up the room now."

"The Waverly House," Clark said. He nodded his agreement with this arrangement.

Vaughn leaned closer and spoke directly to Clark. "My mom said to tell you breakfast is on the house for the duration of Laurence's stay."

"I'll thank her in the morning," Clark said.

I expected a little resistance on the part of Laurence, but he didn't seem to mind us making arrangements on his behalf. He'd regained control of his emotions since the last time I saw him, but his neat appearance was rumpled thanks to his afternoon in a jail cell. His magenta blazer needed, at minimum, a sponge, and preferably a thorough dry-cleaning, and his gray trousers were whiskered at the crotch and knees from sitting for an extended period. Even his white hair, normally combed neatly into place, had released a shock in the front that hung over his forehead. He pushed it back with the palm of his hand, but it returned to his forehead as soon as he let go.

The three of us left the sheriff's office and walked across the street. The door to the Waverly House was propped open. Laurence put his hand on both Vaughn's and my arms to stop us before entering.

"Thank you," he said. "Both of you. I did not know who to call. The sheriff suggested Mr. McMichael."

"Adelaide will make sure you're comfortable here," Vaughn said.

"She's your mother, isn't she?" Laurence asked. After Vaughn nodded, he continued, "I've known Adelaide a long time. I can't imagine a better person to run the Waverly House."

"We can bring some of your belongings to you if you like," I offered spontaneously. "Toothbrush, pajamas, a change of clothes."

"My mom will have toiletries for him," Vaughn said, not seeing through my offer to my true intentions.

Laurence was unfazed by my suggestion. "I hesitate to ask more of you than you've already done, but having a few familiar items would be lovely." He pulled his keys out of his pants pocket and handed them to me then extracted his driver's license and showed us the address.

"I know the place," Vaughn said.

"I thought you might. A week's worth of clothes and pajamas would be much appreciated. My casual attire is in the armoire in the blue bedroom." He patted the pockets of his blazer. "Fresh handkerchiefs, too. They're in the top drawer with my unmentionables. I seem to have lost mine along the way."

"You had it—" I started but bit back my words. I didn't need to bring up the moment we'd found Laurence in the projection booth, the one that had led to him being brought here. I glanced at Vaughn, who furrowed his brow. "We'll bring you some handkerchiefs too."

Adelaide arrived to greet us, and Laurence followed her inside. After the door closed, I turned to Vaughn and twirled the keys around my index finger. "What do you think? Is it too late to get to know one of your neighbors?"

———

WHEN IT CAME to things like following up on leads, Vaughn and I were kindred spirits. The same could be said for our sleep schedules. It was late, and we both had work the next day, but neither of us used it as an excuse not to poke around a murder suspect's home. I didn't believe Laurence Thibodeaux had committed the crime, but it wouldn't hurt to snoop.

Vaughn's car was still in the Waverly House lot, so he offered to drive. Soon we headed in the direction of Laurence's apartment. Vaughn turned off Bonita Avenue onto the side street that led to his place, a penthouse in a tower of art deco apartments.

"Do you know where you're going?" I asked.

"The company that owns my apartment building has three properties. Laurence lives in the oldest of the three. It's about half a mile from mine."

"Weren't you on a wait list to get your apartment?"

"Yes. Not to be indelicate, but Laurence Thibodeaux is almost forty years older than I am. From what I've heard, that property was pretty run-down in the seventies. The property management company that currently owns them said there was a lot of structural damage, not to mention the lack of air conditioning and questionable plumbing."

"I never noticed those things."

"You're a romantic," he said. "You look at buildings and you see what they were. That's what I see too. But the interns who work in my office? They think of the properties as old buildings with no amenities. They can't imagine living in a house that isn't wired with smart technology."

Vaughn took a series of rights and lefts and eventually slowed in front of a tall white building. The words GROSVENOR ARMS were embedded into the facade.

Vaughn parked and unhooked his seatbelt. I got out and leaned on my cane, more because it was there than because I needed it. I'd been faithful in doing my physical therapy, determined to minimize the damage to my ankle. I'd probably never recover from being a klutz, but I wasn't ready to sign up for chronic pain.

We approached the doorman, and Vaughn greeted him. "Hi, Will. Poly and I are here for Laurence Thibodeaux."

"Let me get the guest book."

I pulled the keys out of my pocket and glanced at Vaughn.

He said, "Laurence is staying with a friend for a few days. He asked us to pick up a few things for him. He gave us his key."

"The rules here are the same as the rules at your place. You still have to sign in."

He opened a ledger and set a fat pen on top of it.

Vaughn wrote "McMichael" and "Thibodeaux" into the guest and resident columns and handed the pen back to the doorman.

"Mr. Thibodeaux called ahead to let me know you were coming. It's the penthouse. Go on up. The building's quiet tonight, so if you need some help when you leave, just ask."

"If you already knew we were coming—" I started to say.

Will cut me off with a raised hand. "Rules are rules."

Living in a small town has its benefits. In a city like Los Angeles, we wouldn't have gotten into the lobby, let alone been given the unit number by the doorman. It was part of San Ladrón's charm, but also part of the problem. It was too easy to get where you shouldn't be, to gain access to places that should have been monitored. I thought again of Laurence's key ring at the theater, how he'd said he was the only one with access to the stockroom where we'd found the body of Ben Schaffley. It was the single most damning piece of evidence against him, and eventually, someone was going to use it. Sooner or later, he was going to need an explanation.

Vaughn and I stayed quiet while we rode the elevator to the

top floor. Vaughn unlocked the front door, switched on the lights, and whistled. I stood with my eyes wide. We were standing in the center of an Art Deco masterpiece.

Framed works of art covered the walls, and a hand-painted mural depicting stylized gazelles in stark black against ivory decorated the ceiling. Display cases of vintage glassware lined one wall, overflowing with etched tumblers, old-fashioned glasses, and champagne coupes. A mahogany-wood bar sat in the back corner of the living room, locked with a brass skeleton key accented with a thick ruby tassel. The floors were parquet, warm hues of wood with a pattern of black inlay setting off the border. Inside the border was a worn throw rug woven with an abstract floral pattern that was mimicked in the curtains. I could have stood there studying the room for a week and found something new with each passing minute.

"Wow," I said.

"Decorating goals," Vaughn said. "This place is amazing." He approached a small bronze statue on an end table. "This is a Picasso."

"It can't be." I moved to Vaughn's side. "People don't just set Picassos on their end tables in San Ladrón."

Vaughn picked up the bronze and looked at the underside. A small piece of paper was taped there. *Violinist at Play, Picasso, 1926,* followed by an auction estimate in the five figures.

Vaughn held the base of the figurine so I could read it.

"Do you think all the art in here is real?" I gestured toward the walls.

"It's possible."

"Then Laurence Thibodeaux isn't the tragic figure we thought."

"What about a man in a magenta blazer says 'tragic' to you?"

I laughed and led Vaughn farther into the apartment, looking for the blue bedroom. "He worked at the Villamere for half a century, and he got the same disbursement from the will as ushers who worked there for ten years."

"A minimum of ten years. And it looks to me as if ol' Larry Thibodeaux did pretty well for himself. He hasn't asked once about the money. Not when he'll get it or if he can use the promise of it as collateral for a loan or bail. My office has already fielded half a dozen calls from other people asking questions like that. For all we know, Laurence is going to donate the money to a charity."

"What about Josephine Barkley? The woman who inherited the theater? Have you found her?"

"I'm not supposed to say anything, but I'm going to Nevada to meet with her tomorrow."

"Vegas?"

"Not quite. She lives in Proper City. It's a small desert town just over the state border. With everything else connected to the Villamere Affair, I think it's best I go out there and meet her face to face. This whole thing has taken on crazy proportions."

"The Villamere Affair," I said. "Sounds like a movie."

"Starring Cary Grant and Joan Fontaine."

"Not Cary Grant. He did comedies back then. This would be a mystery."

"Henry Fonda?"

"Oooh! He's good. Henry Fonda and Joan Fontaine."

"And Peter Lorre," Vaughn said. "Everything's better with Peter Lorre."

We forgot all about the murder and the mystery

surrounding the real Villamere Affair and speculated on the plot of our fictional one while Vaughn located an empty bag in Laurence's closet. I opened the top drawer of the armoire. Neatly folded stacks of white cotton undershirts and boxers sat next to pressed handkerchiefs. I removed a stack of each and set them on the bed, then I slid the next drawer open and pulled out a pile of cashmere sweaters.

And then I froze. Because underneath the stack of sweaters was a neatly typed multipage document. The heading on the first page read *Revised Will and Testament of Reginald Villamere*, and it was dated last month.

10

"Vaughn?" I called behind me. "Can you come in here?"

A few seconds later, Vaughn entered the bedroom where I'd been snooping. "Did you find another Picasso?"

"Not exactly." I stood back and pointed at the document in the drawer. "Is that what I think it is?"

Vaughn extracted the sheaf of papers. He scanned the front page then flipped through the pages to the last one. "It is and it isn't."

"That's as clear as mud."

"It looks like a revised will, but it's not signed. Which means it could be legitimate, or it could be fake. If it's presented to the court, they're going to need some pretty thorough evidence to prove it should be allowed at all, let alone replace the will Schaffley, Bozer, and Schmidt had on file."

"You're the executor of the Villamere estate. Shouldn't your office have a copy of the will on file too?"

"Not necessarily. The legal advisors keep wills, and if no executor is named, they step into that role. Any money that's left after the estate is dispersed goes to the executor, but most people include a catch-all somewhere in the language. Something like 'Any and all monies not directly assigned will go toward managing the estate, or the property, or to the family, or be designated for sale at auction and the proceeds directed somewhere.' Phrases like that keep anyone other than the mentioned parties from claiming anything of value."

"Oh." I dropped onto the bed next to the suitcase. "That's a bummer."

"You didn't really expect me to benefit from this, did you?"

"Not that. I knew you were just doing your job. I meant the lawyers. We've been spending so much time talking about Laurence Thibodeaux and whether or not he had it in him to commit murder, but the other half of the picture is Ben Schaffley. Who would want to kill him? Was it because of the Villamere will or some grudge from a former case? I thought maybe, if he was set to inherit a chunk from the estate, he might have made an enemy."

Vaughn sat on the other side of the suitcase. "It's not a bad theory, but it wouldn't work in this case. From what I saw in my brief time working for him, Schaffley was a jerk, but that comes with the territory. Lawyers are the original rule followers. They're bound by precedent and regulations. They have to do things a certain way or risk blowback."

"What blowback?"

"If they don't follow the letter of the law, they can be fined, suspended, held in contempt, or disbarred. In big cases, mistakes have been known to cost law firms millions."

"Not cases like this though, right?"

"This one should have been cut and dried. Reginald Villamere had an old will on file. Nobody came forward to contest it. According to Bozer, his office handled all of

Villamere's legal needs. If Mr. Villamere wanted to update his will, he had ample opportunity to do so."

"So what do we do with that one?" I pointed to the drawer.

Vaughn turned and stared at the newly discovered document. "Nothing for now. All that new will does is make Mr. Thibodeaux look guilty. If we weren't doing him a favor, we never would have found it. Put it back. Let's talk to him first and find out what's what."

It was after midnight when Vaughn dropped me off behind Material Girl. He waited until I was inside before he drove away. We'd agreed it was best for him to hand the suitcase we'd packed over to his mom to deliver to her new tenant. It would be less suspicious all the way around.

The next morning, I slept in until nine thirty. Rays of bright sunlight filtered through sheer voile curtains in my bedroom, hitting me square in the face. I rolled over to escape them, but they were more effective than an alarm. Coupled with the meows of my two furry roommates, my day was destined to start.

After a brief shower, I fed the cats and dressed for the day in black yoga pants and an oversized black hand-knit sweater. I ran my fingers through my bobbed auburn hair and raked my bangs back into place. I had a little over an hour before I was due to open the store, which was enough time for tea and a croissant from Genevieve's tea shop.

Tea Totalers was a French-themed cafe. Genevieve had first moved to San Ladrón with her husband, Phil, who had grown up here. They put their savings into opening the cafe, and Phil drove a delivery route to supplement their income while Genevieve got things going. But it turned out Phil had a side business that included extramarital affairs and attracted the wrong sort of people, and last year it had all caught up with him. Phil was out of the picture permanently, and if you asked anybody in San Ladrón, Genevieve was better off without him.

When I moved to town, I'd had my own set of troubles, and I worked some of them out with a fabric makeover of Genevieve's shop. Every time I entered Tea Totalers, I was reminded of what a little fabric could accomplish when used to its maximum effect.

The interior of the shop was done in shades of deep blue, yellow, and cream in toile and velvet and voile. Gen had spent her nights staining the wooden door frame and baseboards, and she'd rented an industrial buffer to bring out the shine in her wood floors. She'd brought boxes of vintage mugs back from a trip to Paris at the end of last year, and now she served coffee in them for dine-in customers. Coupled with her proprietary tea blends and savory baked goods, she'd created an establishment that people didn't want to leave.

Yesterday at Duke's, she'd intimated that the legal team had overrun the place. Today was no different. Her tables were filled with men and women in suits, hovering over their laptops. Leather satchels and briefcases occupied the space on each table not already taken by a computer, a mug, or a plate.

I approached the counter. "They came back," I said. "Does this mean business is good?"

Genevieve wiped a dusting of flour from the bridge of her nose. "I baked all night. They don't like sugar until after lunch. They wiped me out of my protein bars and high-fiber muffins. I tried to sell my oatmeal raisin cookies, but I got pushback. Evidently, raisins can cause gestational diabetes in pregnant women."

"You learn something new every day." I glanced at her case of baked goods. "I'll take a blondie and a cup of lily bang tea to go."

"One cup of lily bang coming up!" She prepared my tea and put a blondie in a wax bakery bag. She added an oatmeal raisin cookie. "On the house. No sense letting them go to waste."

I patted my tummy. "Not when they can go to waist instead." I stepped away then turned back. "If you need to make some space, I'm sure Adelaide would be happy with a donation."

"I already sent her two dozen cookies."

"Duke?"

"He got a basket of muffins."

"Clark?"

Genevieve sighed. "Good thinking. I forgot he now has employees to feed."

I made it back to Material Girl and opened the gate. It wasn't as if I had droves of customers shopping every day, but if you want to be in business, you fulfill the promise to be open during advertised hours. The shop offered me a distraction from the Villamere Affair, as I'd come to think of it, and my immediate attention was quickly diverted to the task of bringing my custom suit shop to life.

Before my first customer arrived, I picked up where I'd left off the previous day, adding novelty silk fabrics to my cards of suit-lining options. I included the tropical prints Tiki Tom had asked about, along with novelty polka dots, growing the count of swatch cards from four to six. I brought a small round table out of the stockroom and covered it in an ivory tablecloth, then set the lining swatches there. My first customer came into the shop, and I abandoned my project to help her select some indestructible fabric to cover her sofa.

While I worked, Jun Wong, a petite Chinese woman who worked for me on Wednesdays, entered through the back door. She wore a tweed skirtsuit with a crepe blouse, sheer stockings, and low black heels, and she had a jet-black bouffant.

"Good morning, Miss Poly," she said.

"Good morning, Jun. Set up wherever you like. I'll be with you in a moment."

"No need." She held a bulging knitting bag. "I bring work to keep me busy."

Jun Wong was the closest thing I had to a regular employee, though she had her own seamstress business that came first. It turned out that you could own a fabric shop and not be skilled in sewing, but it helped when you had someone to pick up your slack. I didn't know how old she was, but I'd place her in her late sixties. When I'd first met her, she told me she'd learned to sew when she was ten. That was also the age when my great-aunt Millie first showed me the vintage garments she'd purchased from flea markets and deconstructed to make patterns. Ten seems to be a good age for imprinting possibilities on a young mind.

Jun reminded me of the women who worked in the To The Nines workroom back in Los Angeles, and on more than one occasion, when they'd made the trip to San Ladrón to help me out, she'd gotten to work alongside of them. I couldn't wait to tell her about my suit idea and see what she thought. I had a special incentive that I suspected she'd love.

I cut the decorating fabric for my customer and rang up her sale, then joined Jun by the suit table display.

"You have idea?" she asked.

"I do. I'm about to come into possession of a large quantity of superfine wool serge, and I thought we could run a custom suit shop. Have customers make their selections from pattern components, take their measurements, let them choose their fabric combinations." At the tortured look on Jun's face, I asked, "What's wrong?"

I'd expected Jun to be enthusiastic about my idea. She loved to sew and hadn't met a sketch she couldn't turn into a garment. She worked quickly and expertly, and if a scout from a couture house ever came to San Ladrón, they'd snatch her out from under me. But instead of the enthusiasm she usually showed for my ideas, she backed away and put her hands up. "No," she said. "I no make suits for men."

Misunderstanding her, I quickly said, "They won't be just for men. They'll be for women too. Do you remember my friend Charlie? She wants one. I might like one too."

"Men's suit for woman is still men's suit." She shook her head. "I no make suits for men."

"I don't understand. It can't be more difficult than the women's clothes you make, can it?"

She shook her head vehemently. "Is too personal."

I pictured Vaughn standing in the shop while Jun took his measurements. "Because of the measurements?"

"I no make man's suit since my husband died."

"Oh."

I didn't know much about Jun's personal life other than that she lived alone in San Ladrón and ran a dress shop out of her home. Vaughn's company had provided her start-up loan, and he was the one who suggested she come to the fabric store for supplementary hours. I'd been in the middle of making twenty gowns for beauty pageant contestants at the time, and Jun's arrival had been a blessing. Since then, she had worked for me every Wednesday, setting up in my front window so passersby could watch her work. It had brought more than one person into the shop.

Jun had told me about growing up in China, how sewing

was a respectable job for women there. She'd entered her first workroom when she was fourteen, working alongside her mother, aunts, and cousins. I didn't know the details about her coming to the States, when or why. She'd kept her story to herself.

"I'm sorry, Miss Poly. Men's suit not for me." She picked up her bag. "I still work for you in window? Or is that no good anymore?"

"Of course you can still work here. You have a job here as long as you want it. I'll come up with another plan."

"There is someone you could ask. He big loudmouth, but he help you when you ask."

I knew exactly who she meant: my old boss Giovanni. I'd thought I was rid of him, but what's that they say? Just when you think you're out, they find a way to weasel themselves back into your world. Maybe that's not what they say, but in Giovanni's case, it was more than accurate.

11

I DIDN'T CALL GIOVANNI RIGHT AWAY. INSTEAD, I helped a fresh wave of customers who claimed they were just browsing. My eagerness to put off the phone call to my old boss turned me into the kind of employee I hated, hovering too close to people who wanted to be left alone. Each of the customers walked out without making a purchase. Even Pins criticized my actions. He meowed at me then trotted to the other side of the shop.

In addition to acting as a live window display, Jun had learned to work the point-of-sale system, so I left her alone to oversee the shop and went upstairs for a quick bite of lunch before making my phone call. I was delaying the inevitable because favors from Giovanni came with a price.

After I finished a half of a turkey sandwich that had been in my fridge for possibly one day too many and followed up with the blondie I'd purchased that morning, I put on my big-girl panties and called To The Nines. Giovanni answered on the first ring.

"Hi. It's Poly. Do you have a second?"

"Sure. What's up?"

His friendly demeanor made me suspicious. "I've acquired a lot of superfine wool serge," I said, avoiding the details of my inheritance, "and I want to set up a custom suit shop."

"Bespoke?"

"Made to measure." I hesitated. "Why? What's the difference?"

"Bespoke is fully custom. Made-to-measure allows people to make choices from a set of predetermined patterns. You'll save yourself time and money if you go made-to-measure, but you have that wild design hair up your—"

"Made to measure it is," I said hastily.

"Smart choice. What do you need from me?"

I'd expected a comment about me overreaching or not being able to make it on my own. Aside from his dig about my love of design, his tone was cooperative. Friendly, even. But I had worked for Giovanni for long enough to know how he worked, and this could be a trap.

"I know you're probably going to make a comment about my sewing skills, but I oversee the shop, and it really does work better if I have someone handle the sewing."

"Of course. Do you want me to ask the girls if any of them want hours at your store?"

"They're women."

"If you say so." He was silent for a moment. "Poly? Are you still there?"

"Yes."

"Do you want me to ask the women if any of them want hours at your store?"

"Does anybody there have experience with men's suits?"

Giovanni cleared his throat. "One does."

"Who?"

"Me. I grew up working in my uncle's suit shop. Not as big of a profit margin as the dresses we make now, but it's like riding a bike. Once you know what you're doing, the skills don't go away."

"I was hoping for..." I didn't know what I'd been hoping for. Having one of the women from Giovanni's workroom flex to me for hours had sounded like an easy fix, but if I had the opportunity to hire a skilled tailor, wouldn't that be better? And if that situation allowed me to turn the tables on my old boss and assign him work, wasn't that a win-win?

"Tell you what," Giovanni said. "My afternoon is looking light. How about I head your way, and you walk me through what you have in mind. I can be there in about an hour."

"Don't you need to be at the shop?"

"My presence at the shop isn't going to change anything. See you this afternoon."

And with that, he hung up.

I stared at the phone. Needles hopped up onto a kitchen chair and then onto his hind legs, swatting at the paper that had wrapped my half sandwich. He pulled the paper toward him with his orange paw and knocked it onto the floor then jumped down and stuck his nose into it. The foil made a scraping noise against the floor as he pushed it, trying to find a piece of turkey that had fallen out of the sandwich.

I picked up the trash. Needles meowed. I tossed the sandwich paper into the bin and pulled out a small canister of cat treats. I shook the canister, and a few seconds later, Pins charged up the stairs. I rewarded them both for being cute and headed back downstairs, preparing myself for whatever storm Giovanni would bring with him from Los Angeles.

Leaving Jun alone in the store was the best thing I could have done for business. She'd doubled my cash take for the day in the time it took me to eat lunch and call my old boss. I relieved her from the register, and she went to her portable sewing machine.

While I waited for Giovanni's arrival, I got a cart from the stockroom and loaded it with the wool I already had in stock. Flannel and serge, mohair and tonik, and a couple ends-of-bolts of cashmere. The color palette was muted: dove gray, charcoal, black, camel, and brown. One bolt had a peppy windowpane in plum. I rolled the cart to my makeshift suit shop and swapped out the fabrics that were already on display there with this new assortment. These were for suggestion only because I planned to push the Villamere wool once I had it here, but I didn't know how long it would be before that happened.

True to his word, Giovanni arrived about an hour later. He entered through the back door and waved to Jun, then joined me and surveyed the setup.

"This isn't going to work," he said.

"Nice to see you too," I said.

He cast a sideways glance at me. "You don't want men to strip down for measurements in the middle of your shop. They will, and they won't much mind the request, but your regular customers will be put off."

"Who said they had to strip? Can't we get their measurements over the top of their clothes?"

"A made-to-measure suit is an indulgence. You want the entire process to feel that way from start to finish. That includes taking their measurements."

"So we show them the display, they decide to order a suit, and we move them to another part of the store for—what?"

Giovanni shook his head. "No. The display is just the start of the process. Men and women shop differently. A suit isn't like a formal dress. Women like to think they're getting something other women approve of. Men like to think they're in charge." He held up his hand to block any protests of his sexism. "Psychology 101. There are exceptions, but you'll do a lot better if you understand it than if you think you're going to break the mold."

"Go on."

"Men don't browse. If you get the word out about your custom suit clinic, they'll come here specifically for that. You need to remember that if they're in your store, they've already decided to buy. Everything you do from the moment they walk through your doors needs to be informed by the understanding that they have already said yes. Your job is to keep them from changing their mind, because once they leave, they won't come back."

"How do you know all this?"

"I told you. I grew up in my uncle's suit shop."

I pictured the suit shops on the same street as To The Nines. "On Santee Alley?"

"No. On Rodeo Drive in Beverly Hills."

"You never told me you worked in the luxury sector."

"Business is business, Poly. Supply, demand, and location. I thought you knew that by now."

We felt dangerously close to Giovanni giving me a business lesson, and my instincts were to resist that. But I couldn't deny that he knew more about suits than I did. I pushed my pride aside. "What's in the binder?"

"Patterns. Come on, I'll show you."

The last thing I would have predicted when I woke up this morning was that I'd spend my afternoon with my old boss paging through a binder filled with men's suit pattern pieces, but that was exactly what happened. I was so absorbed in the show-and-tell that I lost track of time. Giovanni was a font of knowledge when it came to men's suits, and his willingness to share that knowledge with me was appreciated. Jun brought us two mugs of coffee from the Nespresso machine in the stockroom and set them on the wrap stand next to us.

"Miss Poly, it's time for me to leave." She looked at Giovanni. "Is good for you two to work together after what happened."

Giovanni looked uncomfortable. "It's nothing."

"Is something. Miss Poly has clever idea. Needs help executing. You have time and skills. Is good partnership. Help you keep busy."

Giovanni raised his hand to his face and put his index finger across his lips, almost as if he were asking Jun to be quiet. I moved my eyes back and forth between him and her. Something was going on. Something I didn't know, but Jun did.

"Come with me," I said. "I'll write out your check." I asked Giovanni to wait for me, and I walked Jun to the register. I removed my checkbook from under the cash drawer, checked her hours on the sign-in sheet, and calculated the total for the month. After filling out the check and handing it to her, I lowered my voice. "Is there something you know about Giovanni that I don't?"

"Is not for me to tell," she said mysteriously. She tucked the check into her handbag. "Mr. Giovanni is good man to help you with your idea."

"He'll get something out of it. I know Giovanni better than you do. He hasn't told me what he wants just yet, but he always wants something."

"Is worth it. Sometimes you need, sometimes he needs. Is mutually beneficial relationship."

"I suppose you're right." I pushed Jun's sewing machine to

the back door and watched her leave. When I turned back, I studied Giovanni standing by the suit display. He paused every few seconds to make notes on a lined yellow tablet. He was completely absorbed in the project.

I glanced at the clock on the wall. Hours had passed since my old boss had first arrived, and he'd been nothing but helpful. This was the opposite of Giovanni's classic modus operandi. It wasn't the first time I'd asked him for help since reopening the shop, but it was the first time he agreed to my request without negotiating something for himself first. I watched him work, his lean frame bent over the table, his hands, deeply tanned and gnarled with arthritis, moving deftly between the swatches and his notes.

Jun had said it was a mutually beneficial relationship, and ever since I'd taken over the fabric shop, that had been the case. I had access to fabrics, and Giovanni oversaw a workroom of employees. For all of my complaining about him, I knew she was right—we each had what the other one needed. But there was something different about Giovanni today. Something about the way he'd dropped everything and showed up here an hour after I called, about how he'd come prepared, about how he hadn't yet asked for anything in return for his help. Whatever it was, Jun knew. If Giovanni wasn't going to tell me, I was going to find out some other way.

<h1 style="text-align:center">12</h1>

A couple of last-minute customers came into the shop, and I left Giovanni alone by the suit display to help them. As I drew closer, I recognized members of the legal team that had been at the theater for the reading of the Villamere will. I glanced one more time at Giovanni, expecting to see him watching me. He was busy with the display.

"Hi," I said to the couple. "I'm Poly Monroe. We met yesterday at the theater."

"Right," the man said. He held out his hand. "Mike Bozer. Of Bozer and Schmidt."

I froze in the middle of our handshake. Ben Schaffley had been dead for a day, and already his law firm had dropped his name from their marquee. That felt callous—and fortuitous to the partner whose name now came first. He crushed my fingers in a power handshake. If he noticed my reaction, he didn't show it.

I turned to the woman and held out my hand. "I didn't catch your name."

"Taylor," she said. "I'm part of the legal team."

"Your firm has a big legal team. I didn't know a will reading took so many lawyers."

"We're thorough," Bozer said.

Mike Bozer lacked a warm and fuzzy personality. He pulled his phone out of his pocket and scrolled through his screen. I glanced at it, but from my angle, the screen was black. I assumed the two of them were there for a reason, and it didn't seem as though the reason had anything to do with fabric.

Bozer turned to Taylor. "Give me a minute."

Taylor nodded at him. He distanced himself from us by a few steps.

Up close, Taylor lacked the overall sheen of money that dripped from her boss. I could tell she'd taken care with her appearance, with dark-blond hair cut to a blunt shoulder length and tucked behind her ears and small pearl earrings. She wore a gray flannel suit, the woman's version of the style favored by her bosses, narrow at the waist but by no means revealing or sexy. Instead of a shirt, she wore a thin jewel-neck sweater underneath, along with a thin gold necklace with a single pearl pendant. She reached up and pinched the pearl between her thumb and forefingers and slid it back and forth along its chain.

"Are you here about the will?" I asked.

Bozer looked up and nodded at Taylor and then went back to his screen. She led me to the opposite side of the fabric shop, where we were well out of earshot.

"We got an injunction from the local courts to approve the disbursement of acquisitions that aren't in question. The sheriff's department released the crime scene—" She stopped mid-sentence, and her face lost some of its color. She put one hand on her tummy and the other over her mouth. I grabbed a nearby trash bin that was partially filled with fabric cuttings and held it out to her, but she glanced at the bin and pulled herself together. She waved me off and continued. "I'm sorry. I saw the photos of Ben Schaffley earlier today. I didn't expect there to be so much blood—" Her face turned green again, and this time she grabbed the trash bin and threw up. When she finished, I moved to take the bin from her, but she resisted and hugged it against her torso.

Getting sick wasn't an unusual response to seeing a dead body. If Taylor had been among the drunk and disorderly lawyers rounded up last night, this could be the result of her hangover. The lawyers' behavior made sense—drinking was a temporary way to help them forget their boss's murder. Or maybe, drinking was a way to forget committing the act.

I glanced across the room at Giovanni. He was talking to Mike. I turned back to Taylor. "Are you feeling better? I can get you a cup of tea if you'd like."

"No tea," she said, sticking a hand out in protest. "I think that's what made me sick. That or the gluten-free muffin I ate at that shop."

"I don't think it's the tea or the muffin."

Taylor looked at me with panic in her eyes.

"One of your named partners was murdered yesterday. I'm surprised someone showed you the photos. That's not something that should be passed around."

"I asked to see them," she said with an attempt at bravado. "I didn't believe he was dead."

I guided Taylor to a nearby bench, and we sat. It was after closing time, and unless Tiki Tom showed up two days in a row, I doubted anybody would take advantage of the unlocked gate out front.

"Was Ben Schaffley a good boss?"

"He was a great lawyer. He knew the law like the back of

his hand. He was tough, but we all knew if he chose one of us to work on a case with him, we'd come away learning something new. It was like a treasure hunt, finding something to help him win."

"Did you work on his team much?"

"A few times. The first was a big case, and it was all hands on deck. Ben and I were up all night looking for something to help his client. It was three thirty in the morning when I found a precedent in a volume of case rulings. Baum vs. Baum. Isn't that funny? I still remember it. I read the page three times before I took it to him. I didn't want to make a fool of myself. But I was right; it was exactly what he needed. He poured me a glass of bourbon, and we toasted then and there. He was that confident that I'd found the missing link." She chipped at her fingernail polish. "He was right, too. The judge dismissed the case."

"Sounds like the two of you were close."

"What?" she asked, looking up suddenly. "No. No closer than any of the other assistants. That's the job. I mean, I got a bonus out of it, but that's how it works."

I regarded Giovanni and Mike Bozer across the store. Bozer was facing the wall, and Giovanni was taking his shoulder measurement. Looked as though I'd asked the right person for help!

"I'm not supposed to talk about it," Taylor said in a pinched voice.

I turned back to her. "Your old case? You didn't violate privilege."

"The murder. You won't tell anybody I said anything, will you? They had us all sign non-disclosure agreements before we saw the photos."

"Did everybody sign?"

"Of course. It was that or lose our jobs."

While we sat on the bench, Taylor set down the trash bin. A rancid smell emanated from it. I pulled the plastic liner out of the bin and knotted the top of the bag before the odor could infect the fabrics in the area and stood.

"I'll be right back," I said. I carried the bag out the back door and tossed it in my dumpster. When I came back inside, Taylor stood next to the bench, running her hand over a fat bolt of lemon-yellow fleece. I cleared my throat, and she turned away from the fabric. Any friendly connection we'd had was gone, replaced by an officious nature.

"Can you pretend I didn't say anything about anything? I don't want to get in trouble. We're only here because we're moving forward with the disbursement of the Villamere estate. The sooner you pick up your fabric, the better."

I nodded my understanding of her request, hoping she'd interpret it as a blanket agreement to keep quiet. I still didn't know how exactly I was going to get all that fabric here, but that was my problem, not hers.

Taylor's phone buzzed. She checked the screen. She looked up at her new boss, and he tapped his watch. She hoisted her bag onto her shoulder and headed in his direction. I followed, unsure if our business was concluded but having no other reason for standing in the corner.

"Finished?" Mike asked.

"Yes. She's been advised."

"Did she sign off?"

"I forgot." Taylor pulled a leather folio and a pen out of her tote bag. She opened the folio and clicked the pen then handed me both. "Initial at the tape flags to indicate you understand."

I scanned the page. "This says I have forty-eight hours to take possession of all that fabric. That's not possible. I'm the only one who works here full-time. I can't get there until the weekend." I tried to hand the folio back, but Taylor made no move to take it. I looked at her boss. "Does Vaughn McMichael know about this? He's the executor of the will. I spoke to him last night, and he didn't mention a timetable."

"Mr. McMichael has been tied up with other responsibilities relating to his duties as executor."

The whole time this conversation took place, Giovanni stood a few feet away. To Mike and Taylor, he probably looked as if he were absorbed in his project, but I knew him well enough to know he was eavesdropping. I hadn't told him where the fabric for the suit clinic was coming from, but now it was a matter of time before he knew about my new bounty.

In a spontaneous move, I closed the folio and thrust it back at Taylor. She seemed surprised by my action. She stepped back but instinctively took the folio.

"I'm not signing anything just yet. I'll follow up with the theater. Laurence said there's no rush."

"Who is Laurence?" Taylor asked. She looked at Mike, who stared at me.

"Laurence Thibodeaux. The Villamere theater manager."

"Mr. Thibodeaux has no say in what happens to the theater anymore. If the inheritor can't be located by the end of the weekend, the theater will close while it goes through probate."

I didn't like the sound of that. If nothing else, it gave Laurence even more of a motive for murder.

13

THE LEGAL DUO LEFT THROUGH THE FRONT GATE. I trailed a few feet behind them and locked the gate into place. I turned around and found Giovanni staring at me.

"Okay," I said, holding up both hands. "I'm surprised you didn't ask. The fabric for the suit shop is coming from the Villamere Theater. Reginald Villamere died and left the textiles from the renovation to my great-aunt and -uncle. The will was written before I was born, but now they come to me. It's mostly heavy decorating fabric, for chairs, curtains, things like that, but there are several bolts of superfine wool from when they made the uniforms."

"Condition?" Giovanni asked.

"From what I've seen, good. Mint. The fabric was woven for mass production, not for retail. They're seventy-two-inch width, and they're still sealed in the original heavy plastic in which they were transported."

"How many bolts?"

"Twenty? Fifty? I didn't make a proper inventory yet."

Years of negotiating bulk purchases of cheap fabrics had left Giovanni with a talent for quick yardage calculations. "You're looking at a couple thousand yards of suit-gauge wool. That normally sells for eighty-five dollars a yard plus tariffs if it's imported."

"I know. It's a major score."

Giovanni nodded.

I waited for him to start his negotiations. Truth be told, if I was going to be held to that forty-eight-hour window of time, I'd need someone to help me liquidate the fabric. Giovanni wasn't equipped to use those industrial fabrics either, but his shop was in Los Angeles's fabric district. He knew people. And if he came into a large amount of fabric, he could use it to barter for yardage he could use.

"Fine," I said. "We can work something out."

This time Giovanni held up his hands. "Not necessary." He turned back to the table and glanced at the yellow pad. "But I did get you your first customer."

"He's not my first. I already promised a suit to Vaughn."

"Your rich boyfriend?"

I nodded.

Giovanni sighed. "I suppose it's not the worst idea to have him represent you in his line of work."

"Charlie wants one too. So does Tiki Tom."

Giovanni's forehead creased. "Isn't Charlie your mechanic friend? Why does she want a man's suit?"

"Haven't you ever heard of Marlene Dietrich?"

Giovanni handed me the yellow tablet with Mike Bozer's notes and measurements. A check for a thousand dollars was paperclipped to the page.

"What's this?" I asked, pointing at the check.

"A good-faith deposit. Put it with the others."

"What others?"

"You've taken orders from three people. Are you telling me they haven't given you deposits?"

I stared at Mike Bozer's check. "One thousand dollars?"

"We haven't discussed your prices, so I estimated. For a made-to-measure suit, that's a steal. If you want to do this, do it right. No more orders without a deposit."

Giovanni promised to return tomorrow with his van. I watched him collect his keys from the drawer under the register, and he waved on his way out. Something about my opportunistic former boss was definitely different. Maybe his doctor had put him on Prozac.

On any normal weekday, I'd lock up and meet Genevieve and Charlie at the Broadside, but today didn't feel normal. I called Charlie to cancel.

"You and Genevieve are on your own tonight."

"Nope, I'm flying solo. Frenchy's hands are full with the tea shop. What's your excuse?"

"I need to talk to Vaughn about the will."

"Good luck with that. He had me put his Beemer on the rack this morning before he headed on a road trip to locate somebody in Nevada. Josephine something."

"He's not back yet?"

"Maybe. Why? Are you jealous? Who is she?"

"Josephine is the inheritor of the Villamere estate. Vaughn was going to drive to Nevada to meet with her today. He made it sound like he was headed there and back."

"If I'd known that, I would have invited myself along for the ride."

I told Charlie to get takeout and bring it to my place. It took ten minutes to tally my sales for the day and close the register, and by the time I was done, she was at my gate. I let her in, and she led the way upstairs. I was starting to test my ankle by walking without my cane, but after a long day on my feet, what I wanted more than anything was to sit.

I poured a glass of wine, and Charlie grabbed a beer. Tonight's offerings were salads with blackened chicken and green goddess dressing. It was an odd choice for Charlie, and I said as much.

"Duke's working out some new additions to his menu. These were on the house."

While we crunched our way through the salads, I filled Charlie in on Giovanni's arrival and suspiciously helpful demeanor. "Giovanni always has an angle. It's not like him not to ask for what he wants up front."

"Does he know about the fabric from the theater?"

"One of the lawyers was here. He said I have to get the fabrics out within forty-eight hours. Giovanni heard that, and I may have elaborated on the situation after the lawyer left."

"If you keep making your own problems, you're going to run out of people to blame." She took a swig of her beer. "Your old boss probably wants to see what you get before naming his price. Is he any good at this suit stuff?"

"He got a thousand-dollar deposit from Mike Bozer based on one conversation."

"You're giving me the friends-and-family discount."

"Better than that," I said with a laugh. "You get the working-out-the-kinks discount."

We clinked glasses, and I continued. "Giovanni said he grew up working in his uncle's suit shop on Rodeo Drive, and he talked the lawyer into a custom suit without even having sketches or fabric swatches or a proper display. You want to know what was suspicious?"

"I'm all about suspicious."

"When the lawyer introduced himself, he said he was Mike Bozer of Bozer and Schmidt."

"That's not suspicious. That's how those guys talk."

"Before the murder, it was Schaffley, Bozer, and Schmidt."

At this, Charlie looked surprised. "They already dropped the dead guy's name from their firm?"

"Show a little respect, please."

"People have to earn my respect." She took a swig of her beer. "Just because he's dead doesn't mean he gets preferential treatment. So far nothing I've heard about Ben Schaffley makes me think he deserved it."

We finished our dinner, and Charlie talked me into a spontaneous trip to the Villamere Theater to inventory my fabric. It was eight thirty. I called Genevieve to see if she wanted to join us. I put the call on speaker so Charlie could listen in.

"I'd love to, but I can't," Genevieve said when I called. "I finally worked out a recipe that works for these vultures, but I ran out of organic sugar."

"Isn't all sugar organic?"

"You would think so. No, I need unrefined brown sugar. And unbleached flour. And organic maple syrup."

"Now I know you're pulling my leg."

"Poly, you lived in Los Angeles. Is this how everybody is? Homegrown, farm-to-table, organic, pesticide-free, unfiltered ingredients? I'm all for eating well, but there's such a thing as taking things too far."

"Can you think of this as a creative challenge? Like I did with the wool?"

Charlie's contribution to the conversation: "Edibles."

I shushed her.

"Charlie's with you?" Genevieve continued with her voice

raised. "Charlie, I already told you I'm not baking pot into my brownies! I don't care if it's organic or not. My shop is called Tea Totalers! The last thing people expect is for me to serve happy brownies!"

"From what I've heard about the lawyers, it would be a public service," Charlie said.

"My baked goods are happy enough."

I'd long ago accepted that this was Charlie and Genevieve's way of showing each other love. Genevieve was soft, demure, and learning how to live on her own for the first time in her life. Charlie was rough around the edges and took a metaphorical bat to most interactions. She bullied her way through life and usually came out ahead. They could learn from each other if they'd shut up long enough to listen.

"Are you sure you can't join us?" I asked.

"Poly had two whole glasses of wine and can't drive," Charlie added.

"I can't, but I have an idea," Genevieve said. "Go wait on your sidewalk. Your carriage will be there in five minutes."

"You better send us dessert!" Charlie said before I disconnected.

I cleaned up the kitchen, and Charlie and I headed downstairs. Our driver was waiting for us, just like Genevieve said. I pictured her laughing her way through her next organic recipe.

Our "driver" was Sheriff Clark. The "carriage" was his official county vehicle.

"Frenchy has a funny sense of humor." Charlie said with a scowl. She climbed into the back seat of Clark's sedan. I questioned her willingness to voluntarily get into the back of a cop car and pointed at the front seat.

"Suit yourself," she said. "This isn't a date."

I raised my eyebrows and looked at Clark. He shrugged as if Charlie's actions weren't a surprise.

Clark and Charlie had an on-again, off-again, really off-again relationship, though if she heard me use the R-word to describe them, she'd do something to the engine block of my VW Bug. Not two weeks ago, I'd spotted them dining together in a back booth at the Broadside Tavern, so I knew whatever it was that had turned her sour tonight was temporary. Charlie's default was that she didn't need anybody, and it was entirely possible that this current wave of distance between them was her fear that she was letting him get too close.

"Sheriff Clark," I said in greeting.

"Poly. Charlie." He nodded at each of us in turn.

"Don't 'Charlie' me."

I grinned at him. "You can 'Poly' me as much as you want."

I slid onto the back seat next to Charlie.

"Genevieve said you wanted a ride to the Villamere Theater."

"That depends. Did you release the crime scene?"

"Earlier today. Whoever killed Ben Schaffley did us a favor by committing the crime in that room. The fabrics are all in plastic, so it was easy to check for trace evidence. Once the body was removed, we had a clear view of the scene."

Clark pulled out into traffic. Bonita Avenue was one of the roads that cut through San Ladrón. During the day, it was filled with cars parked alongside the curbs while people shopped or ate at one of the small businesses lining the street. At night, the parking spaces were empty, but the traffic picked up as people headed either into or out of town. Most of us had small lots behind our shops, and we didn't much mind if someone left their car parked out front while they shopped the rest of the street. There had been a proposal to change the city ordinance and make all of the lots communal under city management. It was a good idea in theory, but it was one step closer to paid parking, and if there was one thing I'd learned about business, it was that free parking is a valuable incentive.

"Did you find a murder weapon?" I asked.

"Nothing conclusive."

"How about clues?"

"A partial footprint and a torn piece of paper. Looks like the first page of Reginald Villamere's will. Makes sense that Mr. Schaffley would have it with him, but the tear is suspicious. The will is a matter of public record, so we don't know why someone would forcibly take it from him."

I thought back to the will Vaughn and I had found in Larry Thibodeaux's apartment between layers of cashmere sweaters. It was unsigned. From everything I'd heard, there was no evidence that it existed in the first place. Clark had seemed as if he was on Laurence Thibodeaux's side on the night of his arrest, but what would the presence of a second will do? Might the sheriff see it as motive for the theater manager? If the text on the torn page clutched in the victim's hand matched the text from the copy of the will found in Laurence's dresser, would that be good or bad?

I didn't know why Clark was being so forthcoming with his investigation, but with Charlie doing her bump-on-a-log routine, I kept pressing him. "Anything else?"

"Security camera footage caught movement in the hallway, but the only thing we have to work with is a shadow. I turned it over to the forensic team at the community college to see what they can find."

"That sounds like a big break."

Clark took a sharp turn at a yellow light, and Charlie and I swayed to the left.

"It's something," Clark said. "I don't know if it relates. It could have been a member of the theater staff, or Ben Schaffley, who we already know went into that room. What we don't know is why he went there. It could be he planned to meet someone, or that he was up to something on his own."

14

CLARK, CHARLIE, AND I ARRIVED AT THE THEATER. The parking lot was empty. A smattering of cars were parked at the edges of the lot, probably belonging to employees who'd been instructed to leave the closer spaces open for patrons. Charlie and I followed Clark to the door. He and Charlie entered, but I stopped. A poster that hadn't been there on Monday advertised an all-day 1930s film retrospective for the upcoming weekend to honor Reginald Villamere and his theater.

I pulled out my phone and took a picture of the poster then texted it to Vaughn with a note: *Did you know about this?*

His reply came back almost immediately. *News to me. Want to go?*

Wouldn't miss it for all the tea in Genevieve's shop. I added a smiley face.

It was tempting to stand outside the theater and call Vaughn, who appeared to be available for a chat, but Charlie and Clark were inside the theater, waiting for me. I wasn't used to having the police on my side when I wanted to nose around a crime scene, so I pocketed my phone and joined them before Clark revoked his generosity.

The theater lobby was empty. A handful of employees were scattered about, one behind each of the concession stands and another in the hallway to take tickets and direct patrons to their theater destination. The intoxicating scent of salty popcorn filled the room. Other than the three of us and the employees, the lobby was empty.

A young lanky Black man approached. He had a wide-open face with high cheekbones and a trace of facial hair trimmed to define his jawline. He wore an oversized magenta blazer with gray slacks. It was the same outfit Larry Thibodeaux had worn on the day of the will reading, but unlike Mr. Thibodeaux's neat and tailored appearance, this younger man looked as if he'd raided Hulk Hogan's closet.

"Hi," he said. "I'm Devontay, the acting manager. You missed the start of the second movie, but the theater's empty, so if you want to go in, you can."

"Score," Charlie said. She turned to me. "You in?"

"That's not why we're here," I said.

"Speak for yourself. Come on, Ryan," she said, tipping the energy of the evening by using Clark's first name. "Buy me a popcorn."

"Charlie..."

She crossed her arms.

Clark looked at me. "Technically I'm off the clock."

"Buy me a popcorn too."

Devontay said, "You'll need tickets to see the movie."

"You said it already started," Charlie said.

"We still have to sell tickets. Those are the rules."

"Sheriff Clark?" I said, hoping he was feeling generous.

Clark shook his head. "If I get the concessions, somebody else gets the tickets."

I turned to Charlie. "You heard the man."

She pulled a couple of crumpled twenties out of her pocket and handed them to Devontay. He walked to the box office booth and tapped the screen, then returned with her change.

She turned to Clark. "I want Goobers too. And we're dumping them into the popcorn bucket."

"You know I hate that," Clark said.

"And that's why I'm doing it."

As Charlie and Clark headed to the concession stand, bickering about snacks, I lingered behind with Devontay. "There's really nobody in either theater?"

"No."

"Why bother running the movies?"

"Contractual obligations. Tonight's movies are beamed in via satellite."

I thought back to the day of the will reading, when someone had told Laurence there was a problem with the projector. "If the movies are beamed in, then what do you do with the projection booth?"

"We use the projector when we run films from the studio archives. There's nothing like seeing a movie on the original 70-millimeter film. The equipment needs to be maintained, and it's overdue. Spools of film are becoming more and more fragile, and to defray costs, we started streaming. We keep the booth intact for the rare special event."

"Do you mean when I come here to see a Mae West movie, it's being streamed from some remote location?"

"Sometimes. Or sometimes you're watching a disc. Most theaters break even on ticket sales because movie rentals cost so much. Once the movies are rented and paid for, the show times are programmed. The movies start when they're supposed to start and end when they're supposed to end. Trailers are packaged with the movie, and the studios have to make sure those trailers get shown."

"But there's nobody there to see them."

"That's not the point."

"But if…"

"We make our profit on concessions. Have you noticed how many special events we have?"

"Concerts and stage performances. Yes."

"Rentals, too. Some people rent the theater and play their favorite movie in the background while they mingle. If they arrange for one of our catering packages, we make money on food and drinks."

While we talked, Devontay led me toward the hallway leading to the theater. He handed my ticket to an employee in an usher uniform, who tore it in half and handed me the stub.

"You still go through all of this when nobody else is here?"

Devontay shrugged. "Like I said, these are the rules. It's easier to follow them than to get lax and have to remember what to do when we get a crowd."

I glanced around the interior. "When's the last time the Villamere had a crowd?"

"It's been a long time." We reached the doors to the theater. "Sorry I can't restart the movie for you."

"No problem. I've seen this one before." I reached for the handle and pulled it open. Devontay stepped back and waved as I ducked inside. I let the door fall almost completely back into place and caught before it closed, then I peeked through the crack and watched him retreat down the hallway to the lobby. Watching a movie in an empty theater was one of life's great experiences, but I had something else in mind.

I crept forward in the darkness and scanned the interior. Clark and Charlie were seated next to each other. She plucked a kernel of popcorn out of the bucket and fed it to him. Glory be, they were getting along. Far be it from me to interrupt them. Who knew what their status would be on the drive home?

Returning to the door, I opened it a sliver and peeked through the crack. The hallway was clear. I eased the door open and snuck out. The usher who had torn our tickets sat on a folding chair with his back to me, and another group of ushers stood talking by the popcorn concession stand. White paper bags were lined upon the counter, and the employees took turns dumping scoops of freshly popped popcorn into each of the bags. Somebody was going to benefit from today's slow box office sales.

I had every right to go to the storage closet and assess the fabric. Technically, that was the reason I was here. I could have asked someone to unlock the closet for me, but there was another part of the theater I wanted to see.

It hadn't surprised me to find Laurence Thibodeaux crying in the projection booth the day Clark and I went looking for him. He'd worked at the theater for over half a century, and the will reading must have brought up emotions about his connection to the venue and questions about his future. A person would have to be inhuman not to shed a tear about that.

The projection room had been part of the theater's original design, spacious enough for the projectionist to oversee the reels of film needed to show a movie, but not much more than that. Having learned that the movies were sent to the theater via satellite, I wondered about Laurence's trip to the projection booth. Had he been hiding from us? Or had the message about a problem in the projection booth been a coded message, spoken in quotes to indicate Laurence's need to step away and deal with his emotions in private?

When we'd found Laurence crying in the projection room, he'd had his handkerchief. I remembered him dropping it. If nothing else, I wanted to retrieve it for him.

The red velvet stanchion that restricted access to the hallway had been put back into place. I swung my leg over it and miscalculated, catching my foot and falling forward. The posts tilted but righted themselves. I wasn't so lucky. I landed on my hands and knees, protecting my recently recovered ankle by engaging my thigh muscles to keep that leg in the air. I stood and brushed carpet fibers from my black sweater, then I located the door to the projection booth and entered.

A soiled hanky rested on the floor by the base of the projector next to a series of footprints that disturbed a layer of dust. I turned on my phone's flashlight and aimed it at the ground. The size of the prints indicated men's dress shoes. I expected to have a couple of minutes to poke around and observe the tiny room without being rushed, but that expectation was quickly dashed when the door to the projection booth opened a second time, and someone advanced up the stairs.

15

THE PROBLEM WITH LITTLE ROOMS THAT HAD ONLY one entrance was that they left no way out. Shaking with nerves, I dropped Laurence's handkerchief. The footsteps grew closer. I swooped down and grabbed the monogramed square and stood, hoping handkerchief retrieval was a plausible explanation for my presence. I turned to face my company. It was Devontay, the stand-in theater manager.

"What are you doing up here?" he asked. His demeanor was less friendly than it had been moments ago.

I held up the hanky. "Mr. Thibodeaux dropped this yesterday. He wanted it back. Sentimental value."

"What is it?"

"His handkerchief. He didn't realize he had dropped it until after he left. I figured as long as I was here, I'd be helpful."

The hanky was wadded up in my palm, and the longer I stood there, cornered in the projection booth with an employee who had as much access to the stockroom as anybody else, the more I regretted being there in the first place. I jammed the hanky into my pocket and played my ace card.

"I don't know if you heard about anything from the will reading yesterday, but Mr. Villamere left the textiles in the theater storage closet to my fabric shop."

"That closet in the back hallway where the lawyer was killed? There's something in there?"

Devontay's ignorance temporarily silenced me. Was it plausible that he didn't have access? That he didn't know what was in the theater's storage?

"The room is full of fabric. Textiles for drapes, seat cushions, and staff uniforms."

Devontay put his hands on the lapels of his baggy magenta blazer. "It is?" he asked.

"Yes. I didn't know either, not until the reading of the will. My relatives left me a fabric shop, and Mr. Villamere must have been friends with them. He left the contents of the closet to them. They're deceased, so it all went to me. You really didn't know?"

"I've only worked here for a few years. I was out front while the tenured ushers were in the conference room. When the meeting ended and they came out, all they wanted to talk about was the money Mr. Villamere left them."

Devontay still stood on the staircase. When he'd found me in the booth, he hadn't come any farther inside. His eyes moved over me, head to toe, almost as if *he* suspected *me* of something nefarious.

"Sheriff Clark brought me here so I could take a quick inventory of the closet and figure out what I'll need to transport the textiles to my store," I said, which wasn't exactly the truth, but Clark hadn't spelled out why he agreed to drive me here, so I convinced myself it wasn't exactly a lie either. "Since it's slow tonight, is there any chance you could unlock it for me?"

"Sure," he said. "Follow me." He turned around and descended the stairs.

I swiped the screen of my phone to turn off the flashlight and hit the camera icon instead. My phone made a shutter sound.

Devontay came back up the steps. "What was that?"

"Nothing. I was turning off my flashlight app and hit the camera icon." I jammed my phone into my other pocket. Devontay leaned to the side and looked behind me at the small, cramped room.

"You go ahead," he said and gestured me forward. "I'll get the keys and meet you in the hallway in a moment."

I squeezed past him and turned right, following the carpet until I reached the stockroom door. Since it had been applied, someone had sliced through the crime scene tape to gain access. A piece of paper that documented the evidence collection and the release of the room was taped to the door. Clark's initials were on both lines.

Yesterday, before Laurence had unlocked the room, he'd said he was the only one with the key, but that couldn't be true, not if Laurence was innocent. Ben Schaffley and his killer had somehow gotten inside without the theater manager's knowledge or aid. I pushed aside the nagging thought that there was another explanation for all of that—maybe Laurence wasn't innocent. I had nothing concrete to base my conclusions on, but I couldn't see the kind, elderly theater manager bludgeoning the hotshot lawyer and then leaving his body to bleed out on the floor while he offered the rest of us concessions.

I reached for the doorknob, expecting it to be locked. It turned under my hand. I entered the room and flicked on the lights. My attention went directly to the center of the floor where Ben Schaffley's body had been. The floor was empty, the blood removed. To anybody who hadn't been here yesterday, this wasn't a crime scene, it was a stockroom filled with fabric. And after I transported the fabric away, it would become something else.

A lined yellow pad sat on a shelf of fabric. The pages were blank. A pen dangled from a piece of string tied to the fixture, so I untied the pen and used it to make notes. My original assessment had been correct. Most of the textiles were heavy upholstery fabrics that would be of little use to my shop. I could use the bolts to barter with a distributor or sell them directly to a jobber, though finding a buyer on short notice seemed like a long shot. Even Giovanni would turn down this inventory. Aside from Scarlett O'Hara and Carol Burnett, nobody wanted to wear clothes made from their drapes.

Now that the concept of a suit shop was shaping up in my plans, I was mostly concerned with the quality and content of the wool, so I spent time making a rudimentary inventory of that corner of the stockroom. There was more than enough to get my suit clinic off the ground. I tried to pull one of the bolts off the shelf but succeeded only in moving it about six inches. This was a two-person job. Once again, I saw the value in Giovanni's offer of help.

I tore off my sheet of notes and put the tablet back on the shelf where I'd found it. I retied the pen to the string. Between snooping and taking inventory, I'd been busy for close to two hours. If the movie wasn't over yet, it was bound to end soon.

Charlie and Clark were waiting for me in the lobby. The concession stands were dark, and save for two employees vacuuming the carpet, everyone else had left. I glanced to the left and the right, looking for Devontay's bright-magenta blazer. He wasn't there.

"About time you showed up," Charlie said. "Clark here thought you went the way of Ben Schaffley."

"Charlie," Clark admonished.

"What? That was a good reference."

"He's not wrong," I said quickly to keep the peace. "I was in the stockroom, taking inventory. Extend my gratitude to whoever you hired to clean the crime scene after you released it."

"You can thank the city of Los Angeles for that. Our annual murder count exceeded the standard for city-funded crime-scene cleanup, so now it's covered by them."

I shuddered at the thought. "That probably wasn't one of your goals when you took the job."

Clark shook his head, not in disagreement but at the unfortunate reality of his job. "Small-town sheriff. You think the worst of your job is going to be keeping the peace at backyard cookouts. Etta forwarded a list of crime-scene cleanup companies to the acting theater manager when we released the room."

"They didn't waste any time getting in here."

"Would you have?"

"I guess not."

Behind Clark, an employee held a stack of handouts advertising the film festival this upcoming weekend. The usher saw me watching him. He approached us and handed me a flyer then gave one to Clark. He held one out to Charlie, and she waved him off.

"How long have you been planning this festival?" I asked. "I'm on the mailing list, and I haven't seen it mentioned."

"It's a last-minute thing. Mr. Villamere's death put a spotlight on the theater, and we've been getting a lot of calls about our schedule. We thought it was a good idea to capitalize on the publicity and do something special to honor his memory."

"We?"

"The ushers. None of us thought Mr. Villamere would name us in his will, but that's who he was. He loved this place and encouraged his employees to love it too. The theater was his legacy, so it felt fitting to honor him with movies."

"Or it's a way to make a quick buck," Charlie said. "No judgment."

The usher's face colored, and he averted his gaze down to the carpet. "You're not the first person to say that. Mr. Villamere didn't leave a contingency plan for the theater. He left the estate to a woman nobody ever heard of, and we don't know what she'll want to do. We—some employees—thought if we could raise enough money, we could buy her out. Or, if she's on the fence, it won't hurt to show her what kind of money the theater is capable of pulling in."

To my surprise, Charlie said, "Talk to Vaughn McMichael at McMichael Industries. He takes an interest in small businesses. If you're serious, he's your guy."

She didn't look at me or Clark, and neither of us said anything about her rare foray into helpful advice. Not a lot of people knew that Vaughn was her brother. He worked for his dad, and Charlie and Vic McMichael had a troubled history.

The usher nodded. "I will. Thanks." He glanced down at the flyers in his hand and then back up at us. "Are you guys going to come? The lawyers arranged for us to display items from Mr. Villamere's personal collection of movie memorabilia in the lobby. Someone from the Broadside Tavern is going to serve classic cocktails. We have a great lineup of movies, and there might be an award for best-dressed attendee."

"Will these movies be beamed in via satellite like tonight's movies?" I asked.

"No. We're renting the film reels from studios in Hollywood. There's been some concern about whether or not the projector is in working condition, but we're all hoping it's fine." He held up crossed fingers. "What do you think?"

"We wouldn't miss it," I said, not giving Charlie or Clark a chance to say otherwise.

Satisfied with my response, he set the stack of flyers on our table and emptied the trash from a nearby bin. He headed toward another trash bin and left us alone again.

A row of lights in the back hallway went out, leaving us in a dimly lit lobby.

"You get what you came for?" Clark asked me.

I held up the page I'd torn from the tablet. "Rudimentary inventory of my inheritance. I'll be back in the morning with a truck." I turned to Charlie. "Speaking of which, can I borrow your truck tomorrow?"

"Ever notice how everybody wants what I have?" Charlie asked, which was not an answer. "It's good to be me." She stood and tugged Clark's sleeve. "Date night's over, Sheriff. Let's get Polyester home before she turns into a pumpkin."

"I thought this wasn't a date," I said as we walked out to the car.

"Don't look a gift horse in the mouth. I kept him out of your hair while you snooped, didn't I?"

I grabbed the handle to the back door and climbed in. Charlie got in the front seat next to Clark. I wasn't sure which one of the three of us had just gotten played.

16

Later that night, after I'd plugged in my phone to charge, I swiped through the various apps I'd opened throughout the day. When I came to my photos, it took me a moment to recognize the most recent image as the floor of the projection booth. I used my thumb and index finger to magnify the photo. It showed the dusty floor next to the base of the projector covered in footprints of varying sizes. I already knew Laurence had been up there, and Clark and I had too. The projection booth wasn't part of the crime scene.

I closed the photo app and sent Vaughn a text asking about his trip to Nevada, but I fell asleep before he had a chance to respond. The next morning when I woke, there was still no reply.

———

There are routines to life. Get up, get ready, get to work. Even with the nuances of being self-employed, there are factors on which one can rely: time to open the shop, time to close the shop, and the needs of the business that fall within those tent poles, like helping customers, stocking shelves, tallying sales, and brainstorming ideas for the future. But as time ticked away, a low-level fear ran in the background. No matter how idyllic small-town San Ladrón life was, danger lurked somewhere in the neighborhood. The more time that passed since Ben Schaffley's murder, the more likely that the killer would get away. I wondered if, as a community, we would be able to recover from this without answers through a sort of group amnesia or if we would start to look at each other differently, with questions in our eyes.

I was at the beginning of my routine on Thursday when Giovanni walked into Material Girl with a pink bakery box in one hand and a bottle of orange juice in the other. I was instantly suspicious. Giovanni had never once supplied food for the workroom when I worked for him at To The Nines.

"Morning," he said. "I brought donuts from the shop down the street."

"You went to Lopez Donuts?"

"Yes. They're your friends, right? Thought you'd appreciate that. Where should I set up?"

"There's a table in the stockroom."

"Cups?"

"Mugs are on a shelf above the sink."

Giovanni entered the stockroom, and I watched him until he was out of sight. Maybe I was wrong about him, and he hadn't always been the cheap, opportunistic boss who exploited my design skills. None of that changed the fact that he always had an angle.

He exited the stockroom and wiped his mouth with a napkin then tossed it in the trash. "What's on your agenda for today?"

I thought back to the previous day when Jun had hinted at some trouble Giovanni was experiencing. "Why are you here?"

"You need help getting this suit thing up and running, don't you?"

"Yes, but you have your own business to run."

"You should spend more time worrying about your business than mine."

"It's called consideration."

"Don't sweat it. Your replacement has things well in hand."

I had never once regretted the decision to upend my life and move to San Ladrón to reopen my family's fabric store, not after fighting for my life in the stockroom, or finding a body in a delivery of fabric, or getting mixed up in a beauty pageant that had peripheral ties to a homicide investigation. Even when my ex-boyfriend showed up and revealed his engagement to a ballerina bridezilla, expecting me to make her dress, I knew this life had been the right choice. To The Nines was a small dress shop that made mediocre-quality dresses expected by their purchasers to survive one wearing. There'd been no room for advancement, no opportunities to grow. Yet upon learning that Giovanni had filled my shoes, I felt a pang of regret. One likes to think one is irreplaceable.

"Good," I said to cover my surprise. "Do the workroom women like her? Wait, don't answer that."

Giovanni didn't respond. I couldn't read his expression, but it wasn't a smirk, and that was good enough. It surprised me to realize there was something I missed from my time working for him, something I wasn't getting from working for myself. I shook off the unwelcome thought.

"I'll ask again. What's the plan for today?" Giovanni asked.

"For the next eight hours, we're working in the store. I didn't expect you to get here so early."

He looked around the shop. "Did you get your fabric last night?"

"No."

"Have I taught you nothing? Get the fabric while you can. Do not give anybody a chance to toss it, claim it, damage it, burn it, or accidentally sell it to the highest bidder."

"Speaking from experience?"

"You already know my business relies on my access to low-cost fabrics. Some of those fabrics have questionable provenance."

"That doesn't bother you?"

"Not since you quit," he muttered under his breath. He pulled a set of keys out of his pocket and held them out to me. "Go get your fabric. I'll watch the store."

"The fabric retrieval is a two-person job."

"I'm sure you have at least one friend in this sleepy town who can help you out in a pinch."

"I have a lot of friends in this sleepy town, but they all have their own businesses to run."

"That is your problem. You make fun of me for negotiating what I want in advance, but when there's something in it for both parties, things get done. You live in a world of favors, and now that you need help, you find yourself without anyone to call."

"I called you, didn't I?"

"And I'm here. But if we go retrieve your fabrics from the theater, who do you plan to leave in charge of the store?"

I *hated* when Giovanni had a point.

Wednesdays were under control with Jun working for me, but on any other day I was a one-woman show. That would have been perfectly fine if I didn't have a side hustle to juggle. I pulled out my phone and scrolled through my contacts, deciding on the ones who had the most personal stake in me getting the fabric that had been left to the family store.

"Hi, Dad. Any chance you or Mom can come work in the store today?"

———

MY PARENTS, Helen and John Monroe, lived about half an hour from San Ladrón. They still owned the tract house that I'd grown up in and showed no signs of moving, especially with California real estate prices being what they were. It was a convenient distance when it came to keeping in touch, attending get-togethers on the holidays, and providing favors of the "can you run the store while I go do things?" variety. Both of my parents were retired, and they were amused by the wages I paid them for their hours in the store. So far, I'd funded a new HVAC unit, gutter guards, and a leaf blower. Ah, the glamour of home ownership.

I filled and turned on the water percolator then fixed myself a mug of Genevieve's black ginger sage tea. She experimented regularly with unusual flavors, and I welcomed the role of voluntary taste tester. I took a sip and made some notes on her feedback card, then tucked it back into the basket for when she picked it up. I helped myself to one of the glazed donuts Giovanni had set out. By the time my parents arrived, I was properly caffeinated and sugared up, and I probably could have carried the bolts of fabric out of the Villamere Theater myself.

Anybody who knew anything about Material Girl knew to park in the lot out back, and my parents did one better. Like the theater employees did, they parked in the farthest space from the entrance to leave spots open for paying customers. No sooner had they entered when Pins and Needles charged at them from some undisclosed location within the store. Needles tried to stop and skidded on the polished concrete floor, scrambling to turn around and head back. My dad picked up Pins and scratched his ears. "Hey there, fella." Pins, who wouldn't let anybody else hold him, settled into the crook of my dad's elbow and purred as if he'd found his soul mate.

My mom bent down and stroked Needles then straightened. "Hi, Giovanni. When Poly asked for help, I was under the impression she was alone."

"Giovanni's going to help me pick up fabric from the Villamere Theater," I said.

"That's nice," my mom said. "I trust she offered you something to make it worth your while?"

Giovanni turned to me, and I held up my hand before he could comment. "Giovanni and I will work out a deal. As for you two…"

"We're working for curtains," my mother said proudly.

"Your mother wants new curtains in the living room," my dad explained. "Today's wages go into the fund."

"I admire her streamlined approach." Giovanni turned to me. "Too bad you didn't inherit it."

After a brief discussion, it was decided that Giovanni would work in the store with my mom while my dad and I went to the theater. There had been a contest of the wills between Dad and Giovanni. My dad won, but only after he offered to buy Giovanni dinner at the Waverly House after the store closed for the day.

I drove Giovanni's van to the theater, which was starting to feel like my home away from home. "Why did you want to come with me?" I asked my dad.

"Your mother is worried about Giovanni. There was

something in the paper about him closing the shop for repairs. Didn't he say anything?"

"No. He said he hired my replacement and business was under control."

"Maybe your mother was wrong about what she read."

"Mom's not usually wrong about things like that."

"She's not usually wrong about a lot of things."

We arrived at the Villamere a little after noon. A couple of employees were in the parking lot, replacing the posters in the displays. The new posters announced who we would see that weekend: Marlene Dietrich from her Weimar period, Greta Garbo from her Russian period, and Claudette Colbert from her Egyptian period. The celebration of the Villamere was shaping up to be an international event.

"The Villamere Theater," my dad said, staring at the facade of the building. "I can't believe it's the end of an era."

"It might not be. The ushers are trying to raise money to buy it from Reginald Villamere's family."

My dad released his seatbelt and turned to me. "Reginald Villamere didn't have any family. Who inherited his estate?"

"Josephine Barkley. I haven't met her yet, but she inherited everything."

"That's not possible," he said. "Josephine Barkley doesn't exist."

17

Temporarily taken by surprise, I slammed on the brakes. We were already in the parking lot with no other vehicles around us, but my dad lurched forward against his seatbelt and put his hands out on the dash.

"What do you mean, Josephine Barkley doesn't exist?" I asked my dad. "Vaughn drove to Nevada to meet with her yesterday."

"Josephine Barkley is made up." My dad looked embarrassed. "I'm not even supposed to know about her."

I parked the van and opened the back doors, but this conversation seemed much more important than—well, it wasn't more important than getting my fabric, but in the grand scheme of things, it was right up there. I sometimes forgot that my dad grew up here in San Ladrón, that he knew things about people that I didn't.

"Tell me what you aren't supposed to know."

He turned around and sat inside the van with his legs hanging out the back. "When I was younger, I worked as a lifeguard at Gnarly Waves. I was probably around fifteen or sixteen."

Gnarly Waves was San Ladrón's answer to Water World. It was a theme park with colorful plastic slides, tubes, and pools. Fun for the whole family, assuming the whole family didn't mind getting wet.

"The theme park hired a fifteen-year-old?"

"It was a different time," he said dismissively. "One day, I was working a private party at the pool. I was in the lifeguard chair. Some kids were roughhousing in the Splash Down area. I kept blowing my whistle at them, and they'd stop, but then they started up again. There were a couple of men; they seemed old to me at the time but were probably younger than I am now. They were reclining on deck chairs near me. One of them said something about how awkward it was to be a bachelor. How people asked intrusive questions about his personal life... if he was seeing someone, if there was anyone special, that sort of thing. The other man agreed. I overheard them saying how easy it would be to invent a woman—an imaginary woman who could be their assistant, or their companion, or their ex-wife depending on the situation. They started knocking around names. Geraldine, Josephine, Jacqueline, Joan, Jan—"

"That's a lot of J names."

"Technically Geraldine starts with a G, but I see what you mean."

"You heard them settle on Josephine Barkley?"

"Not exactly. The kids in the pool got out of hand. I knew one of the kids was smaller than the others, and I didn't see him. I panicked. I climbed down from the lifeguard chair. One of the men saw what was going on, and he dove into the pool and broke up the fight."

"Was the smaller kid okay?"

"Yes." He smiled ruefully. "The reason I lost track of him was because he was at the snack bar."

"Did you get in trouble?"

"Almost. After everything cooled down, I overheard my manager telling the other man that I was probably too young to be a lifeguard, and that he'd have to let me go. The man, he told my manager that just last week his girlfriend pointed out to him what an excellent job I did and how I was an asset to the pool. Whenever any of us got a compliment from a patron, the manager would write it up and pin it on the bulletin board in the hallway. He asked for the man's girlfriend's name, and the man said Josephine Barkley. Aunt Millie was so proud she took a picture of the display. There's probably a picture of it in one of our family photo albums."

"Dad, do you know who the man was?"

"I know who both of them were. Reginald Villamere and Laurence Thibodeaux."

"But Mr. Villamere was rich. What would he be doing at Gnarly Waves?"

"The private party was for the Villamere staff and their families. Mr. Villamere hosted it annually. The only reason I was in that lifeguard chair was because another lifeguard called out sick and Gnarly Waves had to get someone to fill his spot."

I stared into the theater lobby while processing my dad's story, trying to figure out what it meant. Vaughn was supposed to meet with Josephine Barkley yesterday, and Charlie had said Vaughn had brought her his car for a once-over before heading out of town for a meeting. All of that pointed to there being a Josephine Barkley, someone who had been identified as the inheritor of Reginald Villamere's estate. She stood to become a multi-millionaire overnight, and only a handful of people even knew she existed. Fewer, it seemed, knew that she didn't.

And now, one of those people was dead. I was more curious than ever about Vaughn's meeting, but now, a sense of fear crept into my curiosity. Vaughn hadn't returned my text last night. If Josephine Barkley didn't exist, then who had he met with?

My dad reminded me that he didn't have all day, so I brushed my questions aside, and we headed into the theater. Ushers in their neat burgundy-and-gray uniforms were handling their stations without complaint: two prepping the concessions stand, one wiping down the counter of the bar on the opposite side of the lobby. Another rolled a magnetic sweeper over the carpet, fluffing the nap and picking up anything the vacuum had missed last night. I'd seen enough businesses that were staffed with resentful employees who barely put in their time to recognize that this team took pride in their jobs. I felt a pang of sadness for the employees who might be facing a career change. If not for the Villamere, there wouldn't be much need for ushers in San Ladrón.

Devontay waved at me from the top of the winding staircase that led to the landing. Laurence's magenta blazer hung from a stanchion, and Devontay was in rolled-up shirt sleeves. He stood next to a female mannequin dressed in a colorful Hilo Hattie Hawaiian dress.

"Hi, Poly," Devontay called. "I thought you'd be back this morning. I unlocked the storage room for you and put a couple bottles of water in there in case you guys get thirsty. I'm going to be busy setting up for the weekend, but let me know when you're done for the day so I can lock the room back up. "

"Sure thing." I pointed to the mannequin. "That doesn't look like it's from *Ninotchka*."

"Tiki Tom lent us his mannequins. He was going to undress them, but we're not getting the costumes until tomorrow, and I don't think parents will appreciate naked mannequins on display until then."

I'd already recognized the garments from Tiki Tom's shop. I'd made a series of muumuus for his mannequins last month. Nice to know the whole community was pitching in to help with the weekend event.

"Could make for an interesting discussion on the ride home," my dad said under his breath.

I turned to him. "You're lucky you and Mom had a girl."

"Did you park out back?" Devontay called down the stairs.

"No, we're in the front lot. There's parking out back?"

He straightened and put his hands on his back then stretched from side to side. "Yes—I mean no, no parking, but there's an exit out back for loading in equipment and access to the dumpster. Pull your van around. It'll be easier than carrying your textiles through the lobby. Shorter distance for you and less disruptive for us."

"Where's the door?"

"Past the last theater. It's painted to match the Art Deco mural on the wall. You probably never noticed it. You'll see it from outside. There's a brick outside with the theater name stenciled on it. Use it to prop the door open."

"I'll move the van," my dad said.

I called a thank-you up to Devontay and headed past the stockroom, past the stanchions, and down the hallway toward the mural. Devontay was right. I'd never known there was a door there. But now that I knew, I spotted a seam in the mural that matched the size of a standard door. I pushed on one side, and nothing happened. I pushed on the other, and the door swung outward into the parking lot. A brick sat a few feet away, and I used it to prop the door open.

The driveway behind the theater was rough, filled with

chunks of broken concrete and loose gravel. It was a short distance from the door to the dumpster, and I covered that distance as I waited for my dad to pull the van around. A sticker on the outside of the dumpster documented the trash pickup schedule and indicated it would have been emptied yesterday, but I braced myself anyway and peeked inside. The only contents of the bin were several knotted-off plastic bags containing empty popcorn buckets, candy boxes, and soda cups. If there had been clues, they were now in the city dump.

My dad pulled the van up in front of the propped-open door. He got out and opened the back doors of the van then followed me inside the theater. He slowed as we neared the crime scene tape affixed to the door frame.

"It's okay, Dad. Sheriff Clark released the scene. I was here last night. A clean-up crew erased all signs of the crime." I peeled the crime scene tape off the door frame and wadded it up into a ball. Tacky residue left behind evidence that it was there, but a swabbing with denatured alcohol would remove that too. "If you didn't see this, you wouldn't even know what happened inside."

I turned the knob and pushed open the door. The room was as neat and organized as I'd left it. Bins lined both sides, stacked with hundreds of bolts of fabric, each individually secured in a thick plastic bag.

My dad stood inside the doorway and whistled. "All of this is yours?"

"Yep." I pulled the folded sheet of yellow paper out of my pocket and handed it to him. "I made a quickie inventory last night. Right now, our main concern is the wool on the right side of the room. I don't know how much of it we can fit in Giovanni's van, but we should take as much as we can."

We spent the next couple of hours working without a

break, pulling bolts down from their bins, each of us taking an end as we carried each bolt out to the van. It was physical labor, and after carrying a dozen bolts, I was ready to sell the store and apply for a job serving coffee instead. I handed my dad a bottle of water from the stash Devontay had left for us, and we sat inside the back of the van while we drank them.

"I can't thank you enough, Dad. This was more work than I expected."

"I trust that will be reflected in my paycheck?"

"Standard wages plus a bonus?"

He looked satisfied. "That should take care of the downstairs windows."

"Dad, you know this fabric is from the Villamere renovation, right? That includes the curtains that cover the screen. You could—"

He held up his hand. "If I allow you to pay me in fabric, your mother will never let me hear the end of it."

"But I don't know what I'm going to do with those fabrics. You'd be doing me a favor."

"Stop. She has her heart set on a mocha shantung she saw in one of her decorating magazines. Do not ask her to settle for heavy burgundy jacquard."

"What about you? What do you want?"

"I want what your mother wants."

"That's not how it used to be. I seem to recall the two of you negotiating over the shade of paint you used in the living room."

"That was before."

"Before what?"

He looked embarrassed. "Before the paint I chose took on an unfortunate green cast when the sun went down."

I stood and closed the back of the van. "Mocha shantung it is."

While my dad drank a second bottle of water, I went back inside the theater to tell Devontay we were done for the day. We'd emptied two full floor-to-ceiling bins, but we'd barely put a dent in the total contents of the stockroom. I looked for the new theater manager but didn't see him anywhere.

A stocky usher approached me. "Poly, right?" I nodded. "Devontay took a break. He asked me to check in with you."

"Tell him we're done for the day. I'll be back tomorrow to get more."

"Not tomorrow. We're having a private reception for employees and their families and then the film festival over the weekend. We're closed on Monday, so you won't be able to get back in until Tuesday. Is that going to be okay?"

"If it works for the theater, it works for me."

"Cool," he said. I turned to leave, and he called after me. "I almost forgot. You left this here the other day." He held out a yellow legal pad. "You might want your notes."

I glanced at the pad. The only yellow tablet I'd used was the one on the shelf in the stockroom. I'd made notes on it and had torn off the page, and now that page was in my back pocket. The notepad I'd used was still sitting where I'd left it inside the stockroom.

People bought yellow pads all the time. But this one wasn't like the one I'd used. This one was legal sized. It was probably nothing. But then again, there'd been a bevy of lawyers in this building for the reading of a millionaire's will, and one of them had been murdered. It didn't feel like nothing.

I thanked the usher and left with the legal pad tucked safely under my arm.

18

On the ride back to Material Girl, I told my dad about the legal pad. "It's probably nothing."

My dad, who had taken the keys for the ride home, took a sharp turn, and the tail of the van swung wide. I double-checked my seatbelt for emphasis, and my dad shook his head at me.

"Did you ever learn about code breaking?"

"A little bit in high school. There's not much need for code-breaking classes in design school. Besides, the notepad is blank." I held it up as evidence.

"It *looks* blank. That doesn't mean it *is* blank." He took another turn, and the fabric in the back shifted again.

"Whoa, Dad! What's the rush?"

"Your mother wants to beat the afternoon traffic."

"You told Giovanni you would treat him to dinner at the Waverly after the store closed for the day."

"I made that offer on your behalf. It seemed like the least you could do."

I knew my dad was right, but that didn't make me any

happier about my parents leaving so soon. "Mom should have told me she had plans when I called."

"Curtains," he reminded me. "Besides, she didn't expect you'd work me for more than an hour. Have you thought about hiring some real employees?"

"So far, I haven't had to."

"You're running a business now, Poly. We're all proud of what you've accomplished, but you can't expect your friends and family to be available whenever you need us."

"I pay you, don't I?"

"Yes, you do. And that's a start. But if you're already willing to pay someone, why not create a real job? Write up a description, conduct interviews, and put your money back into your community."

I slouched down in my seat and didn't say anything. The only one of my friends who didn't have a paid staff was Charlie, and she wasn't exactly the poster child for Community Member of the Year. My resistance didn't come from the idea of being responsible for providing steady wages for someone else like I kept saying. It was really the idea of giving away a piece of what I'd built. Relying on favors from friends and family had gotten me this far, and I'd convinced myself it was a working system. It seemed as if I was fooling myself.

My mom was waiting for us in the parking lot. "What took you so long?"

"Poly is a slave driver," my dad said at the same I said, "Curtains."

My mom waved her keys. "Poly, Venmo us our wages. John, let's go."

"Sorry, boss, she outranks you," my dad said to me. "Think about what I said."

I waved goodbye as they pulled away, then I headed inside

the fabric shop. Giovanni was at the cutting table, measuring silk for a mother and young daughter. He nodded at me and kept working. I climbed the stairs to my apartment and checked for messages. Still nothing from Vaughn. Stinging from my dad's critical advice, I stopped myself from texting Vaughn a third time. He was dealing with his business; I had to deal with mine.

I ordered two turkey sandwiches to be delivered from Earl of Sandwich and returned downstairs. Giovanni was at the button wall with his customer, and the little girl was on the floor, playing with the cats. I left a twenty-dollar bill tucked under the corner of the register with a Post-It that said *for food delivery. Food + tip.* I got a cart from the back room and went outside to tackle the inventory in the van.

Thanks to a combination of gravity and determination, unloading the van was an easier task than loading it had been. It took three trips with carts loaded to capacity to finish the task, and I left the bolts of fabric on their respective carts to be dealt with later. Giovanni, with a sixth sense that kept him from menial labor, found me in the stockroom when the job was all done.

"I'm surprised you haven't hired someone to do that for you," he said.

"Is this a conspiracy?"

Confusion shrouded his face. "This is a business. The boss does what the boss does best and hires out everything else."

"I'm perfectly capable of unloading fabric from a van."

"How much is your time worth?" he asked, his arms crossed over his chest. When I didn't answer him immediately, he asked, "You *do* pay yourself a salary, don't you?"

"I pay my living expenses, and the rest goes back into the shop."

Giovanni shook his head. "Let's assume for a moment you pay yourself what I paid you to be the workroom manager. You produced a portfolio of fresh designs every month. You wrote the schedule for the seamstresses. You negotiated with fabric and trim vendors on my behalf."

"I dealt with staff complaints about upper management."

Giovanni ignored that. "Now I ask you. How would it feel to learn I paid my sixteen-year-old stock boy the same salary I paid you?"

"But you didn't."

"Exactly. Because stock work doesn't require the same skill set or education as lead designer or workroom manager. When you do the grunt work, you equate it with the pressures of overseeing the business. Why are you trading on your valuable experience like that?"

"The work needs to be done."

"You don't need to be the one to do it."

"But I *can* do it."

"You miss my point."

We were interrupted by the lunch delivery. I paid the deliveryman and handed Giovanni a sandwich. "Don't spoil your appetite. You're getting dinner at the Waverly House when we close."

"Not tonight," Giovanni said. "I have to get back to Los Angeles to handle a few things." He grabbed the sandwich. "Thanks for lunch."

I worked out front while Giovanni ate in the stockroom. He'd cleared the cutting station and placed bolts of fabric in a shopping cart to be returned to their rightful displays in the store. I handled that task between customers. By the time he came back out front, I'd added two more sales to the tally. I ran the figures and was impressed to see we'd exceeded my daily sales goal, and we still had hours of business remaining before I closed for the day.

The rest of the day was quiet from a customer standpoint. I showed Giovanni the wool I'd retrieved from the Villamere, and he was suitably impressed with both the quality and quantity.

"Wait here," he said. He went out the back door and returned with an arm full of large white binders. He set them on the suit display table and opened one. Inside were sketches of suit components: lapels, vents, cuff details, and buttonholes. Behind each page were plastic pockets containing neatly folded pattern pieces.

"Are these from your uncle's suit shop?"

"Yes. You're not the only one who inherited something of value."

"Can I make copies?"

"I already did. Those are yours. You might want to make notes on the pattern pieces. The notes are your version of shorthand. They don't have to make sense to anybody other than you. Pattern pieces don't last forever, so you'll just make a new set for the next person. Try not to press as hard as you do when you write. You'll damage the paper."

"I don't press hard when I write."

"Please. You left your notepad on the passenger seat of my van. I could practically read the writing from the indentation on the next page."

I stared at Giovanni. He didn't know he'd just said something important. I left him standing at the suit station and went to his van. I peered through the windows and looked for the notepad, but it wasn't there. When I came back in, Giovanni was where I'd left him.

"What did you do with it?" I asked, my voice lodged in my throat. "The notepad."

"I put it in the drawer under your register."

I raced across the shop. My soles skidded against the polished concrete floor the same way Needles had when he'd greeted my dad, but the wrap stand broke my forward momentum and kept me from falling. I yanked the drawer open and pulled out the legal pad then angled it under the light. As expected, Giovanni had exaggerated about the ease with which he'd read what was written there, but he wasn't lying outright. The indentations of words were faint on the fresh page. I rooted around inside my drawer for a pencil—handy for making cut marks on light fabric when chalk wouldn't show up—and I shaded the page with broad diagonal strokes from the side of the pencil tip.

I revealed two columns of notes: names and inheritances from the Villamere will. At the bottom of the page were additional notes: *felony charges* and *Josephine Barkley* with three question marks behind it. I set the tablet down and looked at Giovanni, who had less of an idea of what it meant than I did.

Giovanni pointed at the page. "Something else is written at the bottom."

I picked up the pencil and shaded over the rest of the page. *Inheritance contested by Wallis Wilson at historical society. Claims another will.*

"That doesn't look like your handwriting," Giovanni said.

"It's not."

"Then whose is it?"

"I don't know. This needs to go to Sheriff Clark." I tapped the page. "I think it might be connected to the murder."

19

GIOVANNI DIDN'T STICK AROUND TO HEAR HOW THAT conversation went with Sheriff Clark. Whatever business he had to deal with back in Los Angeles couldn't wait. He wished me luck and left with a promise to return the next day. Giovanni's interest in my shop seemed to be centered around the suit project. I welcomed his help, but I was pretty sure there was more to him showing up than the usual tit for tat. It was almost as if he was avoiding his own store.

On top of everything else, I needed to know what was up with To The Nines. I was hesitant to build my new business idea around Giovanni's expertise if there was a chance he would leave me in the lurch when his problems resolved.

I pushed thoughts of Giovanni's suspicious generosity aside and called the sheriff's mobile unit. Etta fielded the call.

"Sheriff Clark isn't here." In the background, I heard a file cabinet door slam shut. "The local high school is having a career assembly, and he's talking to the students about a career in law enforcement. He's coming back after it's done to catch up on paperwork tonight. If you drop something off, I'll make sure he sees it."

I stared at the legal pad. Now that I'd decimated the page with my pencil rubbing, it needed context. "I'll come to the mobile unit after I close today."

The rest of the day passed slowly. About an hour before closing, my cell pinged with a text message from my dad. *Found it!*

A second text pinged through. It was a blurry photo of a cork board at Gnarly Waves. The borders of the board were decorated with wavy blue paper, and the center of the board held cut-out words that read EMPLOYEE COMMENDATIONS. Cut-out water drops had been thumbtacked to the cork, each one featuring a compliment from a pool member about one of the lifeguards. The compliments were all written in the same handwriting, which pointed to the manager having written them up. In the center of the snapshot was a compliment that read, "John Monroe is an asset to this pool!" The compliment was attributed to Josephine Barkley.

Not for the first time, something about the identity of the Villamere heir seemed hinky. Josephine Barkley hadn't attended the reading of the will on Monday, and to the residents of San Ladrón and neighboring counties, that will reading had been the most exciting event to take place all year. My dad's first-person account of the conversation between Laurence and Reginald Villamere by the side of the pool might have been easy to dismiss if it came from anyone other than him, and this photographic proof showed me that at least in one scenario, the men had trotted out their imaginary friend to convey information. And now, a multi-million-dollar estate had been left to her, a possibly fictional woman.

Why would Reginald Villamere do that? Was Josephine

Barkley his secret love child? A pseudonym? Some other relation?

Josephine Barkley's name wasn't the only questionable piece of information on the legal pad. I pushed my suspicions about the heiress aside. What would it mean if Wallis Wilson contested the will?

I needed to talk about this. The second the clock hit six, I called Vaughn.

"Hey," he answered. "Sorry I haven't called you back. I spent most of today on the road."

"Did you find Josephine Barkley?"

"Yes. She's at Reginald Villamere's house now."

"You found her? You met her?"

"She rode back with me. Why?"

"Where are you?"

"The Waverly House. What's with all the questions, Poly?"

Something didn't jibe. I glanced at the legal pad. Somebody had been researching something related to the Villamere estate, but I still wasn't sure which way these notes pointed. This was the first mention of felony charges, and the question marks behind Josephine's name suggested I wasn't the only one who wanted answers about her identity.

The notes also mentioned the historical society and another will. Maybe no one else would consider a scribble at the bottom of a forgotten legal tablet an implication, but I'd seen another will. Vaughn and I both had. Yet since then, not a soul had mentioned it.

"I told Sheriff Clark I was bringing him something, but I'd like to show it to you first. Wait there. I'll be over in five minutes."

I climbed my steps and fed the cats, then grabbed my

handbag and called Genevieve to cancel our standing after-work dinner.

"It's Poly. I'm headed to the Waverly House instead of Duke's."

"Great idea! I'll tell Charlie."

"No, Gen, that's not what I meant." My protest fell on deaf ears. She'd already disconnected.

I called Vaughn back. "Charlie and Genevieve are headed over too."

"Great. Tiki Tom just walked in. It's turning into a party. I'll tell Chef to leave the kitchen open."

My hopes that I'd have an opportunity to grill Vaughn about his day dissolved like a scoop of Marshmallow Fluff in a mug of Clark's hot chocolate. I put the yellow legal pad in a discreet plastic bag and left. By the time I arrived at the Waverly House, the dining room was crowded with fellow Bonita Avenue business owners.

I looked around the room. It was a gathering of friends, neighbors, people who defined San Ladrón thanks to their independent businesses. We'd repeated this routine, this meet-up in the dining room of the Waverly House many, many times before, but what no one was saying was that tonight, it was different. There was a killer in San Ladrón and nobody knew who or what they wanted. The murder could be tied to a disgruntled employee of the theater, or a passed-over connection to Reginald Villamere's past. It could have been brought on by the lawyers, some old case that had a less-than-satisfying resolution. Considering the disparate possibilities left me feeling anxious, not settled.

I wedged myself into an empty seat between Genevieve and Vaughn. "Where's Charlie?"

"She got a better offer," Genevieve said. "She's across the street with Clark. I think they're on again."

"They seemed to find some common ground last night at the Villamere," I said.

Genevieve excused herself to go to the ladies' room, leaving Vaughn and me alone at the table.

"When did you go back to the Villamere?" he asked.

"Wednesday. It wasn't planned. Charlie was at my place for dinner. Genevieve sent Clark over to give us a ride."

"Why did you need a ride?"

"There was wine involved."

Vaughn chuckled.

"I caught Charlie and Clark cozied up in an empty theater, so I left them alone and checked out the projection booth."

"They just let you in there?"

"I didn't ask permission."

"And did you find anything?"

"Just Laurence's handkerchief." I paused, embarrassed by this next part. "Devontay, the acting theater manager, caught me in the act."

Vaughn laughed out loud this time. "I give you credit for trying."

I switched gears. "Let's talk about your day. You said you located Josephine Barkley?"

"Maybe we should talk about that later too."

I dropped my voice so low it was barely above a whisper. I put my lips close to Vaughn's ear to ensure nobody else could hear us. "Josephine Barkley isn't real."

"She wasn't a figment of my imagination."

I remembered again the surprise I'd felt when my dad told me about his days working at the local pool, and I rushed to share this new information with Vaughn. "My dad was a lifeguard at Gnarly Waves when he was a teenager. He overheard Reginald Villamere and Laurence Thibodeaux talking about how much easier their lives would be if they invented a companion. A fictional woman wouldn't show up at the will reading—"

Vaughn sat back and smiled. "You're as bad as the conspiracy theorists I met earlier today. Ms. Barkley didn't show at the will reading because she didn't *know* about the will reading. When I introduced myself and told her why I was there, she was shocked."

I continued as if Vaughn hadn't interrupted me. "They said she could be an assistant, or an ex-wife or girlfriend, or an employee. And later that day, Laurence told my dad's boss that Josephine Barkley had praised his job performance. The manager wrote up the compliment and tacked it on the bulletin board."

"It sounds like the men knew your dad was eavesdropping and decided to have some fun at his expense."

"Then tell me. What's this woman's connection to Reginald Villamere? Why did he leave her his estate?"

"It's not on him to explain his whims, and it's not on her to know."

"Yes, but she inherited a multi-million-dollar estate. Did that surprise her? That's a lot of money. She obviously didn't know he died, or she would have attended the reading. How did she react when you told her?"

"I didn't tell her. There are a couple of steps between tracking her down and cutting her a seven-figure check. I told her I was the executor of the Villamere estate and that she was named in the will. I asked if she was able to come to San Ladrón with me. She's meeting with Bozer and Schmidt tomorrow to start the process, but in cases like this where there's a lot of money involved, a transfer of the estate won't happen quickly."

I leaned in closer. "Have you seen Wallis today?"

"My mom said she was in earlier. Why?"

I kept my voice low. "Did you tell anybody about the will we found at Laurence's apartment?"

He shook his head.

"Wallis says there's a more recent version of the will. You're the executor. Did you hear anything about that?"

"I've been on the road all day." He glanced around the table. "I left word at the office that unless something urgent came up, I'd handle it tomorrow. How'd you hear about it?"

The impromptu party swirled around us, letting Vaughn and I share our findings without attracting attention.

I pulled the legal pad out of the plastic bag and handed it to Vaughn. "One of the ushers found this in the Villamere stockroom where my fabric is. He thought it was the one I made notes on, but that one wasn't legal sized. You might need more light to read it, but it says right there that Wallis contested the will."

Vaughn picked up a small tea light candle from the table and held it above the page for illumination. "It could be a stall tactic. There's nothing to indicate the will we saw at Laurence Thibodeaux's apartment is real. Right now, we're working on the assumption that the only will is the one from the nineties. Very few people knew where I went today or why I went there. If Wallis wants to put up a fight about the Villamere, she might slow down proceedings with accusations and claims, but that doesn't mean she's going to be successful. If there was another will, the legal team would know. Maybe one of them did. Maybe he was killed to keep that other will a secret."

20

Vaughn returned his attention to the tablet and scanned the rest of the page. "It also says something on here about felony charges. Any idea who that refers to?"

"No," I said.

"Have you shown this to Clark?"

"Clark wasn't available when I called to tell him. Giovanni was with me when I revealed the writing."

Genevieve came back to the table, and Vaughn gave the tablet back to me. I jammed it into my tote and pushed it under my chair.

"Did you order?" she asked. "I just passed the kitchen and saw Chef making the most incredible pot of lobster mac and cheese. I can't possibly eat it all by myself. Anybody want to split?"

Our conversation was put on hold while Vaughn gestured to a waiter. We went around the table placing our orders. The rich mac and cheese was accompanied by three orders for steak frites and two for sautéed spinach. The bartender sent over an open bottle of red Sancerre, less well known than its white counterpart, which was light and bright and made the perfect counterpoint to the rich meal.

Genevieve ordered a dish of guava gelato for dessert, and Vaughn and I opted for Vietnamese coffees in lieu of dessert. The layered beverage consisted of sweetened, condensed milk on the bottom, espresso in the middle, and a layer of foam on top.

"You two are going to regret that," Genevieve said. "Caffeine at dinner keeps me up all night."

Vaughn and I glanced at each other. He pressed his lips into a forced smile. I wasn't planning to sleep anytime soon, and it seemed as if he shared that thought.

As the after-work dinner wound down, Adelaide breezed into the dining room. She was dressed in a light wool suit and floral blouse, a more businesslike appearance than she usually favored. She came over to our table, and Vaughn rose to greet her with a kiss.

"Hello, everyone. Did I know you were coming tonight?"

"No, this was a spontaneous decision," Vaughn said. "I planned to surprise you, but someone said you went out to dinner with a friend."

"Friends, and we didn't go out, we dined in a private room. Don't sound so suspicious. The Waverly House gets plenty of my time and attention."

"Who were the friends? Anybody we know?" I asked.

Vaughn cast me a quick glance.

If Adelaide thought there was anything suspicious about my question, she didn't say so. "Two. Laurence Thibodeaux and Wallis Wilson. I've known both for decades, and I thought they should meet."

Genevieve surprised me by speaking up. "Wallis runs the historical society, doesn't she? She came into Tea Totalers earlier today. Did you know she worked for Henry Kissinger?"

"Wallis has a colorful past, that is true," Adelaide said. "She was the most driven of my acquaintances. Always had her eye on what was next."

"And now instead of looking at what's next, she's in charge of what was," I said.

"Don't let her involvement at the Historical Society fool you, Poly. Wallis has made big moves for them in a short amount of time. There are some people in this town who considered tearing down the glorious Art Deco apartment buildings that give San Ladrón its style, but she put an end to those inquiries with an architectural oversight committee. The Waverly House used to be an independent property, yes, but she petitioned for our acquisition. She made a compelling case, too."

"I don't understand that decision," I said. "The Waverly House has been the crown jewel of San Ladrón for a very long time. People come from all over to have their dedicated events here, and the annual garden party gets national attention. Why would you want to get folded into the historical society's holdings?"

"It's become increasingly difficult to rely on donations and rental income to cover our expenses. The Historical Society guarantees that we will be operational for decades to come regardless of who is at the helm."

"Mom, you're not planning on retiring, are you?" Vaughn asked.

"No, dear. The Waverly is in my blood. But that doesn't mean I can't minimize my hours and start looking for a replacement to train. No matter how much I love this place, I'm certain of one thing. I'm not going to live forever."

I sat quietly, trying to figure out how to steer the conversation away from the Waverly House's future and onto the details of Adelaide's lunch, but Genevieve, who didn't know I was ferreting out information, was eager to chat with Adelaide about a tea collaboration.

My phone pinged with a text from Vaughn. *Call me*

I looked at him across the table. He nodded. I pressed his name on my speed dial and his phone rang. He swiped to answer and listened. "Now?" he said. "Sure. Give me twenty minutes." He disconnected. "Sorry, Mom, I have to go to the office."

"I suppose Poly has to go with you?" Adelaide asked with a twinkle in her eye.

"That's right."

I hopped up and grabbed my bag. "Genevieve?"

She waved me off. "Don't worry about me. I'm a businesswoman with a captive audience. I'm not leaving until Adelaide gives me a yes." She glanced at Adelaide, probably checking to make sure she hadn't overstepped her boundaries. Genevieve's cheeks were flushed pink. It would be near impossible to say no to her when she looked as angelic as she did now. Adelaide smiled, and Genevieve's smile grew wider. "See you two at the film festival tomorrow night!"

We were halfway to the exit when Adelaide called after us. "Poly, you can hang up on my son now."

Busted.

Once Vaughn and I were outside, we did a bit of negotiating.

"Clark should see the notepad," I said.

"The notepad implicates my mom's friend."

"If your mom's friend has something to do with a murder, don't you want Clark to be on board?"

"You don't think Wallis Wilson killed the lawyer, do you? She's on the board of half a dozen companies between here and Los Angeles. She's not a murderer."

"She worked for the government."

"What does that mean?"

I waved him off. "I don't know. Something shady. She probably knows who killed Kennedy."

Vaughn laughed. "You'd *definitely* like those conspiracy theorists I met today."

Over the past year, I'd made myself a slight nuisance at the sheriff's office. It was the same reason he still took my calls. When I found evidence related to a crime, I took it to Sheriff Clark. That ended up being the winning chip in deciding where we went next. That and the fact that the sheriff's mobile unit was right across the street.

When we entered the sheriff's unit, we found Clark and Charlie playing cards at Etta's desk. Two towers of colorful poker chips sat in front of Clark, and two green poker chips sat in front of Charlie. A messy pile of chips sat between them.

"I'd ask who's winning, but the answer seems obvious," Vaughn said.

Charlie looked up at us. "I'm letting him get comfortable with a new power dynamic. I'll win it back before we're done playing."

"You keep saying that," Clark said.

"You might be done playing now." I pulled the legal pad out from the plastic bag I'd carried it in and handed it to Clark. "I found this in the stockroom at the Villamere. I thought it was the one I'd used to make notes about my fabric, but somebody else used it."

Clark took the tablet and scanned the page. "Who did this?"

"The pencil? That was me."

"If this turns out to be evidence of anything, it's now inadmissible."

"Why?"

"Chain of custody."

"You sound like a lawyer."

"What do you think happens to the cases we solve? They go to the district attorney's office. They won't prosecute unless they know they'll win. A confession works. So does a smoking gun. But a notepad that was in a public place, that shows—what?—evidence that somebody wrote something on a now-missing page, that's no smoking gun."

"It could mean something. Those notes—"

"You could have made them yourself and torn off the page."

"But I didn't. It's not my handwriting."

"The tablet was in your possession."

"Because it was in the stockroom with the fabric that I was told I had to pick up today."

Our conversation was interrupted by the door banging open. Mike Bozer, of Bozer and Schmidt, stumbled in. His face was bruised, and one of his eyes was rapidly swelling shut. A trickle of blood ran down his forehead. He clutched a small black revolver in his left hand.

"I need to report a shooting," he said then collapsed on the wooden floor.

21

Mike Bozer lay motionless on the floor. His left arm was splayed out with the pistol in his hand, and his right arm was trapped under his body. His blazer was torn by the shoulder seam. His fingers were clean and pink.

Clark bent down and checked the lawyer's pulse at his wrist. "He's alive. Poly, call an ambulance. Vaughn, help me move him to the cot in the cage." Clark pried the pistol from Mike's fingers and set it on his desk.

Mike stirred. He rolled over and pushed himself up to a sitting position. He turned and leaned against the base of Clark's desk. His breathing was labored. Whatever had happened, he looked as if he'd barely made it out alive.

He held up both hands. "I'm okay," he said.

"You don't look okay," I said.

I glanced at Clark. He nodded at me. I called the hospital, relaying the need for an EMT at the sheriff's office. Vaughn and Clark helped Mike move to a chair. Clark handed him a paper cup of water from the cooler in the corner.

"What happened?" Clark asked.

"I was jumped outside my office. Someone was waiting for me. I think I shot him." He looked away from Clark and stared at his shoes.

"Walk me through your night."

Bozer took a moment before speaking. "I was the last person to leave the office. My car was at the edge of the lot. I thought I saw somebody in the shadows, so I pulled out my gun."

"Do you have a permit for that?" Clark asked.

Bozer nodded. "Safety precaution. People don't like lawyers." He allowed a wry laugh. "I guess you know that already."

"What next?"

"I reached my car. He came up from behind and knocked me down. I remember pointing behind me and pulling the trigger before I hit my head on the bumper. I tried to stand, but he hit me again. Everything went black. I don't think I was out long, but it was long enough for him to get out of there."

"Did you get a look at him?"

Mike shook his head. "He had on one of those ski masks." He moved his hand up and down by his face, as if to indicate the mask's coverage. "Black knit. Only showed his eyes and nose."

"Did you notice anything else about him? Skin color, tattoos, shoes?"

"No. White sneakers, maybe. It was dark out. I wasn't paying attention to the lot. I was checking my email on my phone."

"While you were carrying your gun?" I asked.

All faces turned to mine. Clark's expression indicated a mix of what-are-you-still-doing-here and stay-out-of-this.

"How'd you get here?" Clark asked Bozer, not pressing him to answer what I thought was an astute question.

"I drove," Bozer said. "I think there's something wrong with my car. The steering felt funny."

Sheriff Clark nodded along with Mike's narrative. Vaughn returned from the men's room with a handful of damp paper towels that he handed to the lawyer, who pressed them to his forehead.

The front door opened, and a man in a blue windbreaker strode in with a medical kit. He looked at us. I pointed at Mike, but Clark waved the man to him. They conversed briefly, and Clark left the EMT and approached us.

"Show's over," Clark said. "Mr. Bozer is going to the hospital to make sure he doesn't have a concussion. I'm headed to his offices to check out the lot to see if there's any evidence. You have to leave."

"Aren't you going to follow up on that potential shooting victim?" I asked. "Maybe call the hospital and see if anybody with a flesh wound came to the ER?"

Clark glared at me. After an uncomfortable number of seconds, he shifted his attention to Charlie. She was the only one of us who hadn't jumped to attention when Mike burst through the doors.

She laid her poker hand on the table. "Full house." She corralled the messy pile of chips to her side of the desk. "Looks like it's not your night, Sheriff."

I tried to press Sheriff Clark into keeping me in the loop, but he was distracted. The three of us headed to the door. Clark asked Charlie to stay behind. I assumed it had something to do with the number of poker chips she'd just claimed.

Vaughn and I stepped into the cool evening air. The sky was a deep shade of midnight blue dotted with stars. The streets were mostly empty, the sign of a small-town ecosystem having wound down for the night. An ambulance was parked alongside the curb with lights flashing. An older man and woman watched us from the corner—possibly their evening walk was interrupted by some unexpected excitement, or possibly they were doing reconnaissance for their next Senior Patrol meeting. If anybody from our dinner was still at the Waverly House, it was a matter of time before they came out to investigate the scene too.

Charlie joined us. "Clark wants me to tow Bozer's car to my auto shop and give it a once-over. You guys calling it a night?"

"In a minute," Vaughn said. He turned to me. "Who told you that you had to pick up your fabric today?"

"Mike Bozer," I said. "He and his legal assistant came to my shop yesterday. They said I had forty-eight hours to claim my inheritance."

"That's not true," Vaughn said. "The Villamere might ask you to remove your inheritance, but there's no rush from a legal angle."

"Then why would they give me a deadline?" I asked, my radar on alert.

"Bozer's team probably wants to wrap this up," Charlie said. "If somebody murdered a mechanic, I'd feel the same way. Right now it looks like open season on lawyers."

From the moment we'd discovered Ben Schaffley's body at the theater, I'd assumed the murder was connected to the Villamere estate. It seemed like too much of a coincidence that someone had been murdered at that location twenty-four hours after the will had been read, and I couldn't imagine that the two acts weren't related. But this attack on a second named partner at the law firm shed a different light on things. Was it possible that Ben Schaffley's murder had nothing to do with the Villamere will, and the theater had merely been a convenient location for a crime?

The yellow legal pad with the potentially incriminating transfer of writing that I'd brought for Clark still sat on his desk. If Bozer hadn't stumbled into the sheriff's office when he did, Clark might have met that clue with more enthusiasm, but now, even I wasn't sure if it meant anything. I also hadn't had a chance to tell him what my dad said about Josephine Barkley, but according to Vaughn, Josephine Barkley not only existed but was currently holed up at Reginald Villamere's house. The arrows that had previously pointed one way now looked like a tangle of conflicting directions.

Charlie headed to her shop on foot. Vaughn and I matched strides on the walk to Vaughn's car in the Waverly House parking lot. At five foot nine inches, I was taller than most of my friends, but Vaughn was a few inches taller than I was, and it felt good to temporarily shed the self-consciousness I sometimes felt about my height.

It also felt good to stretch my legs. My ankle was fully recovered, and I walked with confidence—or as much confidence as a lifelong klutz can muster. Working in the store used a certain set of muscles, those involved in standing or walking short distances in quick bursts, or lifting bolts of fabric and carrying them to the cutting table. But unless I made an effort to complete laps of the shop's perimeter between customers—which I'd tried a few months ago when I was obsessed with getting in ten thousand steps a day—my job provided minimal daily exercise.

"Do you want to come to the shop?" I asked Vaughn. "Giovanni brought suit pattern pieces so you can make your selections."

"To be honest, I spent six hours in a car, and I'm looking forward to a thirty-minute-long shower."

"Haven't you heard? California's had a water shortage for the past decade."

"I won't tell the governor if you won't." He pantomimed pleading with me.

I pinched my nose. "I suppose you're due."

"I'm going to be tied up in meetings all day tomorrow, but about the film festival at the Villamere on Saturday—do you want to attend together?"

"Absolutely. What time does it start?"

"The doors open at five thirty. The reception starts at six. I don't know what your store hours look like, but there's a contest for best-dressed at six thirty that might be fun if you can make it." He glanced at me from under his long eyelashes, and I smiled.

"I'm looking forward to seeing how San Ladrón cleans up. I close the store at five on Saturday. That'll give me half an hour to get ready before you pick me up at six."

"You can get ready in half an hour?"

"Standing on my head."

"Impressive."

I got into Vaughn's car, and he drove me the short distance home. His normally clean Mercedes showed signs of his road trip: empty water bottles and coffee cups, a takeout bag from In-N-Out. I moved a newspaper called *Spicy Acorn* from the front seat to the back and smiled to myself at the atypical mess but didn't say a word.

———

THE NEXT MORNING, I was on my own. Fridays could be hit or miss when it came to sales. Sometimes people wanted to spend their weekend working on a project, and that meant procuring their materials ahead of time. I'd already called in all the favors I could, so once I opened, there would be no running around town sleuthing until closing time.

After I completed my store-opening ritual, I checked my email. A newsletter about the film festival, sent from the Villamere Theater, was at the top of my inbox. The communication didn't surprise me. San Ladrón's relative proximity to Hollywood made it easy for the theater to get the word out through a network of lovers of classic films, and the news story surrounding Reginald Villamere's estate had gone national. I expected tomorrow night's reception at the theater to be full of hipsters who didn't care about the reception or the fashion show but were there for the venue. The future of the theater was still in question, and depending on what happened next, this might be their last chance to patronize the place.

Another email from the theater came in while I was reading the first. It was from Devontay, asking if I'd allow them to use some of the fabric in the storage closet for the night. I replied by pointing out that until the will was fully executed, the fabric still belonged to them, but it was fine by me, then I added a P.S. *Please don't use the wool!*

Sales were intermittent, and between customers, I kept myself occupied with my suit idea. I'd initially thought I could set it up at the front of the store, but Giovanni had put the kibosh on that idea. *Women like to think they're getting something other women approve of. Men like to think they're in charge.* It was my default to correct Giovanni when he made blanket statements that showed off his misogyny, but maybe he had a point about this. I already had orders for four custom suits, and each one had been easy. Vaughn, Tiki Tom, Mike Bozer—each had verbally committed to an order based on the idea alone. They hadn't needed a sales pitch. Even Charlie had jumped at the idea, though when it came to her habits, she was in a category of her own.

Charlie might be in a category of her own, but I called her anyway. Her apparent reconciliation with Clark had kept her from showing up on my doorstep as often as usual, and I was curious about what she'd found when she inspected Mike Bozer's car. There was a fifty-fifty chance she would answer.

"Yo, Polyester. 'Sup?"

"Have you heard from Clark?"

"Not since last night. You have plans tonight?"

"Nope."

"Stay where you are. I'll be there in five."

While I waited for Charlie, I started a list of ideas to get the word out about my new business idea. It wasn't an easy task to woo a person in the market for a custom suit to enter a fabric store, especially one called Material Girl, but not easy wasn't the same as impossible. I'd need to plan events. What kind? Maybe a bourbon tasting. I could partner with Duke and the Broadside Tavern. I turned around and stared at the interior of my shop. It was a big warehouse space, walls lined with bolts of fabric, large wooden tables loaded with different fabrics taking up the middle. A few cutting stations and the register area. No matter what event I came up with, once people walked in, it would be a challenge to make them forget they were in anything other than a fabric store.

By the time Charlie arrived at my door, I'd filled a fresh notepad with ideas about how to create a men's club—in style, not in exclusionary practices—in a cordoned-off corner of my shop. The key would be to incentivize prospective customers to walk in my doors.

Charlie's arrival pierced the solitude of my thoughts with a bang of my gate and heavy footsteps across my floor. Under her motorcycle jacket she wore a deconstructed sweater, and long strands of yarn hung down from the hem. The cats materialized out of nowhere and trailed her like she was the Pied Piper, occasionally hopping up and trying to swat at what must have looked to them like a tail.

"Brought you a present." She pulled a file folder out from the back of her waistband and extended it to me.

"What is it?"

"Ben Schaffley's file from the forensic lab."

22

"You stole case notes from Clark?" I asked, pushing them back toward her.

"Not stolen. Copied." Charlie hoisted herself up on my wrap stand and kicked her heels against the white laminate exterior. Smudges of black transferred onto the surface next to handprints from kids who had accompanied their parents. It was time to clean.

"Charlie..."

"You want to know the cause of death or not?" She hopped down and squatted by the cats, greeting them in turn. "The contents of that file are a matter of public record. They came from the public records office. The name of the office itself implies I broke no rules, though they probably charge a per-page copying fee. If it soothes your conscience, I'll slide a couple of bucks under their door."

"Does Clark know you have this?" I asked Charlie, flapping the thick folder under her nose.

"How do you think that conversation would go? 'Hi,

Ryan, want to chat about the autopsy reports over hot chocolate?'"

"I know Clark drinks hot chocolate, but you never seemed the type."

"I make mine Irish."

Charlie and I both knew I was going to read the file, so I wasted no more time. I flipped it open. The first page of many showed a cartoon drawing of a male body. Notes were handwritten alongside the rendering with an arrow pointing to the back of his head. *Blunt force trauma*, it said. *Possible weapon characteristics: heavy and flat. No identifying ridges.*

I scanned the rest of the document. It included Ben Schaffley's name, height, weight, and gender, description of his body, and any other identifiers. Under "Type of Death," two boxes were ticked: *Sudden When in Apparent Health* and *Found Dead.*

"What's it say?" Charlie asked.

"You didn't look?"

"No time."

"It says here Ben Schaffley was bonked on the head. Not poisoned, shot, or strangled."

"Spontaneous, heat-of-passion stuff."

"Not just spontaneous. It sounds like he had his back turned to his attacker. That lines up with what Bozer said, right? He said he was attacked from behind in the parking lot." I scanned the rest of the notes, but nothing jumped out at me. "I keep thinking I'm missing something. We're all missing something. If someone's targeting the named partners of the law firm, then Clark should look closer at their cases and employees."

"And put Schmidt of Schaffley, Bozer, and Schmidt under

protective custody," Charlie said. Needles meowed his agreement.

"Clark acted like Ben Schaffley's murder had something to do with the Villamere will. He even arrested Laurence Thibodeaux."

"He released him the next day."

"On bail. With Laurence agreeing to wear an ankle monitor to track his whereabouts. Laurence is free to come and go to a degree, but he's not out of the woods yet." I strummed my fingers on my lips. "I wish I could poke around the Villamere. Laurence Thibodeaux seems like a nice old man, but there must be something we're missing if Clark's keeping an eye on him."

"The Villamere is going to be hopping tomorrow night. The film festival is a good opportunity to snoop."

"Yes, but Clark's going to have eyes and ears on the crowd."

"I'll create a distraction. Leave Clark to me."

Needles jumped up on the wrap stand, and Charlie scratched his orange ears. While she was distracted, I reflected on the case notes again. The medical examiner's drawing indicated a wound at the back of Ben Schaffley's head. If you were facing someone, you wouldn't be able to hit them there. It was possible Ben hadn't even seen his killer before being struck.

I closed the file and set it next to Charlie. "Did you find anything odd with Mike Bozer's car?"

"Loose lug nuts on his back tires. Dent in the bumper. Nothing major."

"Is that what you told Clark?"

"Yeah. If the guy didn't look like he was jumped in a dark alley, I'd say a couple of local kids played a prank on him."

Business hours were over, and if I kept reading notes about a murder, I'd kill my appetite for dinner. I closed the gate out front and beckoned for Charlie to follow me upstairs. I put a pot of water on to boil and pulled a package of fresh pasta out of the fridge along with a container of frozen meatballs and sauce that I'd picked up at the farmer's market last week. I cooked up the pasta and tossed it with the red sauce then doled out two equally generous portions and carried them to the table. Charlie pulled hers close and speared a meatball with her fork.

"Why do you want a suit?" I asked, shifting gears to a more suitably dinner-appropriate topic.

"I don't have a suit."

"Yes, but you haven't seen the patterns, you haven't seen the fabric. Don't you want a consultation, or a review of your choices, before you commit?"

"I don't go in for that 'how can I help you' crap. I know what I want, and I get it. Life's a lot easier when you live that way."

"Yes, but where are you going to wear a suit?"

"Why does that matter?"

"I'm trying to understand my demographic. I thought it was about making men's suits, but you threw me off."

"Don't change your business model because of me. I'm an outlier."

"I don't think outliers are supposed to think of themselves as outliers."

"Your problem here is the same as your problem out there. You let the world dictate rules to you that you had no part writing. Why are custom suits for men? Why have you bought into that? Because some retailer saw a potential market opportunity and taught women to want something new every year. And why is that? Because women were bored. And why was that? Because women weren't allowed to have things like bank accounts and pockets."

"You know things have changed since women couldn't have... pockets."

"My point is your brain"—at this point she flicked my forehead—"has been wired by somebody else. You're on the verge of seeing it, but you're still playing by their rules."

"I already have four orders for custom suits, and all I've done is mention the idea to people. Vaughn, okay, I did sell him on the concept, but what do you, Tiki Tom, and Mike Bozer have in common?"

"We all know what we want?"

"But how do I use that to attract future business? Of the four orders I have, only two wear suits with any regularity, and they probably buy them at some suit store."

"Come at the idea a different way. Half of your customers find it preferable to get what they want instead of what somebody else has to offer. That's your hook. Freedom of choice. Market that. And don't give it a cutesy name like Suit Yourself. You'll chase your target market to Men's Warehouse."

"If it's about choices, then it's about letting the customer pick out exactly what they want. Tiki Tom is getting a suit with a Hawaiian-printed lining that he gets to select from my inventory and you... I don't know what you want, but I know you'll get it."

Charlie sat back in her chair. "Hallelujah, she sees the light. There's hope for you yet, Polyester."

THE NEXT MORNING, I rose early and made a hearty breakfast of eggs and rosemary potatoes and a cup of

Genevieve's lily bang tea. The normally cloying scent of lilies was a pale imitation of itself when dried into tea leaves, and it turned out to be a perfect counterpoint to the sharpness of the gunpowder blended with tea leaves. I ate my breakfast while Pins and Needles munched their can of salmon noisily next to me. The cats remained upstairs when I went down to open for business. Apparently, they were taking the weekend off.

As often happened when there was an event in town, business was slow. I spent the day neatening the shop after a week of robust business, returning bolts of fabric left next to the cutting station to their rightful display spaces, thankful that I'd already made my sales numbers for the week and didn't have to wish for Saturday shoppers with money to burn.

At around four thirty, Tiki Tom called into the store from the sidewalk. "Hey, Poly. Why are you still open?"

"I don't close until five."

"You must have missed the memo. The rest of us closed at four. Most everybody's getting ready for the big shindig at the Villamere tonight."

I met him at the door. "Are you going?"

"Nah, I'm headed to the South Bay for a surf guitar showcase." He looked to his right. "I just came by to loan you these mannequins." He stepped back, and I looked outside. Three male torso forms were lined up on the sidewalk next to him. "Eddie, Paul, and Dick at your service."

I wrapped my arms around the closest one and carried him into the store. "How'd you name them?"

"Eddie Bertrand, Paul Johnson, and Dick Dale. Three California surf music gods. I retrofitted each of them with Bluetooth speakers, so if you sync up your phone, you can play music through them."

"How do they feel about Motown?"

Tiki Tom shrugged. "Everybody needs a palate cleanser."

It took a couple of minutes to get the torsos inside the shop, and in that time, I confirmed what Tiki Tom had said. The street was empty, and an unusual number of parking spaces were vacant. The shop fronts across the street had Closed signs in their windows.

In a small town that relies on foot traffic, there exists a one-for-all and all-for-one mentality. A shopper who heads out for Hawaiian ephemera at Tiki Tom's might pick up some fabric from me and vice versa. Flowers in the Attic, the antique shop on the other side of Material Girl, attracted a similar customer base too. We cross-promoted each other's shops, and most store owners were up for event collaborations. I was a little miffed that no one had told me about the amended store hours today, but not enough to make a federal case of it.

I pulled the gate closed behind Tiki Tom and secured it, then headed upstairs to get ready for the night.

Most days, I wore black. What it didn't hide was the orange and gray cat hair that evaded my vacuum cleaner. I glanced down at my sweater and noticed little pieces of fur embedded in the weave. I tossed the sweater on a growing mound of black in a wicker basket in the corner. Laundry day was approaching.

I pulled on a vintage silk robe and flipped through garment bags in my closet until I reached the one I wanted. I lowered the zipper and pulled out a hanger with a black velvet blazer, a sheer black blouse with accordion-pleated collar, and wide-legged pants made from layers of black lace. I closed the door to the bedroom to keep the cats from having their way with the vintage fabrics, laid the garments on the bedspread, and then stripped off the rest of today's outfit.

The extra time from closing early allowed for a quick shower, which revived me considerably. By five twenty-five, I stood admiring the reflection of Aunt Millie's outfit in the full-length mirror. The pants would have been too long on most people, but not me. My feet weren't visible under the pants, but I slipped on a pair of vintage-inspired black pumps anyway. I adjusted the bow at my collar and smoothed the nap of the velvet blazer. I had just finished touching up my deep-ruby lipstick when my phone buzzed with a text from Vaughn announcing his arrival out front.

I tossed my essentials into a beaded handbag, kissed the cats goodbye, and went downstairs. Vaughn was at the back door. He wore a tuxedo—not vintage, but with all the necessary hallmarks of the era. He whistled when he saw me, and I felt heat climb my cheeks.

"All credit goes to Aunt Millie."

"Not all of it." Vaughn put his hands in a circle around my waist. "Not everybody could fit in those pants."

"Not everybody would want to," said Charlie, who I hadn't noticed at first. She followed her comment with a grin. "Just kidding, Polyester. You look good." She held her open palm out to Vaughn. "I'll drive. You two can cuddle in the back seat."

Vaughn's keys changed hands. Charlie strode away, and Vaughn turned back to me. "You don't mind if she comes with us, do you? She said she didn't want to walk in alone."

"She's never cared about that before. I wasn't even sure she was going to go."

"Maybe she's finally ready to be part of the San Ladrón community."

"I wouldn't go *too* far."

Vaughn guided me to his car. I climbed into the back, and Vaughn followed. Charlie, in rare fashion, drove at a respectable pace. Before long we arrived at the theater.

It had been smart to carpool. The parking lot was packed, with the closest spaces occupied by a row of vintage cars. Normally, car shows were filled with muscle cars from the fifties and sixties era, but tonight, a different era of automotive style was represented. Fat vehicles with curved lines and no apparent concerns about the difficulties of parallel parking occupied the row of spaces by the front door. I counted a taupe-and-ivory Bentley, two black Model As, and one cobalt-blue roadster that put me in mind of Nancy Drew.

Large spotlights were aimed into the sky, drawing attention to the theater. Villamere employees in their burgundy-and-gray uniforms attended to patrons as they arrived. A temporary valet stand had been set up in front of the theater next to a red carpet, but Charlie blew past it and parked in the farthest corner of the lot.

"You're here to observe, right?" she said as she turned the engine off. "Eyes on the prize, Polyester. Look at the big picture before you get too close to see what's right in front of your face."

I glanced at Vaughn, who was amused at Charlie doling out advice.

"Right," I said. "So far, I see a crowd of people who came out to see classic movies at a theater that may not be in business next month. A bigger crowd than I've ever seen here before. If we don't get in soon, we're going to miss the movies."

"Not to worry," Vaughn said. "When I heard about the sell-out crowd, I arranged for a private screening on Monday when the theater is closed to the public. Like Charlie said, tonight is about observation." He kissed the tip of my nose. "I didn't want you to miss the movies because you were busy... observing."

It wasn't the first time I'd benefited from Vaughn's largesse.

He had never been one to throw his money around, but there were occasions when his solutions to problems were ones I never would have considered.

"How much does something like that cost?"

"Poly…"

I held up my hands. "You're right. Not my concern. Thank you for making those arrangements."

We were far enough away that I could still take in the entirety of it: the theater marquee, the blinking bulbs that set off the name VILLAMERE THEATER, and the flurry of people entering the building. Half an hour ago, I couldn't wait to get here, find a seat, and take in the rare screening schedule, but with the movies rescheduled for Monday, new questions were cropping up.

"Why didn't you come with Clark?" I asked Charlie. "Did he find out about the file? He's not mad about you copying that file, is he?"

"Clark's on the payroll tonight. He'll be around."

As we neared the theater, I spotted the sheriff talking with an unfamiliar woman on the red carpet. "Clark's over there. Who's the woman?"

Charlie shrugged. "Probably some rando asking for directions to the bathroom."

Vaughn followed the direction I pointed. "That's not a rando. That's Josephine Barkley, Mr. Villamere's missing heir. Come on, I'll introduce you."

23

I wasn't going to pretend that, on some level, I hadn't been hoping for this very opportunity. On any agenda I might have mentally planned for the night, meeting Josephine Barkley would have jumped to the top. I'd observed every person involved in the inheritance of Reginald Villamere's estate save for one. I didn't know whether Ben Schaffley's murder had anything to do with the will, or whether he'd been killed over some other lawyerly thing, but my eyes and ears were open. And right now, I was about to make a new best friend.

Interestingly, Charlie remained by my side. The three of us cut through the crowd (against a not-small number of protests). Clark saw us, but he wore his poker face, and if he had thoughts about our approach, they didn't show in his expression.

"Vaughn, Poly, Charlie," Clark said in greeting. "I thought you would have gotten here early to reserve your seats."

"We're here for the costume contest," Charlie said.

"You aren't—" Clark said. He looked uncomfortable.

"I am," Charlie said confidently. I was getting a bad feeling about Charlie's agreeable nature tonight. Usually, she was a force of opposition, protesting for the sake of being contrary. Charlie had never met a rule she didn't rally against, and if she ever fought the law, she'd win. It hadn't led to a charmed life, but it was a life lived on her terms, and after everything she'd been through, that was how she wanted it.

Vaughn, sensing the moment called for a distraction, jumped in with the promised introduction. "Josephine, this is Charlie Brooks and Poly Monroe. Poly and Charlie, this is Josephine Barkley."

Up close, I had a better opportunity to assess the inheritor of the Villamere estate. The woman in question looked to be in her forties. Her hair was cut in a soft layered style that she'd tucked behind her ears. She wore gold button earrings and a black wool cape that cloaked the majority of her outfit underneath. Gold silk peeked out from under the cape, falling below her knees. There was nothing remarkable about her, but nothing threatening either. She could have been a CEO or the president of the PTA.

I extended my hand and shook Josephine's.

Charlie nodded and said, "You're probably the most popular woman in San Ladrón."

Josephine glanced at Vaughn. "They know who I am?"

"Your name was kept out of the media, but enough people were at the reading of the will to know who you are."

"Do you live around here?" I asked.

"No," she said. "I live in a small town outside of Las Vegas. I was as surprised to hear about Mr. Villamere's will as anybody."

"I doubt that," Charlie said under her breath.

"Charlie," Clark, Vaughn, and I all said at the same time.

"What? You were all thinking it." Charlie turned to Josephine. "What's your connection to Reginald Villamere? Uncle? Sugar daddy? Love child?"

"Charlie!" Clark, Vaughn, and I all said at the same time.

One of the ushers poked his head out the door and called for participants in the costume contest.

When he was finished and went back inside, Charlie picked up as if we hadn't been interrupted. "You're going to start a lot of rumors around here. These three are solid, so you don't have to worry about them, but if I were you, I'd watch out for everybody else. Now, if you'll excuse me, I have places to be. Be careful what you wish for, Sheriff. You just might get it." She blew Clark a kiss and left us to wonder what she was up to.

Clark had turned an unflattering shade of red. He hooked his finger into the collar of his uniform and tugged on the fabric. "I should have arrested her for something."

The longer Clark and Josephine stayed near Vaughn and me, the more I put together that for Clark, "working the event" meant staying close to the recently located, soon-to-be multi-millionaire. Even though the attack on Mike Bozer had redirected the focus of the case from the theater to the legal team, the theater was still a crime scene. No matter how festive the Villamere Theater appeared to be, a murder was at the center of the Villamere Affair—or maybe it wasn't the center. Maybe the murder was Villamere Affair-adjacent. If something about the will had led to the aggression against the lawyers, then anybody involved in the execution of the estate could be in danger.

That meant Vaughn was in danger, too. I glanced at him. He took my hand and held tight. Ah. It wasn't an accident that we'd run into Sheriff Clark. This chance run-in on the red carpet had been prearranged.

The lobby of the theater was considerably warmer than the red carpet outside thanks to the crowds of people now hovering around us. Tickets were being collected at the door, but once inside, people moved to either the concession stand or the bar. A separate bar had been set up along the wall by the high-tops, and a line of people dressed in a range of styles from jeans and Clippers T-shirts to vintage ensembles milled about. A couple of people had misjudged the era and represented the forties, fifties, and sixties.

"Does anybody want popcorn?" Vaughn asked. "Or a drink?"

"Give it a couple of minutes," Clark said. "The lines are ridiculous right now."

"I'll take some popcorn," I said.

Vaughn looked back and forth between Clark's and my faces. "I'm going in." Vaughn disappeared into the crowd.

In the parking lot, he had reminded me I was there to observe, so that was what I did. I scanned the crowd, picking out Maria and Big Joe Lopez, the co-owners of Lopez Donuts. Maria was resplendent in a simple silver-and-gold gown I'd made her when she was asked to judge a local beauty contest. Big Joe was wearing a suit and tie. Genevieve sat on a stool by the bar. She caught my eye and waved. At first I thought she was alone, until I spotted Duke in his wheelchair next to her and Sam, his regular bartender, mixing old fashioneds and pouring martinis behind the bar.

If the lobby was any indication, the event was a success. The ushers stayed busy, all hands on deck, and as people left the concession stand with their buckets of popcorn and boxes of candy, they headed toward the roped-off display of items from Reggie Villamere's personal collection of Hollywood memorabilia. A beaded and fringed dress was on a bust form next to a case that displayed a tiara, a cigarette holder, and an assortment of necklaces, bracelets, and rings. Next to that was a mounted movie poster on an easel, and next to that was another display case filled with scripts.

"Where did all of this come from?" I asked no one in particular.

Josephine answered. "The theater manager asked me to choose things from Reginald Villamere's house."

"You made the perfect choices. Costumes and posters and props. I wouldn't be surprised if some theaters in Hollywood ask for the display to go on loan to them. If they're rented out, that could mean more money."

Josephine looked uncomfortable. She held up her hands. "I'm not looking for more money."

"I meant for the theater. This whole event was planned to raise money—" I stopped right before saying "for a possible buyout" and said, "to keep it open."

"Why would anybody close the theater?" she asked.

"New ownership," I said gently. "You. A lot of people are waiting to see what you'll do with the Villamere. Have you given any thought to that?"

I didn't think it was possible for Josephine to look more out of place, but at this question, she did. Instead of answering me, she said, "Would you excuse me? I need to find a ladies' room." She disappeared into the crowd without waiting for an answer.

I glanced at Clark, unsure if he wanted me to follow her. His attention was on the landing above us. A row of twelve people stood on the platform. Each one held a number mounted on a stick, and each was wrapped in a large swath of curtain fabric from the stockroom. The last person in the line looked suspiciously like Charlie, but that couldn't be, because that would imply that Charlie was participating in an activity arranged by something that had to do with the San Ladrón community, and Charlie protected her status as outsider as if it were a rare and precious diamond.

Devontay, in his ill-fitting magenta blazer, took his place at the front of the landing and welcomed the crowd.

"We at the Villamere would like tonight to be a celebration of what Reginald Villamere brought to San Ladrón. From the moment he opened this theater in 1933, he brought glamour. I wasn't here at the time, but that's what I've heard." The crowd chuckled at this impromptu comment. "The staff thought it was fitting to kick off tonight's event with the glamour you brought with you."

He turned to the woman at the front of the line and nodded. She fumbled with the fabric wrapped around her. The man behind her took the edge, and she spun out of it, sending ripples of laughter through the crowd. She wore a long red bias-cut gown with handkerchief sleeves and a narrow empire waist. To descend the staircase safely, she held up her hem, revealing matching red suede shoes.

Polite applause met her descent and continued as the fellow behind her revealed a black cutaway tuxedo and spats. The third and fourth participants were women, one in a tea-length dress with a narrow belt, and the next wearing a navy-blue long-sleeved gown with a plunging back. A few more tuxedos followed.

And then there was Charlie.

I'd once seen a picture of her in her office. She was barely recognizable, dressed in a short white sailor's outfit, smiling broadly and saluting the camera. She'd brushed it off as having done some modeling in her younger years, and the image in the photo gave the impression that someone had set out to recreate famous pinup art—because the truth was, underneath the coveralls and motor oil, an edge of that pinup girl still lurked below Charlie's surface. Tonight it wasn't lurking; it was fully on display.

I didn't know how long ago the picture in her office had been taken, but the outfit still fit. Unlike the rest of the attendees in formal wear, Charlie's outfit was ninety percent skin. Her cropped white sailor top revealed her taut tummy above high-waisted shorts, both of which were trimmed in navy-blue piping and decorated with gold buttons. Her hair was swept off to the side, and a white sailor's cap was perched on her head. She wore her trademark dark-red lipstick and a pair of high, strappy red shoes. She had a round white Styrofoam life preserver tucked under her arm.

The crowd went wild. A combination of wolf whistles and applause met her descent. She stopped halfway down the staircase, looked directly at Clark, and winked.

If Clark was Superman, Charlie was his kryptonite. The whole scenario would have been hilarious—and would no doubt be talked about many, many, *many* times from here on out—but there was one thing nobody in the room appeared to be thinking about, and that was the whereabouts of Josephine Barkley. She'd excused herself to go to the ladies' room before the show had started, and she hadn't returned. And as fun as it was to watch Charlie's rare foray into the limelight, I had to make sure the heiress was okay.

With some strategic elbow use, I made my way through the crowd. When I entered the restroom, it was empty.

"Josephine?" I called. I walked past ten stalls, each with their doors partially open. "Are you in here?" I reached the last stall. The restroom was definitely empty.

I turned to leave and noticed a small white stick jutting out of the top of the trash bin. I moved closer and recognized it for what it was—a pregnancy test. Using a fresh paper towel, I grabbed the end of it and moved it to the edge of the sink. A plus sign showed in the indicator window.

The results were positive. I didn't know who would take a pregnancy test in a public restroom, but I strongly suspected one thing. Whoever it was didn't want the results to become public.

24

THE LAST THING I'D EXPECTED TO NEED TONIGHT was a plastic bag to secure a used pregnancy test until I could hand it off to Clark. I was standing immobile, trying to decide if it was evidence of anything, when two women came in. I threw a paper towel over the plastic stick and turned on a blast of water, and I washed my hands for well over the recommended two minutes advised by a sign on the wall while I waited for the women to lock themselves into stalls.

When I was alone again, I pulled out my phone and photographed the stick, making sure to get close enough to capture the indicator window, and then I gently set it back in the trash and took pictures of it there too. I buried it under several more paper towels, washed my hands again, and left in search of Clark. I was still missing one heiress.

The crowd in the lobby had thinned. I glanced to my right and saw a stream of people flowing toward the movie theaters. The scent of popcorn was impossible to ignore, and I hoped that, if nothing else, Vaughn had been successful in his trip to the concession stand.

I spotted him at a high-top near the memorabilia display and made my way toward him. Clark and Charlie weren't with him, which could have been either good or bad, neither of which pertained to the case.

I joined him. "You won't believe what I just found."

"I thought you went to the ladies' room. That was a cover story?"

"No. I went to the ladies' room. I found a pregnancy test." I paused for emphasis. "A *used* pregnancy test." I set my beaded handbag on the table and unsnapped the clasp.

"Poly, you didn't—"

"Have some faith." I pulled out my phone and enlarged the first of the photos I'd taken, then handed my phone to Vaughn. "There are about six pictures. The first one might be blurry. A couple of women came in, and I had to hurry." I looked around. "Where's Sheriff Clark? I'd like to show him and find out what he wants me to do."

Vaughn swiped through the photos and handed my phone back. "I hate to say this, but I don't think Clark is going to be interested. Don't get me wrong. I agree, it's suspicious timing. But there's no actual connection to Ben Schaffley's murder. This event is packed, and half of the attendees are women. That could belong to anybody."

The phrase "Ben Schaffley's murder" had the opposite effect of what Vaughn probably intended. "What if the lawyer slept with someone and got her pregnant? What if it wasn't consensual? What if she used the pregnancy to trap him? Extort him? Maybe his murder was blackmail gone wrong." I waved my phone around. "If we knew who took the test, we'd know *something*."

"You're forgetting the attack on his partner outside their law firm. How would that tie in? Besides, a pregnancy test tossed into a public trash can seems to indicate the taker doesn't want their identity known."

"It also suggests the test taker is here." I lowered my voice. "The scene of the crime."

"You could make an argument that the killer wouldn't risk returning to the scene of the crime."

"You could also make an argument that the killer thought a wide cross section of people would be here tonight and it would be easy to stay lost in a crowd. Maybe the killer left evidence behind and had to come back to try to retrieve it. Or they wanted to gloat about having gotten away with it." Once again, I glanced around the room. "Where is Sheriff Clark, anyway?"

"After the costume contest, he disappeared."

"With Charlie?"

"Sheriff Clark is a lot of things, but he's not the sort of law enforcement to abandon his job for a quickie in the projection booth."

"Vaughn!"

"You were thinking it," he said with a grin. "But no. He took Josephine back to Reginald's house. She's been overwhelmed by all of this. I don't know what her connection to Reginald Villamere is, but from the moment I located her, she was like a deer in the headlights. She wasn't expecting this level of attention, that's for sure."

I thought back to my brief meeting with Josephine. "Do you know how old she is?"

"Thirty-nine. I had to confirm her identity earlier today."

"That's not too old to get pregnant, is it?"

"You think Josephine Barkley is carrying Reginald Villamere's secret love child?" Vaughn waggled his eyebrows, something I'd never seen him do before. I tossed a piece of popcorn at him.

"When you put it like that, it does sound farfetched."

His expression turned pensive. "She *did* go to the restroom before she left."

I narrowed my eyes and gauged whether Vaughn was toying with me.

He held up both hands. "What? I'm trying to be objective about your theories."

One of my favorite reasons for spending time with Vaughn was the easy camaraderie we shared. Somehow, we never ran out of conversation. Aside from a couple of understandable false starts when I first moved to San Ladrón, we were usually on the same page.

Tonight was no different. With the importance of the pregnancy-test discovery temporarily sidelined, we were free to relax and enjoy the evening. I held our table while Vaughn had the concession stand refill our popcorn. Just because we wouldn't be watching the movies until Monday didn't mean we couldn't enjoy the rest of what the Villamere had to offer.

There was only one thing keeping me from completely relaxing, and that was opportunity. With Clark temporarily out of the building, my chance to snoop was now or never.

We weren't the only people who decided to skip the first movie, so while the crowd had thinned, it wasn't nonexistent. We put a hit on our popcorn while we watched visitors to San Ladrón circle through the exhibit, posing by costumes and posters for pictures for their social media feeds. Theater employees stayed busy keeping the lobby clean. About half an hour after the first movie started, Maria Lopez came out of the restroom and spotted us. Instead of heading toward the theater, she came our way. She put her hand on the back of her neck and massaged herself.

"It's a madhouse in the theater. We ended up in the front row. I'm going to have a stiff neck tomorrow."

My brow furrowed, and I looked at Vaughn. "Didn't you invite Maria and Big Joe to join us?"

Maria waved my question off before Vaughn had a chance to answer. "Of course he did. I appreciate the invitation, but we can't take a night off. Weeknights are when we prepare the donuts for the next day. We have about twenty standing delivery orders to fulfill before we even think about walk-in customers. Donuts are recession-proof." She looked embarrassed by this statement. "Sorry, I forgot you're a shop owner too. How's your business?"

"It's okay. I'm working on offering custom suits."

"Like blazers and pants?"

"Yes. Big Joe doesn't need a new suit, does he?" I asked hopefully. With height that put him literally head and shoulders above most crowds, Big Joe was a prime candidate for a custom suit.

"He bought his last suit from the Big and Tall department at JC Penney."

"And the boys?"

"Poly, you don't think I'd be foolish enough to order custom suits for two boys who grow an inch a day, do you?"

"I guess not."

"Is that why your old boss has been around lately?"

"Partially. Jun Wong helps me on Wednesdays, but she doesn't want to work on men's suits. Giovanni has experience making them. He brought me his pattern books, and he's been spending more time here." My voice trailed off as I thought about Giovanni. "I hate to say this, but I'm worried about him."

"What did he do?"

"He's been helpful."

Vaughn laughed. "I never worked for the man, but I know him well enough to understand why that raises your antennae."

Maria scooped a handful of popcorn out of our rapidly dwindling bucket. "If you're curious about his intentions, why not ask him?" She pointed across the lobby. "He's right over there."

I stared across the lobby. My old boss stood next to a young woman with his hand on the small of her back. She was shorter in stature. She asked him something, and when he nodded, she turned back to the concession counter and pointed at the candy boxes. The usher pulled out a box of Sno-Caps and set them next to a giant soda cup. Giovanni pulled out his wallet and handed the cashier a couple of bills then waved off his change.

In one transaction, I'd cataloged about seven behaviors that didn't fit Giovanni's profile. I watched from across the room as he guided the woman into the hallway. He held the theater door open for her, and she went in first. He looked side to side, as if checking to see if anyone was watching them, then followed her inside.

"What the heck was that?" I asked.

"Don't you mean who?"

"No, I mean what. What was that scene we just watched? Giovanni paid for something. He left a tip. He looked like he was on a date with a much, much, *much* younger woman."

"I hate to say this, but it might not be what it seems."

"Right. Maybe aliens abducted my former boss and replaced him with a pod person."

Vaughn cracked a smile. "That is one possible explanation."

"You don't understand. I worked for that man for years. I know him. I *know him* know him. He doesn't do things like that."

"Didn't you learn some things about him after you moved here? When he helped out with the beauty contest last year?"

"Yes, but—"

"And didn't he surprise you with his knowledge of the suit business?"

"Yes, but—"

"And didn't you change up your life when you moved here?"

"Yes, but—" When Vaughn didn't immediately say anything, I kept going. "But I'm still the same person. I moved, and I have a new job and new kittens and a new relationship, but I didn't change my identity. I'm still me."

"Maybe Giovanni will surprise you."

I stared down the hallway after my old boss and his young date. Nothing about the scene made sense. The movie had started half an hour ago, and the theater would be packed. No way were they going to waltz in there and get seats together now.

But it wasn't just the behavior I'd just observed that I questioned. Giovanni's recent availability had worked to my benefit, and he hadn't asked for anything in return. That itself was suspicious, but I'd assumed it was a matter of time until the other shoe dropped. In my experience, the bigger the favor Giovanni did for me, the bigger the ask would be in return. For all I knew, he was waiting to see if my suit clinic succeeded before naming his price because that would put my debt to him in a whole different light.

Now I had second thoughts about accepting his help. During the time we'd spent together at Material Girl, Giovanni hadn't said anything about coming to the film festival. When I'd asked if he wanted to attend, he'd said he had plans. He must have thought I was already seated somewhere in the theater. Why else would he sneak around after the movie started? And why was he here with a woman who looked half his age?

Something was definitely up with him. I might have lost traction on the Schaffley murder, but Giovanni was a mystery I intended to solve.

25

Sunday morning arrived with a thick gray fog, affecting the saturation of the colors outside my window. It wasn't unusual for mornings to be shaded by a palette of gray, but experience had taught me that the sun would burn away the cloud cover by eleven. I dressed in my usual black: sweatshirt, track pants, and sneakers, and walked to Tea Totalers for my morning cup of brew and something unexpected from Genevieve's Sunday morning test kitchen.

The line to order was short, and I was at the counter moments after I first arrived. As usual, Genevieve was the face of her business. Her strawberry-blond hair was pulled back in a stubby ponytail, and she wore a taupe-and-blue toile apron over her clothes.

"Hi, Poly, sorry I didn't have a chance to talk to you last night. Vaughn invited us to his private viewing tomorrow, and I wasn't feeling well, so I left after the costume contest."

"You weren't feeling well? Are you sick?"

"Tummy thing. I think something's going around. One of those lawyers—" The man behind me cleared his throat noisily.

Genevieve looked past me and apologized. "Looks like you brought the crowd with you. I'll come talk to you when the rush is over."

Genevieve suggested a strawberry blondie, and I added a Cortado. Genevieve frowned at my drink order. "You don't want tea?"

"I've been drinking lily bang almost every day for a week. I wanted something different."

"I'll give you different. Take a seat." She handed me a number, and I made way for the next guy.

Tea Totalers wasn't a huge cafe, but it was large enough to accommodate several dine-in tables. A counter ran the perimeter of the shop, and during the week, self-employed and remote workers jockeyed for the best spots to plug in and caffeinate to jumpstart their productivity. More than a few novels had been written here, and a small shelf by the northern window held titles with dedications: *To Genevieve Girard at Tea Totalers*. One even referred to her as the author's muse. It was quite the turnaround after being married to a dirtbag, but I didn't say that to her face. I left that for Charlie.

I assumed one of Gen's employees would deliver my order to my table, but a few minutes after I selected my seat, Genevieve carried a tray to me herself. She pulled out a chair and sat down. A college-aged boy had taken over at the register.

"Between business school and baking, I need a break." She picked up my blondie and took a bite then set it back on my plate. "Mmmmmm. Excellent choice."

"Thanks," I said sarcastically. I took the next bite and savored the flavors. "Mmmmmm. You're right."

"Try your beverage."

I took a sip of the steaming beverage. Hot and sweet notes

hit my tongue in layers, as did an unexpected spice. "What is this?"

"I call it a Ready Steady Go. It's two bags of Earl Grey poured over a base of sweetened condensed milk, topped off with a sprinkle of cayenne pepper. I nestled one caramel chip in the bottom of the mug before pouring in the hot tea, so that flavor releases as the chip melts."

"How do you come up with these things? Do you have a hidden recipe book?"

"If you follow somebody else's instructions, you'll get somebody else's results. I do the same thing you do with all that fabric. I use my imagination. You never know when an unexpected combination will lead to perfection."

I took another bite of my blondie, and Gen stared at it wistfully. She turned to the counter, pointed at my blondie, and held up two fingers. Her employee nodded and brought us two more. She handed me one and set it on my plate. "You're going to need more food in your tummy to absorb all that caffeine and sugar."

"What's your excuse?" I teased.

"Somebody has to do quality control. I've had three Ready Steady Gos already today."

We chitchatted about the event the previous night, about Charlie's big reveal during the costume contest, and about the odds of her and Clark staying on good terms through the weekend. A new crowd of customers came in, so Genevieve excused herself and returned to the counter. I was about to vacate the table when I spotted Mike Bozer in the line.

The lawyer's injuries had faded since Friday night. Two butterfly Band-Aids were stuck to his head by his hairline, barely visible thanks to a shock of hair that fell onto his forehead. The swelling around his eye was gone, leaving behind a greenish-yellow cast. The inside corner of his eye socket was purple, and a small cut split his lower lip. Aside from that, he looked the part of a successful litigator.

I still found it difficult to disconnect the violence aimed at the legal team representing Reginald Villamere's estate from the reading of the will. The attack on Mike outside his law firm suggested that a disgruntled former client was seeking vengeance, but I wasn't willing to rule against the two things being connected.

Mike reached the front of the line and ordered a double espresso. He paid by tapping his phone against a small computer screen. He stood off to the side while his beverage was brewed and thumbed through emails or social media posts or something that required very little attention. Before I had a chance for second thoughts, I called out his name.

He looked up and scanned the interior of Tea Totalers, eventually spotting me. I waved him over. He didn't look particularly happy about the invitation, but he joined me anyway.

"I was just getting ready to leave, so if you want a table, you can have mine," I offered.

"Not eating here. I'm picking up a tray for the office."

"I'm surprised you didn't ask your assistant Taylor to do that for you."

"Normally, I would, but she's out sick today."

"I heard there was something going around."

"I'm fairly sure it's the hangover flu. The legal assistants overdid it at the theater last night."

"Not surprising, I guess, what with—" I stopped myself before saying "the murder" and instead said, "what happened to your firm. People probably need an outlet."

"My firm deals with the execution of estates. Death is a

foundational cornerstone of our business. Our employees know how to push aside their personal feelings and do their jobs."

"I didn't just mean Ben Schaffley. I meant you too."

"Me?"

I touched my forehead and shifted my eyes to his wound. He reached up and placed his hand on the butterfly Band-Aid. "Oh. Right."

"I just meant maybe you're working them too hard."

"You don't know a lot of lawyers, do you?"

I didn't answer, not immediately, not because he was right, but because his emotionless answers were telling. The staff of the law firm had lost a boss. Not twenty-four hours after the murder, Ben Schaffley's name had been stripped from the company. A few days later, Mike had been accosted in the parking lot. Lawyers were a cold bunch, but more and more, I suspected something was up with their firm.

Mike interpreted my silence as confirmation. "Legal work is demanding. Long hours are expected. Relationships are not. Personal drama takes a back seat to work, and choices have consequences. It's better for interns and legal assistants to learn that early so they can get out if the job isn't a good fit."

"Has a lawyer ever decided the job wasn't a good fit? After he or she got their name on the wall?"

"Named partner is the goal. That's what builds reputations. The only way to lose that status is by getting disbarred. I'm not sure how it works in your world, Ms. Monroe, but in mine, once you arrive at the party, you don't leave early."

Genevieve called Mike's name. He rapped his knuckles against my table and left me alone to think about the underlying meaning of what he'd just said. For someone who'd just been attacked in the lot outside of his law firm, Mike Bozer had made a striking miscalculation. There were two ways for a name to be removed from a law firm. Disbarment—and death.

After finishing my second blondie, I put a lid on my Ready Steady Go and headed back to Material Girl to open for the day.

I stopped at the Circle K and bought a copy of the *San Ladrón Daily Ledger*. The small-town newspaper had recently returned from indefinite hiatus. From what I'd heard, that hiatus had started out as a vacation, but the managing editor had left the doors closed indefinitely when he lost the better part of his operating budget at a nearby casino. He'd shopped the paper, but no one had been interested. Shortly thereafter, as was the plight of most local newspapers, it had gotten folded into a larger operation, and more than half of the stories were fed to the staff from the parent office. Circulation plummeted when the front page reported on national stories instead of ones of local interest, and the presses eventually stopped without someone commanding them to do so.

Three months ago, a retiree had used a portion of his golden parachute to restart the presses. I'd heard that the first new issue, with the front-page headline about a pack of wild geese establishing residency by the pond behind the Broadside, had broken all previous sales records.

I didn't want to risk tripping over a crack in the sidewalk by reading the paper while I walked, so I tucked it under my arm and went home, took it up to my dine-in kitchen, and spread the pages out on the table, looking for something of interest.

Local news was on a two-day delay thanks to printing and transportation factors, so save for an advertisement for the film festival, there was no mention of the event last night. I flipped past the first few pages of the paper and reached the local-interest stories. I didn't know why it hadn't occurred to me to check the paper until today, because the leading story was about Reginald Villamere's legacy. Before I dove into the story, I flipped through the rest of the section. Buried on the back page, in a section called "Local Crimes," was a brief mention of Ben Schaffley's murder after a story about a break-in at the public records office. It felt as if someone had wanted to bury the lede.

My heart pounded at a heightened rate, and it wasn't just because of the news. Genevieve hadn't been joking about the effects of her Ready Steady Go. I left the paper on the table and fixed myself a bowl of mandarin oranges and cottage cheese, which I ate over the sink. I rinsed my bowl and followed my second breakfast of the day with a glass of water. When I turned back to the table, Pins was sprawled across the center of the newsprint. He looked up at me as if daring me to move him. He stretched one gray paw out in my direction and yawned, revealing fangs befitting a baby vampire. I fell under his spell and stroked his fur.

"What do you make of this whole thing?"

He tipped his head, angling for a little more attention by his ears. I gave him what he wanted, and within seconds, he purred his appreciation. The response was equal parts deeply gratifying and lacking in anything that forwarded my investigation. Like most cats, Pins was only in it for himself.

I had a few spare minutes, so I called Sheriff Clark. It was the weekend, and Etta had the day off. Clark answered after a few rings.

"Sheriff Clark, it's Poly. I ran into Mike Bozer this morning. He seems to be recovering from his attack. Have you had any luck finding who jumped him?"

"Not yet. Etta and Sack called every hospital and vet clinic in a fifty-mile radius to find someone asking to be treated for a gunshot wound. We have a couple of long shots but nothing concrete. I sent Sack to check them out today. Charlie found a bullet hole in Mr. Bozer's bumper, which supports his story that the gun discharged. It's possible he didn't hit anybody."

"Will you tell me if you find anything out?"

"You know the drill, Poly."

26

Talking to Sheriff Clark about an open investigation was like trying to hop onto a moving train. Some days the jump and the doors lined up perfectly. Other days, I was shut out. I was beyond pouting over the sheriff adhering to his own set of rules. I thanked him for the information he'd been willing to share and hung up.

Pins stayed on the newspaper and bathed himself, and Needles, who had been suspiciously absent from the kitchen lovefest, followed me downstairs. I retracted the gate, and he plopped down in a patch of sunlight by the door. I turned the Closed sign to Open and added a second one that said Beware of Cat.

The shop owners of Bonita Avenue were of two minds when it came to Sunday business. Some felt it should be their day off. A time to rest, recharge, hang with family, and enjoy what was left of the weekend. Foot traffic was slower than on Saturday, and there existed an unspoken agreement among some owners that the more businesses that stayed closed, the fewer people would come to San Ladrón. Sundays would become a self-fulfilling prophecy of slow sales, which would encourage the more stubborn businesses to fall in line.

I fell into the opposing group. I hadn't reopened the store after ten years just to close it for half of the weekend. Shortened hours allowed me a little flexibility on Sunday mornings and more time to relax on Sunday night before my day off on Monday. When other things tugged at my attention span, the five hours in between were a minor inconvenience, but when I felt as if I were standing in front of a blank wall, they also provided a welcome distraction. I pushed thoughts of Ben Schaffley and Reginald Villamere out of my mind and focused on business.

———

As was often the case after a big event in town, Sunday business was even slower than usual, but I welcomed the time to attend to my suit shop. So far, I had a small round table with Giovanni's binders of pattern pieces, Tiki Tom's torsos to display garments, and wool from Reginald Villamere's estate. This project was infused with testosterone. I appreciated the generosity that I'd benefited from so far, but I needed a way to make it my own.

The idea came to me around two. I pulled the gate closed and placed a *Back in Five Minutes* sign with the hands of the clock positioned at two-oh-five onto it, then went upstairs. A whisper of discomfort glanced through my ankle, but I dismissed it. In my bedroom, I pushed my and Aunt Millie's clothes to the side, revealing five garment bags that had belonged to my Uncle Marius.

There was a romance to the shop that had lingered after my aunt and uncle had each gone to the great fabric store in the sky. Some of that romance was due to the styles of their era, and some was due to the love they'd poured into the store. Tragedy had hung over the shop for a decade before I'd inherited it, and that was the main reason I'd ended up changing the name. They'd sung "Material Girl" to me when I was a baby, and the song name was my connection to them, to what they'd passed down to me. The shop wasn't a hand-me-down or a burden. It was a lump of clay for me to do with as I wished.

I often dug through Aunt Millie's side of the closet, incorporating vintage items that she'd constructed into my wardrobe, but today I wanted Uncle Marius's suits. I slung his garment bags over my left arm, straining against the weight of the heavy fabrics, and lugged them downstairs.

I laid them on the closest cutting table and reopened the gate, finding Adelaide Brooks standing on the sidewalk. She was dressed more casually than usual in a pale-blue turtleneck and cardigan over camel-colored corduroy trousers and matching loafers. Her gray hair was secured at the back of her head, and her reading glasses hung on a thin gold chain around her neck like a piece of jewelry.

"I was starting to worry," she said.

I checked my watch. It was two-oh-seven. "I took my time coming down the stairs."

"A wise move with your history." Adelaide followed me into the shop, carrying a large take-out bag. "It's sandwich day at the Waverly. Chef made up extras for those who couldn't join us."

"You'll have to thank him for me."

I set the take-out bag on the stairs, and then I had second thoughts when Pins appeared on the landing. I moved the bag to the wrap stand and left it next to the register. Adelaide stopped by the suit station and was flipping through one of Giovanni's binders of patterns.

"My son mentioned your latest idea. How's it coming?"

"Until about ten minutes ago, it was a mismatch of donations volunteered to me by others." I swept my hand to take in the torsos, the binders, and the cart of wool that sat nearby.

"What happened ten minutes ago?"

"I got the idea to use Uncle Marius's vintage suits for the display."

Adelaide's eyes sparkled. "That's a splendid idea. Where are they?"

I pointed to the garment bags on the cutting table nearby.

"You always manage to find a way to make an idea your own. I applaud that about you."

"I was just about to unpack them. Do you want to see?"

She shook her head. "For you, they represent family. For me, they represent friends from a chapter of my life that ended a long time ago." She put her hand on my wrist. "But that's what history is, isn't it? Something different for each of us. It's easier to appreciate when it's not knotted up with baggage."

"Adelaide, you run one of the most historically significant properties outside of Los Angeles. Heck, even counting Los Angeles. People come from all over to have their celebrations at the Waverly House."

"Poly, I'm not so old that I was alive when the Waverly House was built. That era is to me what the thirties are to you. I'm able to see what the rest of the world will love about that time and exploit its historical qualities because I wasn't there to experience it first-hand. That's the main point of contention between me and the historical society."

I leaned against the cutting table and crossed my arms over

my chest. "I always thought once a property was added to the historic registry, there were rules you had to follow about how to maintain it. Is that true?"

"Yes. We're not allowed to modernize the infrastructure. We have to preserve the architectural details of the building, and our color palette is defined by historical photos that document the building's original decor. Currently, a debate is taking place over the use of modern technology. It's one thing to preserve a property, but for a property like the Waverly, we rely on rentals of our award-winning landscaping and gardens to bring in income. Wallis and I are in a battle of wills over whether Chef can use the panini press we added to the kitchen last month."

At the mention of the head of the historical society, I sensed an opportunity. "How come I never met Wallis before?"

"Wallis was appointed to this position six months ago. Until recently, she worked at the public records office, overseeing the archives. It made her the perfect candidate when her current position opened up, but I question if she has the patience for that line of work."

"Why would patience have anything to with it?"

Adelaide smiled warmly. "You're a go-getter, Poly, and that suits your business, but preserving history is a patience game. To even be eligible for historical designation, a property must provide certified plans of their original design along with documentation of any renovations that have taken place and a detailed budget for maintaining the property indefinitely. Occasionally, a landmark will qualify for certification but lack the income stream for upkeep, or the owners will request the certification but want to keep their ownership privatized."

"I never knew there was so much involved in it."

"You don't know the half of it. Sometimes renovations

have to take place to restore a building so it's up to code, and sometimes those renovations are too costly to offset the value of the completed project. The Historical Society deals in certification and preservation, but as a not-for-profit, when they add properties to their real estate holdings, they need ones that can not only sustain their required upkeep, but can also bring in income for them to use for their own operating expenses."

"What about the Villamere Theater?"

"That's a tricky question. Thanks to Reggie Villamere's efforts, the theater has maintained much of its original design. It's still operational, which illustrates a potential revenue stream, but you've seen the effects of neglect yourself. Technology has taken over the movie business. The Historical Society would put an end to movies streamed via satellite. The theater would have to hire a full-time projectionist, and the manager would have to work with the movie studios on rentals, climate-controlled transportation of fragile film reels, and the expenses that come with. Those types of things could eat away at any profit the theater currently shows."

"What would be in it for the theater?"

"An infusion of cash. A safety net to ensure the theater will remain in business regardless of Reggie's passing. A guard dog to protect them from opportunistic buyers and construction firms that offer to swoop in and handle upgrades for a cost."

At this last threat, both Adelaide and I went silent. When I'd first learned of my fabric store inheritance, I'd had a life in Los Angeles. Moving to San Ladrón to become a business owner hadn't been part of my plan. I'd been pressured to sell the store, and rumors at the time had been that the prospective buyer wanted to knock down all of the businesses along Bonita Avenue and build a big-box store.

There were arguments both for and against that action, but ultimately, my decision to dig in, to not only keep the store but move here and reopen it, had put the debate at a standstill. The prospective buyer had been Vaughn's dad, and since then, he'd seemed to recognize the value of our quirky community. It was foolish to think he'd be the only investor to consider buying property to develop in San Ladrón, though, also foolishly, I hadn't considered that until right now.

"If there were opportunistic buyers and construction firms looking to acquire the Villamere, who would they talk to?"

"Whoever inherited the theater."

"What about before the will is fully executed?"

"I imagine that's a matter for the legal team to sort."

Ah. So the employees who had planned the film festival on short notice had a ticking clock before the theater ownership fell to Josephine and she decided their fate.

"Between an opportunistic historical society and an opportunistic investor, I'd side with the historical society every time. Why would anybody say no?"

"The owner would lose creative control of their business." Adelaide stared at the small suit display in progress. "You, Poly, thrive on your ideas. Many of the businesses on Bonita Avenue do, some of them because you're generous with your ideas. I know you, and I know this suit clinic will be up and running by the end of the month—by the end of the week if you keep drinking those Ready Steady Go beverages your friend at the tea shop makes. If you were backed by the historical society, you'd have to petition them for permission to incorporate your ideas, and sometimes those petitions go unanswered for months. You would gain financial security, but you would give up the ability to handle everything on your own."

"You said Wallis lacked the patience to work for the

historical society, but it sounds like she's exactly what the historical society needs. If petitions go unanswered for months, wouldn't it be good to have someone in there who gets results?"

"I'm not concerned about Wallis's ability to get results internally. But wooing a property owner takes time. Finesse. I don't like to think about what would happen if someone got in her way."

27

"You're not suggesting Wallis would harm someone, are you?" I asked. I expected her to admonish me, but she didn't.

"No. I'm worried that she might pay less attention to the Waverly House and what I built." Adelaide paused then added, "But you and I have both seen enough of human nature to know people are often motivated to do things we don't believe they're capable of doing."

I walked her to the door. I'd learned a lot in a short amount of time, but I had one more question. "Did you fight the historical society's efforts to acquire the Waverly House?"

Adelaide smiled. "No. The Waverly has always been a home for the history of San Ladrón. Managing the property has been my life's work, but it doesn't get easier. Wallis and I have discussed historic certification over the years before she took this position. I've never acted upon her suggestion. But you saw what happened last year when it was time for our annual fundraiser, the risks involved if we had fallen short of our goal. After that experience, I felt it was better for the historical society to have our back and to follow their rules than let some investment firm snatch us up and turn us into a moneymaking machine."

Adelaide was too polite to acknowledge that "some investment firm" meant her ex-husband, but we both knew if it wasn't his firm, it would have been another. There was always somebody sniffing around the perimeter of a potential cash cow. It was both a blessing and a slight against my business acumen that nobody had offered to buy out Material Girl since I'd reopened.

Adelaide bid me farewell, and I turned my attention back to the suit project. A last-minute customer came in, raising my hopes that I'd prove the closed-on-Sunday crowd wrong with a large sale. She left with three spools of thread for $6.98. Some days you win. Some days you don't.

———

THE LACK of customers meant a lack of mess to clean when I closed. I packed up the pattern pieces and rolled up the wool. The cats had long since abandoned their felt mice and were back upstairs.

Adelaide had run the Waverly House for longer than I'd been alive, and she'd seen a lot of changes in that time. Our conversation had been interesting, but aside from what she'd said about Wallis, she appeared to be confident that the Waverly House's future was in good hands.

I carried the sandwiches upstairs and made a few phone calls to see if any of my friends wanted to join me for dinner.

Each of my calls landed on someone's voice mail.

Resigned to dining alone, I unwrapped a sandwich, opened a bag of kale chips, and sat down to eat. The newspaper was still open on the table, its pages shifted from Pins's nap earlier. I reread the notice about Ben Schaffley, learning nothing new. I was about to put the paper in my recycle bin when I lingered over the article above it that mentioned the break-in at the public records office.

That was where Adelaide had said Wallis had worked for years before taking over the historical society. It felt like a red flag.

I set my sandwich down and called Sheriff Clark.

"Hi," I said. I conserved valuable police resources and got straight to the point. "Did you investigate the break-in at the records office yesterday?"

"Friday," Clark corrected. "How'd you hear about that?"

"It's in today's paper."

"Yo, Polyester, the only thing around here that moves slower than the cops is the paper," Charlie's voice said in the background. Things between Clark and Charlie were still on. It must be a full moon.

Clark continued. "What do you want to know about the break-in?"

"Do you know who did it? Did they take anything or just vandalize the place?"

Charlie's voice in the background spoke again. "Why do you care about the break-in? I thought you were sniffing out the lawyer's murderer."

"Charlie," Clark said. "That's enough."

"And that's my cue to leave."

"No, wait!" I said quickly. I wasn't in the mood to be alone, and if Charlie was ready to walk out, then she and Clark didn't have any romantic plans for the foreseeable future. "Adelaide dropped off a bag of sandwiches from Chef. If you two didn't eat, I can bring them over."

"We'll talk when you get here," Clark said and disconnected abruptly.

I pulled a black jacket over my sweatshirt, rewrapped my sandwich and put it in the bag with the others, and then left for the sheriff's mobile unit. There was twice as much lighting on Bonita as there was in the alley, and every once in a while a voice whispered a reminder that there was a murderer out there and it paid to take some safety precautions. That also explained the small can of Mace in the bottom of my handbag, a Christmas present from Sheriff Clark.

I reached the sheriff's office without event. The front door was open, with only the screen in place.

Clark was at his desk, scanning notes in a file in front of him. He gestured toward the chair on the opposite side of his desk. "Charlie just left. The seat's probably still warm."

"She's not avoiding me, is she?" I asked.

"More like she's avoiding everybody. Her performance last night turned her into Miss Popularity, and that's not a role she's used to inhabiting. I could have trumped up a charge and locked her in the cage, and she wouldn't have resisted."

"What was up with last night? It's not like her to join in when it comes to town events."

"You'll have to ask her about that."

I pulled two sandwiches out of the bag and gave Clark his choice of chicken pesto or steak au poivre. He chose the steak and got two bottles of water from his mini fridge. We spent the next few minutes eating in silence.

When we were finished and the trash had been cleared, Clark sat back down and tapped the folder on his desk. "These are the notes of the records office break-in. The call came in on Friday. Sack investigated. The employee said his key didn't work when he arrived. He went in through the back and didn't notice anything missing. Two hours later he went to print a file and found the printer jammed." Clark handed me a sheet of partially printed paper. "From what I can make out, those are records from an old court case. No names on the paper, only a couple of details. The records office agreed to stay closed until I can get in there and nose around, but what with Mr. Schaffley's murder, I haven't had the time. Not sure it would help if I don't know what I'm looking for."

"When's the last time you had a break-in at the records office?" I asked.

Clark shook his head. "Not sure we've ever had one. Records are public. If somebody wants something, they can walk in and request it. No point stealing any, either. The records are backed up in the cloud."

"You're saying if somebody wanted to know something about an old case, they can just go in and ask to see it?"

Clark nodded.

"And if somebody stole a file and shredded it, there would still be a record of the information in the computer system?"

Clark nodded again.

"Is there a big need for public records? Is the public records office busy?"

"No. There's one employee, Cooper Hutchinson. He's worked there for longer than I've been in San Ladrón. He called in the vandalism. No reason to suspect him of anything. Even he thought it was a bogus reason for calling the cops. Nothing I can do but make a note of it."

"You said this happened on Friday?"

Clark nodded again. He was starting to resemble a bobblehead.

"If they're a public office, then they're closed on the weekends, right?"

"What are you getting at?"

"Is there any way you can get me in so I can take a look around?"

"What do you think you're going to find?"

"I don't know. But it can't hurt, right?"

Clark pushed his chair back and stood. "Might as well. Nothing else going on tonight."

I didn't stand at first. I stared at Clark. "You normally won't talk about active investigations. Why is this one different?"

"You're asking about a break-in at the public records office. That investigation isn't exactly active. I'm just happy you're not here to talk about Mr. Villamere, Mr. Thibodeaux, Mr. Bozer, or Mr. Schaffley."

Based on that, I kept any suspicions I had about the crimes being connected to myself. Clark was right. Vandalism at the public records office could be indicative of a rising crime rate and nothing more. In addition to my friends and fellow business owners, there was a rougher element in town, and I'd had a couple of interactions with them myself when I first moved here. The misdemeanors could be a distraction or a way to overwhelm the understaffed sheriff's office. Or they could be connected to the Schaffley case. It was not crazy to think there might be an overlap between a murdered lawyer and stolen records about a previously committed crime.

The same rising crime rate that had brought Clark's increased payroll budget had brought a fully functioning forensics lab. I wondered if that lab included a computer that could tell us something about our partially printed piece of paper. As Clark drove the mile or so to the records office, I asked him.

"Already thought of that. I had Hutch search his database

for any string of words that he could identify from the paper that was jammed in the printer. Unfortunately, the part that printed was standard legalese. There were too many hits to narrow our search."

He parked alongside the curb behind a dirty silver Hyundai. A middle-aged man with a florid face waited at the doors, having trouble with his key.

"I thought the lock was broken," I said to Clark.

"The locksmith was here on Friday after I took the call. That's Hutch. I asked him to meet us here to let us in."

Cooper Hutchinson was stocky and nervous. He looked as if he'd just finished running several blocks, and from the color of his face, I hoped his doctor had him on blood pressure medicine. He unlocked the doors and held them open for us, and I entered behind Clark. The old lock sat on the counter in front of us. Clark aimed his flashlight at the pile of metal and illuminated a series of dings on the side.

"Can we turn on the lights?"

"Better if we don't. Lights will alert the residents in the area, and my office will get flooded with calls. Responding to them will keep me from moving on to another investigation."

"I guess having a town of residents who want to help can get in your way."

"You don't know the half of it." Clark grinned to let me know that, at least for the moment, he was only kidding.

We walked through the records office. A glass jar for business cards sat on the counter under a sign to enter for a free lunch at Earl of Sandwich. I doubted it was approved by the city, but good for Earl for convincing Hutch to let him place it there. Behind the counter was a chair and another counter that held the printer. Next to that was a small wire bin stacked with file folders.

I moved toward the bin and then stopped. "Do I need to wear gloves in here?"

"This isn't a fingerprint evidence kind of case, but you should stay out front."

Clark went behind the counter. I lingered in the lobby, removing the folders from the bin and glancing at the documents inside. It felt like a violation of people's privacy, looking at petitions for divorce, applications for marriage licenses, and deeds of ownership.

"Are you sure it's okay for me to look at these?" I asked Hutch, who hovered between the front room where I was and the back room where Clark had gone.

"Public records are available to the public. Nothing here is a secret. Most people are so worried about their own secrets they don't stop to think about how much information is freely available for the taking. The only repeat business I get is from the media when they're looking for background on a story."

"Why are these folders here?"

"That's new paperwork to be filed. I work on filing during the day between document requests that come in through our website."

If the files here were all available to the public, then why would someone break in? What would be worth stealing that couldn't be requested during regular hours?

As I wrestled with that question, my eyes settled on Earl's sandwich raffle. There were only a handful of cards inside, but one of them stood out: Ben Schaffley of Schaffley, Bozer, and Schmidt.

A new question pushed the others out of my mind: if Ben had been murdered on Tuesday, who had dropped his card in the bowl after that?

28

"Sheriff Clark? I found something," I said.

Clark and Hutch joined me out front.

I pointed at the glass jar. "Ben Schaffley's card is in that bowl. I don't know when Earl empties it, but there are only five cards in it, so that makes it seem like he emptied it sometime this week."

"We don't get a lot of foot traffic," Hutch said. "Most requests come in through our website. Earl usually picks the cards up on Tuesdays, but that's not a rule. Sometimes the cards sit there for a month."

"The lawyers met for the reading of Reginald Villamere's will on Monday. Ben Schaffley was found dead on Tuesday morning. Ben's card in there is suspicious no matter how you look at it. Those lawyers are here from Los Angeles. Ben was either in San Ladrón before he said he was, or someone else came here after he was killed and put his card in the bowl for who knows what reason."

"Dump it," Clark instructed.

I tipped the glass jar and fanned the business cards on the counter. Clark picked up Ben Schaffley's card.

"There's something written on the back," I said.

Clark flipped the card over. On the back, the name Taylor was written in ink.

Before Clark could ask, I volunteered what I knew. "Taylor is the paralegal who works at Bozer and Schmidt. Someone at the law firm must have sent her here to pick up records."

Clark pocketed the card. "I'll follow up with her tomorrow."

Clark might have thought the card wasn't important, but I wasn't so willing to dismiss its clue-worthiness. The card placed an employee from the law firm at the public records office sometime between the murder of Ben and the records office break-in. My theory about a past case serving as the motive for murder was starting to shape up.

Until now, I hadn't shared my theory with Clark, but I floated it to him now. Unfortunately, now that there was evidence that connected the murder and the break-in, he took me seriously, and his generosity regarding case information evaporated.

"I'm going to need you to leave. Hutch, can you give Poly a ride back to her place?"

"Sure."

"And keep the office closed tomorrow. I'll get a team out here."

Hutch nodded. He pulled a set of keys out of his windbreaker and headed toward the exit. I didn't know if I should thank Clark or curse him. Maybe I should call Charlie; this was how she usually felt about him. Maybe we could start a club.

Hutch dropped me off at home. It was a short drive, and he

blasted the radio the entire time. Maybe he really liked progressive rock. Maybe he wanted to keep me from asking him questions.

Between dinner and sleuthing, a few hours had passed, and it was now after eight. The cats were asleep in the middle of my bedspread, curled together in a Yin-Yang formation, but it was too early for me to join them. I wandered around, picking up shoes and jackets that I'd left scattered in the living room and on the backs of chairs and putting everything away. The more I tried not to think about the case, the more certain I was that I knew more than I thought I did. It was a frustrating place to be. Maybe if I'd been given the chance to look at the records room with Clark, I might have noticed something, but now, thanks to my own observational skills, the records room was off limits.

I was annoyed enough with Clark to call Charlie.

"Yo, Polyester. I thought you were occupied for the night."

"Clark's your boyfriend, not mine."

"There's a reason you get away with more than anybody else around here. Don't make me revoke your privileges."

"About that. Clark's not my favorite person at the moment, so I thought I'd call you."

"Nothing like being second choice." She paused long enough for me to think maybe I had offended her, and then she asked, "What did he do this time?"

"He took me to a crime scene, and then, after I found a clue, he sent me home."

"Yeah, Clark doesn't put out on a first date."

That was what I loved about Charlie. She didn't allow petty things like traditional gender roles to inhibit her responses.

We made plans to meet at the Broadside Tavern for a

discussion of Clark's flaws—at least that was what I told Charlie. Sunday night for regular folks meant turning in early and prepping for the work week, but Sunday was my Saturday, and tonight was my night to blow off steam. After a day mostly by myself, I was open for company.

Ten minutes later, Charlie and I were seated side by side at the bar. A group of men shot pool and threw darts behind us, creating a general din that made it difficult to quietly discuss the finer details of the case. Faces looked familiar, but I couldn't place where I recognized them from.

"Speak up," Charlie said. "Nobody here cares if you talk about a murder case. Half the dudes in here were probably accessories to a crime before they turned eighteen."

"Don't let Duke hear you talk about his regulars like that."

"Like what?" Duke asked from behind the bar. He had a bucket of ice on his lap, and an unopened bottle of something was submerged in the ice, as were two champagne flutes. He rolled the wheels of his wheelchair until he reached us. "Are you insulting my clientele again?"

"Again? Who said I insulted them before?"

"I hear things." He repositioned his wheelchair by rolling a few inches back and then forward. "Those guys are just blowing off steam. It's been a long week for the Villamere."

"They work at the theater?"

"Worked. Those are ushers. From what I heard, the future of the theater is being decided by a bunch of suits, but it doesn't look good for these guys. Best case, they'll show movies on the weekend. Worst case, the theater will become a pile of rubble."

"Says who?"

"One of the lawyers was in here earlier today. He broke a pool cue the other night when he got into a brawl and wanted to 'make restitution.'" He shook his head at the phrase. "I wish everybody was that considerate."

"One of the lawyers got into a brawl?" I asked. "Did you catch his name?"

"Nope. Gave me a wad of cash to cover the damages. Between you, me, and the pool table, those lawyers are good for business." He patted the arms of his wheelchair. "And for gossip. People seem to think this chair compromises my ability to eavesdrop. You wouldn't believe the things I hear."

"I'll pay you top dollar for the secrets of San Ladrón," Charlie offered.

"Nah," Duke said. "I wouldn't want to be responsible for your actions after you hear them."

I looked more closely at the men shooting pool. Out of uniform, they looked like every other group of men who came to the Broadside: sweatshirts and jeans and tattoos and facial hair. It had been wise to institute and maintain a dress code for the Villamere staff. It lent an air of respectability to all parties involved.

"You two here for the night?" Duke asked.

"Maybe," Charlie said. "Why?"

"You gotta help me out with this Cava. I asked my distributor to add a couple cases of bubbly to my delivery order so Genevieve would have something to drink when she comes to the bar. I figured he would get me the good stuff, but he tried to save me a couple of bucks and gave me this one from Spain. Genevieve's a tried-and-true Francophile, and she rejected it on principle."

Duke held out the flutes of champagne, and I took them. Charlie, who tended to order drinks called Car Bomb—ironic in view of her being a mechanic—wasn't bothered by the Spanish lineage of the beverage. She bent over the bar and snagged the bucket of ice with the bottle in it from Duke's lap. Behind us, someone whistled. She held her middle finger up to the nameless crowd and then sat back down and removed the foil from the bottle.

"Is this on the house?" she asked.

"Might as well be. It'll go flat once it's open, and the rest of my customers won't touch the stuff." He pointed his finger at her. "Nice to see you participate in something last night."

"Mention it again and the contents of this bottle will go over your head."

Duke held up both hands. "Have it your way." He rolled himself back into his office, chuckling along the way.

Charlie filled each of our flutes to the brim and jammed the bottle back into the ice. She slid off her stool and grabbed the bucket handle. "You carry the flutes. A booth just opened up, and we're due for some privacy."

I followed her to a vacant booth in the corner. Charlie loosened the bulb in the lamp over our heads until it went out, leaving our corner dark and mysterious.

After we settled in, Charlie asked, "What happened with Clark tonight?"

"The usual. He took me to a crime scene, but as soon as I found a clue, it was so long, Poly."

"Usually it's so long, Charlie."

"I thought usually it was so long, Clark."

"That's true. But since you lack the ability to get him to fall in line like I do, walk me through your night, and I'll see what I can do."

I told Charlie about the records office and the business cards in Earl's sandwich raffle.

"That's it? That's your big clue—people who entered to win a free lunch?"

"It's not the prize that got me thinking. It's the card. Ben Schaffley's card was in the bowl, but it had Taylor's name written on the back. That puts her at the records office sometime around the murder." I remembered something that hadn't seemed important at the time. "You mentioned the records office not long ago. Schaffley's autopsy results. Something about them being public records?"

"They are. I saved some time and money by copying the report from Clark's files, but if I were the law-abiding citizen everybody wants me to be, I could have gone to see Hutch, filled out a records requisition, paid for the copy, and gotten the same information."

"Tell me again why you took that file? And don't say you did it for me. You're not that generous."

"Maybe you're not the only person around here who's curious about this murder."

"What's your connection to it?"

"This town used to feel like a known entity. I could run my business and do my thing, and people respected my desire for privacy. But now, there's this new element. We're not such an insular small town anymore. The mayor hired a publicist to Gilmore up San Ladrón, and now we're a destination."

"With all due respect, San Ladrón has always been a little Gilmore-y."

"Yes, but nobody knew it. Think back to when you inherited the fabric store. Vic McMichael wanted to buy it out from under you and level the stores on that street to make room for a big-box retailer. It's been, what, a year since then?"

"Something like that," I said.

"And the crime rate has risen by double digits. Los Angeles county raised the payroll budget for Clark's office so he could hire help. McMichael put his money into a forensic lab.

There's enough news here to keep the new *San Ladrón Daily Ledger* printing for years."

"You're saying you pulled that autopsy report because you don't believe Clark is getting the job done."

"Clark's good at his job. I wouldn't give him the time of day if he wasn't. But he has tunnel vision. And you think outside the box."

"There's something else, isn't there?"

"I like to keep an eye on my records, make sure nobody's adding to my file." She sipped her Cava. The bubbles made it prohibitive to chug the beverage, forcing her to pace herself. "Now, back to you and your clue. Do you really think that business card means something?"

"It's not what I think that matters."

Charlie refilled her flute and topped mine off. "Tell me about this Taylor person. Is he a go-fer or a hungry dog?"

"He's a she. Taylor is the paralegal helping to handle the Villamere case. Or she was. I don't think she's cut out to handle the dark side of case law. She said she saw the photos of the crime scene, and then she got sick."

"When?"

"Friday. She came to Material Girl with one of her bosses and threw up in my trash can. I ran into her boss at Tea Totalers this morning, and he said the legal assistants called out sick with the hangover flu. Taylor was at the theater last night, but I don't know a ton about her."

"This Taylor person. Thin, blond, twenties?"

"Yes. Why?"

"I don't think it's the dark side of case law that's giving her a problem."

As soon as Charlie said it, I saw a pattern emerge. I'd forgotten all about the pregnancy test I'd found in the

Villamere trash last night, but now, disparate threads were knitting themselves together in a way I hadn't seen before. The more I thought about it, the more I wondered about Taylor, about her relationship with her now-deceased boss, and what had really happened that night when they'd stayed behind at the office to celebrate—and if it was the kind of thing that drove a young, scared, single, and pregnant woman to murder.

29

"Clark said he was going to follow up with Taylor tomorrow," I said. "The business card puts her at the public records office, but the name of the building implies—confirmed by Hutch—that the records that lie within are public. Anything anybody wants is available with a request. Why would Taylor break in? If she wanted to know something about somebody, why not just request it through their website?"

"Are you thinking out loud, or are you asking?" Charlie asked.

"That depends. Do you have an answer?"

"You're looking at this as if somebody broke in to get information. Maybe they broke in to destroy it."

Two flutes of Cava were enough to turn me silly. Three were enough to turn all thoughts of the murder investigation into a frizzy blob of details that bumped and popped against each other, leaving empty space in their wake. Restraint crept in somewhere after Charlie poured me a fourth, which went untouched. I blamed Duke for giving us the bottle, Genevieve for being a Francophile, and Charlie for being the enabler who kept refilling my glass.

Duke showed up at our table with two complimentary charbroiled burgers and fries. "You two are louder than the rest of my crowd combined. I thought you were meeting friends. Give me your car keys. You both live close enough to walk home. I never should have given Charlie that whole bottle."

"Live and learn," Charlie said, and hiccupped. "That's my motto."

I woke on Monday with a headache. If not for the two meowing alarm clocks on the coverlet, I would have delayed getting out of bed, but that's the price you pay for live-in mouse patrol. I stumbled to the kitchen to feed Pins and Needles. I put on a pot of coffee and made a skillet of scrambled eggs, rosemary potatoes, and toast, along with enough noise to wake Charlie, who had crashed on my sofa.

"You know what they say about payback," I said when she plopped into a kitchen chair. I spooned half of the food onto her plate, put the other half on mine, and set the skillet back on a cork trivet in the middle of the table. I carried two mugs to the table and sat across from her.

"What's the plan today?" she asked.

"I'm going to pay a visit to the law offices of Bozer and Schmidt."

Charlie held up both hands. "You're flying solo on that one, Polyester. Rule followers aren't my jam."

After breakfast, Charlie left. Yesterday I'd been looking forward to spending time in the store, dressing the torsos in Uncle Marius's vintage suits and organizing the wool I'd inherited, but today, I couldn't shake the feeling that the suit clinic was just a distraction from something bigger. One week ago, I'd been in a room at the Villamere, along with everybody else who'd played a part in the execution of Reginald Villamere's will: tenured ushers, Laurence Thibodeaux, and a team of lawyers. Since then, a man had been murdered, a mysterious heir had been located, and a possibly related break-in at the records office had taken place. Suspicion had been cast on the head of the historical society. And Vaughn and I had found a new will hidden at Mr. Thibodeaux's house, but curiously, not one person had suggested in public that it existed —including Mr. Thibodeaux, who had the most to gain if it was real.

I wouldn't have minded company for my visit to the law office, but it was just as well that Charlie had recused herself. She wasn't the most subtle of my friends. If Taylor had something to hide—besides a suspected pregnancy—it would be best to catch her off guard. That would take a gentle touch. Best if I went by myself, especially if I intended to pass off my arrival as business pertaining to the Villamere estate.

I showered and changed into a black Brooks Brothers suit and loafers, checked the address for Bozer and Schmidt, and left. My VW Bug was too old to have GPS, but my phone did the job, directing me away from the quiet camaraderie of Bonita Avenue to the industrial park of the city. The closer I got to my destination, the more traffic I encountered. The distance was less than five miles, but by the time I arrived, I felt as if I'd entered an entirely different world.

Lawyers must keep decorators on retainer. Ben Schaffley's name was gone from the sign out front, the sign in the lobby, and the sign on the wall by their elevator wells. It was as if the deceased lawyer had never existed.

I approached the receptionist. "Hi, I'm Poly Monroe. Is Taylor available?"

"Do you have an appointment?" she asked.

"No, but this is in regard to the Villamere estate. She has some paperwork she wanted me to sign." I smiled warmly, hoping to gain her trust.

I'd been prepared for a brush-off, but Taylor wasn't in as much demand as the lawyers were. The receptionist called her while I stood there, relayed the stated nature of my business, and hung up. "Taylor will be out shortly."

Moments later, Taylor came down the hall toward me. She hugged a leather folio to her chest. Her complexion was washed out. Her suit jacket was buttoned, but the fabric strained at her waist. "I thought you weren't going to sign the paperwork. What changed your mind?"

"Is there somewhere private we can talk?" I asked.

"Sure." She glanced at the receptionist, who made no secret of the fact that she was listening to us. She pointed the end of her pen at the conference room behind us. Taylor nodded and led the way.

The walls of the conference room were thick glass, making it impossible to get away with anything while inside. It also made my job of confronting Taylor with what I suspected, getting a confession, and testing her animosity toward her old boss more of a challenge than I'd thought. I needed time to gather my thoughts.

Taylor set the folio on the conference table. She pulled out a sheet of paper, set it on the table, and scanned it. "It's already been more than forty-eight hours. I'll change that to seventy-two, but we'll both have to initial over my changes."

"I've spoken to the executor of the will, and he said there's no rush on me getting my fabric. The opposite, all things considered. If that forty-eight-hour timeframe is coming from someone at the law firm, I'd like to know why."

Taylor looked pale. Considering what I suspected about

her condition, maybe I was coming on too strong. "I tell you what. Let's take a coffee break and talk this over."

"I'm sorry," she said. If it were possible, her face went even more pale. "I'm off caffeine."

There was no more point beating around the bush. "You're pregnant. You weren't sick from something you ate at Tea Totalers, and you didn't have the hangover flu. You took a pregnancy test at the Villamere Theater on Saturday night and left it in the bathroom trash."

"Are you spying on me?"

"No. I just put it all together. Tea Totalers was bustling with customers on Monday, and you're the only person who claimed to have gotten sick. You told the owner something about raisins causing gestational diabetes in pregnant women, which didn't stand out at the time, but now it does seem like an unusual thing for a not-pregnant person to say. And after you threw up at my fabric store, when I came back from taking the trash out, I saw the way you looked at the yellow fleece. Up to then, you carried yourself like the rest of the lawyers, cold and hard and just the facts, but in that moment, you were... soft. Your mind was a hundred miles from legal stuff. The hangover flu was a convenient excuse to tell your boss, wasn't it?"

"I didn't even tell him that," she said. She sank into one of the empty chairs. Purple half-moons under her eyes stood out in contrast to her wan complexion. "I didn't need to take that test to know I was pregnant. There were signs, you know?"

"I don't."

"Morning sickness. Mood swings. Plus, I was two weeks late. I don't know why I took that pregnancy test at the Villamere except I knew a lot of people would be there so I could get away with relative anonymity." Taylor forced a laugh. "So much for that."

Whatever poise she'd had left her body, as if she'd been possessed by a ghost who'd moved on to greener pastures. "I told Mike I wasn't feeling well, and that was true. I didn't even know he was attacked. The interns were the ones who went out drinking. He just assumed I was out with them, and I didn't say anything to convince him otherwise." Taylor looked up at me, and this time her anger was gone. "What are you going to do about it? What do you want?" she asked.

I sat in the chair catty-corner across from hers. "How about the truth?"

Taylor looked at her fingers. She'd repainted the polish since she'd chipped it off at Material Girl, but the habit seemed to be compulsive because she started in again. I didn't love having this conversation in a conference room where everybody could see us, but you play the hand you're dealt.

"When I got the job offer from Schaffley, Bozer, and Schmidt, I thought I was on my way. There aren't a lot of law firms in the area, but it was either this or move to Los Angeles. My boyfriend had a job here, so I thought it was a sign." She'd destroyed the nail polish on her thumb and moved onto her index finger. "We broke up a month after I started working here, and he moved back to Akron."

"When was this?" I asked, worried that there might be a perfectly reasonable explanation for her pregnancy and instantly chastising myself for having that thought.

"A couple of years ago."

Relief returned. I chastised myself for that too.

"When I started working here, the firm felt friendly, but I quickly learned there was an unofficial hierarchy, and I was on the bottom. I didn't want to get involved in office politics, so I did my job as best as I could. The problems came when I started doing it too well."

"What do you mean?"

"I found things. Precedents for cases, legal loopholes. Because of the break-up, I didn't have a social life, so I spent my free time—nights and weekends—here. I drafted paperwork for the lawyers, and when the partners saw the quality of my work, they started to request me for their cases. I got fast-tracked without even trying, and my colleagues hated me for it."

"What was your relationship with Ben Schaffley?"

"Ben and Mike both wanted me to work on their cases. It got to the point where other legal assistants started to harass me. At first, it was unimportant things. Using up all the cream for the coffee before I had any, drinking the bottled water I put in the community fridge. Taking a bite out of the sandwich I'd packed for lunch and wrapping it back up, so I would find it when I took my break. I started bringing my own coffee and having lunch delivered, but it got worse. Case notes went missing from my desk. My alphabetical files got rearranged at random. When one of the partners asked for something, I couldn't find it."

"Did you tell anybody?"

"I told Ben. We were working late on an important case. He was the only partner who stuck with me after the mistakes started, and I wanted to show him he made the right choice. I found what we needed at two thirty in the morning, and we broke out the champagne. After our second bottle, do you know what he said?"

I shook my head.

"He said, it was about time I got my head back in the game. I was buzzing from the alcohol and the euphoria of having found what we needed to win, and it spilled out, what the other assistants had done."

"What did he say?"

"He went still. Our entire celebration went away in a flash. He thanked me for the work I'd done on the case and called a driver to take me home."

"You and he didn't...?"

"No. The next day he asked me if I'd told anybody else about what happened, and I said no. He told me to keep it to myself. He said he'd put a stop to it. I was promoted by the end of the week, and nothing like that happened again."

Taylor sniffled and swiped at her nose with the back of her hand. I pulled a tissue out of my handbag and extended it to her. She pushed it away and glanced at the glass walls to make sure nobody was watching us.

"I never told anybody. But with Ben gone, I'm afraid it's going to start again."

The story helped me understand her a little bit more, but there was one detail we hadn't covered. I reached out to put my hand on hers, and she recoiled. I remembered the glass walls and sat up straighter. "Taylor, did something else happen between you and Ben? Did he pressure you for... anything... in return for his help?"

"You think he's the father, don't you?"

"Isn't he?"

"You were so smart about everything else, I just figured you knew that too." She shook her head. "Ben isn't the father. Mike is."

30

"MIKE IS THE OTHER SENIOR PARTNER," I SAID, unnecessarily since I was speaking with a member of the firm staff.

"Technically there are two other senior partners. Mike Bozer and Paul Schmidt. Paul mostly handles divorce settlements, so I don't interact with him often."

"And Mike? Did he make you—"

"Every workplace romance isn't a 'me too' situation. I like him. He likes me. We keep things quiet because of how it would look to everybody else."

I couldn't help notice her use of the present tense. "Does he know about..." I pointed at her tummy.

"Not yet. I had suspicions, but I wasn't sure myself until Saturday night." She turned her attention back to her chipped fingernail polish. "I figured there would be a lot of people at the theater, and nobody would put two and two together. You won't say anything, will you?" This time when she looked up, her eyes were wide and pleading.

I tapped the document on the table. "Can you give me more time to get my fabric?"

She smiled in relief. "How does an extra week sound?"

I smiled. "Done."

I stood and glanced out the windows, not the ones that faced the building, but the ones overlooking the parking lot. A sedan from the sheriff's fleet pulled into the lot. It slowed as it passed my VW Bug. This was the real problem with individuality—it put a crimp in undercover work.

I'd been so absorbed in my conversation with Taylor, learning the truth and ferreting out her secret, that I'd forgotten all about why I was there, but the arrival of Clark put me back on track.

"Taylor, Sheriff Clark just arrived. He's going to come up here and ask you about your trip to the public records office last week. Is there anything you can tell me about why you were there?"

"The public records office?" she repeated. Her face contorted, with a pattern of creases appearing like an imprint on her forehead. It looked as if she'd fallen asleep face down on a towel. "I was checking background information on anybody named in the will. It's standard procedure in an estate of this size."

"Did you find anything out about me?" I asked.

"You?"

"I was named in the will."

"Your aunt and uncle were. They're both deceased. I confirmed that you inherited their fabric store."

"So that's all you have to tell me?"

"I think I've already told you plenty."

There was no point trying to sneak out of the building. Taylor walked me to the elevators, and the doors opened to reveal Sheriff Clark. A five-minute difference and I could have made a clean getaway.

"Sheriff," I said by way of greeting.

"Poly," he said. "Business with the law firm?"

"I stopped by to sign some paperwork related to the Villamere estate. Would you like to see a copy?"

Clark's eyes shifted from me to Taylor, to her leather folio, and back to me. Taylor opened the folio and flipped through a couple of pages.

"I trust your business with the law firm is complete?" he asked.

I looked at Taylor. She had no reason to think I was nosing into Ben Schaffley's murder. She probably thought I was the town busybody. "For now, yes."

"Good. I don't want to find out you're halting the wheels of justice." He allowed enough of a smile to indicate he was kidding, but not so much that I didn't know there was some truth behind his concerns.

I said goodbye, breezed into the newly vacated elevator, and jabbed the door-close button. My one lead had turned into little more than an office scandal, which would break the moment Taylor's pregnancy started to show.

Everything Taylor had told me sounded plausible, everything except the assault on Mike. The breakup with her boyfriend. The long hours that resulted in her being fast-tracked and targeted by the other legal assistants. Her account of things had Ben Schaffley looking like a good guy. Everybody likes to celebrate the guy who stops bullying behavior. Was that why he'd been killed? He stood up to the wrong bully?

It bothered me that he'd told Taylor to keep the situation to herself. If there was a problem at the law firm, someone willing to mess with case files to make her look bad, then wouldn't a named partner have a bigger issue than protecting a legal assistant, no matter how good she was turning out to be? It was one thing to drink someone's water or take a bite out of their sandwich. Messing with case files was the sort of prank that could have much bigger implications for the firm. It was almost as if Ben knew who was behind the torment, and he knew how to shut it down for good.

I got into my car and sat behind the wheel before starting the engine. Ben Schaffley had been at the Villamere for the reading of the will. I'd interacted with him. Nothing about him had seemed like the good guy who stands up for the little people. He'd been brusque, dismissive even. He and his team had been there to represent the will, but Vaughn had been the executor. Ben had sidelined him too.

This was the first time anybody had told me anything about Ben Schaffley. A week had passed since he'd been murdered, and there'd been no gossip, no rumors, no praise, and no dirt. There'd been nobody saying he deserved what was coming to him, or what a shame he'd been killed, or how horrible to be the victim of a random act of violence. Nobody was pressuring Sheriff Clark to find the killer and make our community safe again. The staff of the Villamere had organized an entire film festival in under a week to honor Reginald Villamere and what he'd built, but not a single person had mentioned a service or memorial for Ben Schaffley.

I started my car and left the lot before Clark returned from his visit upstairs. I wasn't up for a Q and A session, not now. Aside from Taylor's pregnancy, every piece of information I'd discovered about these visiting lawyers and their L.A. Law ways had gone straight to Clark in an effort to help his investigation. And he'd acted on some of that information too. He'd agreed to move Laurence Thibodeaux to the Waverly House, and he'd taken me to the records office. He'd answered some of my questions. It wasn't until last night that he started to treat me as something more than a concerned citizen.

It was a beautiful day. I called around to see if any of my friends were free, but they were all busy with their own things. Genevieve was experimenting with a new batch of herbs from Hawaii, Charlie had four oil changes lined up, and Vaughn was working on paperwork related to the Villamere estate. My brain circled around the events of the past week, and I wanted to talk things out, but I didn't know where to start.

Actually, I did. There was one person who knew more than anybody else, one person who'd already been arrested and released on bail. One person who had an alternate will buried under layers of cashmere sweaters in his wardrobe.

Laurence Thibodeaux.

After Mike Bozer was attacked while Laurence was having dinner with Wallis and Adelaide, the district attorney had had no choice but to drop the charges against him. There was no reason for him to stay at the Waverly House, so I drove to Grosvenor Arms and asked the security officer to see if the mature theater manager was available for a visit. A few minutes later, the elevator bell sounded, and Laurence greeted me in the lobby.

"Ms. Monroe. What a pleasant surprise. Is Mr. McMichael with you?"

"No, it's just me."

"All the better for me. Shall we go up?"

"Lead the way."

Laurence kept up a patter of polite small talk on the way to his apartment, telling stories about units formerly rented by celebrities who had wanted to escape Hollywood after their careers had gone quiet. We arrived at his place, and I followed him in.

"I'm afraid I've just finished an early lunch, but I can make you a sandwich if you like."

"That's not necessary."

Laurence filled two glasses with iced tea and set them on a tray, then carried the tray to his living room. I sat in one of the tweed club chairs opposite his with a round table between us.

After we each took a sip of tea, Laurence said, "Is this a purely social call, or has Adelaide Brooks sent you to check up on me? She was not pleased when I told her I was going to return home."

"It's mostly a social visit." I cupped my iced tea with both hands and stared at the ice in the glass. I couldn't just sit in his apartment, drinking his tea and making small talk. I had to come clean about what I knew.

I looked back up at Laurence. "My dad was a lifeguard at Gnarly Waves when he was a teenager. He worked a private party one year when Reginald Villamere rented the water park out for the employees of the Villamere and their families. He overheard you and Mr. Villamere talking about how much easier your lives would be if you invented a woman—an ex-wife, or a girlfriend, or an assistant—"

Laurence stared into his tea as if he knew the inevitable end of my story.

I set down my glass. "After an altercation between some of the kids, the pool manager told you my dad was probably too young to be a lifeguard. You told him your girlfriend had mentioned just the previous week what a good job he was doing." I cued up my dad's text and showed Laurence the photo. "My dad got a commendation on the pool bulletin board, and my grandparents took a picture of it. Your girlfriend's name was Josephine Barkley."

Laurence looked at my phone as if he were looking into a window through to the past. He set his iced tea on the tray and leaned back against his chair. The tweed wingback appeared to hug him on either side of his shoulders.

"Well. I suppose if you've found out all of that, then you've earned yourself an explanation."

I sat quietly and gave Laurence the space to decide how much or how little he wanted to tell me. Clark was certain enough that Laurence wasn't the killer that I wasn't worried for my safety. Even if Clark had thought he was the killer, I would have known Clark was wrong. Nothing about any of this pointed at Laurence except for his key to the storage closet where the body was found, but I had a theory about that too.

"Reginald Villamere and I were companions," Laurence said. "At the time, people called us bachelors. The world was not as accepting as it is now, and it was easier to go along with the assumptions that were assigned to us than to risk judgment. Reggie gave so much to this town. It was his wish to be remembered as he was to them. I see no reason to change that for my own selfish reasons."

"Who is Josephine Barkley to Reginald Villamere?" I asked.

"She is what you thought she was. A fictional woman to make certain situations easier for each of us. She was, at times, a secretary, an employee, an aunt, a niece, and an ex-girlfriend. Reggie flirted with the idea of promoting her to ex-wife, but he never quite got there." He smiled to himself at a memory.

"If she's fictional, then why did Reggie leave her the theater and his estate? Was that some sort of code to really leave it all to you but keep your close relationship a secret?"

"No." I watched the rise and fall of his chest. His breathing deepened. He placed his hand on his heart and closed his eyes for a few seconds and then opened them. "About twenty years after we put Josephine Barkley into play, Reggie started to worry that we hadn't chosen an unusual enough name. He hired a private investigator to find Josephine Barkley. He gave minimal information and waited to see what would turn up. The PI located a few women, nobody local. Each of them were married with families of their own, living far enough away from us that the odds of them ever hearing one of us use that name were slim. We were about to retire the name when the investigator reported that a baby girl named Josephine Barkley had been born in Proper City, Nevada. That's when Reggie first got the idea."

I leaned forward. "What idea?"

"When Josie turned twenty-one, we set out on a road trip to meet her. Reggie told her the whole story so that if it ever came up, she would know the truth. They struck up a friendship. He left his estate to her as a thank-you for giving him freedom to live in a world that may not have otherwise accepted him."

"What about the will?"

Laurence looked at me. "I've made wise investments with my money over the years. I live a comfortable life, and I have more than enough to enjoy what life I have left. The estate should go to someone who is young enough to enjoy it."

"No, I don't mean that will. I mean the other one. The one Vaughn and I found here."

Laurence's eyebrows pulled together. He had been sitting back against his tweed chair, but at this he leaned forward. "There is no other will."

"Yes, there is. Vaughn and I found it the night we came here to get your clothes." I felt a flutter of butterflies in my tummy. "Remember, you gave me your key and asked me to bring you a few things while you were staying at the Waverly House—"

He flapped his hand to silence me, and he stood. "You offered to do me a favor, and I took you up on that offer. None of that is in question. But tell me about this will."

I stood too. "It's in your armoire, under several cashmere sweaters. Vaughn and I saw it, but we didn't know what to do about it. You had just been arrested, and it wasn't signed, and neither of us wanted to make trouble for you—"

Laurence had already turned away from me. He headed into his bedroom, and I followed. By the time I reached the room, the drawer was open, and a pile of cashmere sweaters now sat on the bed.

Laurence turned to me. "Where did you say this will was?"

I checked the now empty drawer then turned to the sweater pile. I flipped through the soft cashmere, toppling the neat piles onto the bedspread. The will that Vaughn and I had seen the other day was gone.

"It was here," I said.

Laurence nodded, a bittersweet smile on his face, as if he regretted allowing himself to believe me. One by one, he lifted his sweaters and replaced them in his drawer. His actions were mechanical, as if his mind was miles away and his body was completing the task on autopilot. When he finished, he eased the drawer closed.

"Has anyone else been here while you were staying at the Waverly House?"

"No. Just you, Mr. McMichael, and Devontay."

My antennae went up. "Devontay from the Villamere?"

"Yes. I was unable to fulfill my duties as theater manager, and I asked him if he would assume my responsibilities. I told him where my spare magenta blazer was. Devontay knew where I kept my key ring in the office."

"Is that the same key ring that has the key that unlocks the storage closet?"

"Yes. Why?"

"Laurence, someone had access to your keys. Someone unlocked the storage closet at the Villamere and killed Ben Schaffley, and now it looks like someone used your keys to gain entry to your apartment. You told me you were the only one with the key, but maybe if you left your keys in your office, someone who knew where you kept them used them."

"No," Laurence said. "That's not possible."

"I know you don't want to believe it, but it could have happened—"

"No," he said again. "It couldn't have happened that way because my keys weren't in my office. I already told the sheriff, but I assume he didn't think it was information worth repeating. I did loan my keys out that morning, and I've regretted it ever since."

"Who borrowed them?" I asked. I pushed away thoughts that Clark already knew this piece of information, and for some reason, he didn't think the person in question could have committed the murder. I studied Laurence, who wrung his hands in apparent anguish. I sensed I was losing Laurence to that troublesome part of our brains that imagines alternate endings to our fateful actions, and I nudged him. "Laurence, who did you loan your keys to on Tuesday?"

He looked up. "I loaned them to Ben Schaffley, the lawyer who was murdered."

31

THE TEMPERATURE IN LAURENCE'S BEDROOM instantly felt a few degrees cooler. Next to us, thick shantung curtains shielded the golden sunlight outside his windows. The apartment was so quiet that I could hear the kitchen clock tick away the seconds while I held Laurence's stare.

"Ben Schaffley borrowed your keys," I stated. "Did anyone find them?"

"No," he said. "Devontay found them in the hallway next to an overturned stanchion. He assumed that I'd dropped them, and he returned them to my desk drawer."

I didn't like what this said about Devontay. It looked like he'd had access to the key to the stockroom. His story placed him in the hallway where the stanchion had been knocked down. I'd been in that hallway too. I'd seen the knocked-over stanchion, and I hadn't seen any keys.

Devontay hadn't worked at the theater long enough to be at the will reading, but he'd been there the day I'd found Ben's body. But why would Devontay plant a new will? Why would Devontay murder a lawyer?

Laurence must have correctly interpreted the expression on my face. He put his hand on my wrist. "No. Do not accuse that boy of murder."

"I'm not. But someone was there. And someone was here. Someone planted a new will in your apartment. I saw it. Someone had access to your keys. The police arrested you, and if they had come here to search your house for evidence, they would have seen it too. You just acknowledged that Devontay had access. Maybe there's something you don't know about him."

Laurence sank onto the side of his bed. I waited for a long stretch, willing Laurence to provide context. Eventually, he spoke. "Devontay got himself into some trouble when he was younger."

"What trouble?"

"It's not my place to say. I always believed the boy was merely in the wrong place at the wrong time. I firmly believe in second chances, and it meant a lot to me that he came clean about his record when he applied for the job."

I sat next to Laurence, and this time I put my hand on his. "If Devontay did something illegal, it won't help him to protect him now."

"There are standards of confidentiality that we must uphold. It is what separates us from the barbarians."

———

I SAID goodbye to Laurence and left the Grosvenor Arms. My day off was turning into a series of dead ends, and I was no closer to discovering anything than I'd been yesterday. Storm clouds marched across the sky, dark gray like steel wool. I hadn't heard anything about rain on the forecast, and

I hoped the clouds would pass and find another city to drench.

I went back to Material Girl. When faced with a problem I can't work out, I've found it helpful to turn to creative projects. My custom suit idea was the perfect diversion.

I positioned the bust forms next to the small display table. I removed seven bolts of fabric from the temporary displays and replaced them with wool from the Villamere, lightest on the top to darkest shades on the bottom. I moved my laptop into the store and customized a template to use as an order form with spaces for measurements and fabric choices. I'd had no idea how many aspects of a man's suit could be customized until I flipped through Giovanni's notebook—lapels, vents, buttonholes, and more.

Mike Bozer had left his measurements written on a sheet of paper, and Giovanni had made notations next to them. I hoisted a bolt of wool onto my shoulder and carried it to the cutting station then flipped through the book of pattern pieces to find the corresponding elements. I preferred to have my sketches put into production by a seamstress, but I could do this. I'd worked with patterns before.

I rolled out a bolt of wool and placed the pattern pieces along the selvage edge. Small weights filled with buckshot, placed at the corners of the pattern, kept the fabric from shifting as I positioned additional pattern pieces. I laid out a sleeve, a lapel, and a pocket, and then just stopped and stared at the project on my cutting table. That was when reality came crashing down.

This project was too big for me. I didn't know how to make a suit. I might never know how to make a suit. I had the raw materials, but I didn't have a clue where to start.

It was one thing to sell fabric and patterns. Hiring Jun to

work for me one day a week had solved some of my problems. She made garments for people who weren't interested in making things themselves. My success at To The Nines had been predicated on my knowledge of vintage fashions, not my sewing ability. I made sketches, and the workroom produced them... after Giovanni simplified my ideas into cost-effective designs.

No wonder Giovanni was able to replace me so easily.

At the thought of Giovanni, I felt even worse. Giovanni was a cheapskate and a slave driver, but he'd turned a profit at To The Nines for decades *and* he'd offered to help me. He was responsible for the employment of an entire workroom of seamstresses. He'd not only trained me, but he'd already hired my replacement. I wasn't even willing to put a Help Wanted ad in the paper. I thought being the boss meant doing everything myself.

From the moment Giovanni had turned up here at the store, ready and willing to help without the promise of anything in return, I'd sensed something was up with him. My parents had said they'd seen something in the paper about To The Nines. Whether it was the suit project that freed my mind from details regarding the murder or my willingness to wallow in my situation, a different mystery tugged at my brain.

I hoisted myself up on a corner of the cutting table and called my parents. My mom answered the phone.

"Did your father tell you to call right now?"

"Um... no?"

"John, did you ask Poly to call to get you out of measuring the windows?" she asked, presumably not to me.

"Yes," my dad's voice replied in the background. "Our daughter and I have a psychic connection."

"Don't be cute. Keep measuring. We're ordering those curtains today. Poly? Are you there?"

"Hi, Mom. You know there are people out there who will come to your house and measure things for you."

"I'm fully capable of using a tape measure. What's up?"

"Dad said you saw an article in the paper about Giovanni's store. Do you remember what it was about?"

"Yes," she said. "There was an accident in the store. Dad saved the article for you, but you can probably read about it online."

"Can you give me the highlights?"

"If I remember correctly, a pipe burst in the shop. It destroyed most of the equipment in the workroom. It happened at night, so no one was hurt, but the shop will remain closed while repairs are being made. That's probably why Giovanni has free time to help you. He didn't mention it?"

"No, but my seamstress, Jun, did. And then Giovanni showed up at the Villamere Theater last night with a woman half his age."

"Are you happy running Material Girl?" my mom asked.

"Yes. Why?"

"Then why do you care who Giovanni hires to replace you?"

"Replace me? She was his date."

"Poly, the man runs a business. He's entitled to hire whoever he sees fit."

"But she was young, Mom. I don't even know if she's legal. And he took her to a social event on a Saturday night. Doesn't that seem strange to you?"

"How old were you when you started at To The Nines?"

"Twenty-two."

"Legal for a whole year," my mom said with a sarcastic tone. "You're right. Giovanni's behavior is highly suspicious. It's not as if the man has a history of hiring women straight out of design school or anything."

"Mom—"

"Did she seem like she was there under duress?"

"I didn't talk to her."

"Why not? You already know the best way to get the truth is to go straight to the source. No, John, that's not level. Poly, I have to go. If I leave your father in charge, our curtains are going to be crooked."

I left my parents to their project and returned to mine. I thought about the question my mom had posed. Was I happy running Material Girl? I'd thought so. But then why did I keep making up excuses to get someone else to cover the store while I ran around town? And why did I continue to drag my feet on making any long-term plans for the store's success?

Forty-five minutes later I was deeper into a hole of self-pity and might have bottomed out if the back door hadn't banged open.

Giovanni strode inside. I was so surprised by his arrival that I knocked over the bust form. It clattered to the floor and scared Pins, who had been bathing nearby.

"Tuesdays and Thursdays," Giovanni announced instead of the more traditional "hello."

"Hi, Giovanni, how are you this fine afternoon?"

He flapped his hand. "You asked what I wanted. I want to work at your store two days a week. You already have a seamstress who comes here on Wednesdays, and you're closed on Monday. I'd rather not battle weekend traffic, so I'll take Tuesdays and Thursdays."

I picked up the bust form and pushed it into place then

turned to Giovanni and put my hands my hips. "You want to *work* for me?"

"*Somebody* has to. You can't keep calling your parents for help."

"What about you? Don't you have a business to run?"

"I don't know." He pulled up a chair and collapsed into it. "Two weeks ago, a sewage pipe burst in the workroom during the night. Not only did it take out the fabric cage, but by the time we came in the next morning, the machines were destroyed."

My heart went out to him. I searched for the appropriate supportive response. "Something like that must be covered by your insurance, right?"

He looked away.

This time I prodded for a response. "Right, Giovanni? If a pipe bursts in the building you rent, then you can't be held responsible for it. You've called your landlord, haven't you?"

"I'm the landlord. I bought the building when Los Angeles real estate prices dipped."

"Okay, so contact your insurance carrier."

He inspected his fingernails. "I let the policy lapse."

This time I went quiet. For all of the playful criticism Giovanni received, when it came to how he managed To The Nines, he knew what he was doing. When he lectured me about how I ran Material Girl, it wasn't about things like insurance policies, it was about buying low and selling high, or managing costs to ensure profit. It never occurred to me that he would make such a novice mistake. Unless—

I felt dread blossom in my belly. "Was it an oversight because you were here helping me?"

"As much as I'd love to have someone to blame, it was my

responsibility. I let the policy lapse six months ago to save a couple of bucks. That's the same reason I've been training my niece to take over your job."

Giovanni's *niece*. He'd taken his niece to the film festival. And suddenly, it all made sense.

How many times had I thrown in his face that my designs were rooted in the style of the thirties? How many times had I gotten annoyed with him when he took off the luxurious details I envisioned in my designs so he could increase his profit margin? Giovanni knew how to get fabric. He knew how to maximize productivity, sometimes by purchasing fabric with a factory defect (or in one case creating the "defect" himself and negotiating a discount), and even though I didn't like when he changed my designs, I'd come to see that the clients who bought dresses at To The Nines were looking for a garment they would wear once, not an heirloom to hand down through multiple generations. Giovanni bringing an underage woman to the film festival wasn't inappropriate. It was for her to get inspiration.

I felt something constrict in my chest, and it took a moment to realize it was sympathy. Giovanni had had a good thing going at To the Nines before I quit to move to San Ladrón, and my choice to leave and take over the fabric shop had had repercussions. Giovanni had helped me out more than once since I took over the shop and always asked for something in return, but like he said, that was business. Favors from friends were great, but you couldn't build a business plan on them.

"Who's going to train her?" I asked.

"One of the girls in the workroom."

I grinned to myself. It was like going back in time.

"Women, Giovanni," I said. "They're women, not girls. Your niece, though, you can call her a girl for the next few years, at least."

32

After that, negotiations happened easily. Something about the idea of having Giovanni work for me felt —not just right, but smart. I looked at the fabric laid out. I didn't know what to do with it, but Giovanni did. He'd brought the binders of patterns, and he had experience. The reason things worked at To The Nines was that we'd each had our roles. Maybe that could work here too.

Giovanni and I hammered out the details over mugs of Ready Steady Go in my stockroom then returned out front to discuss the status of the suit shop. Giovanni proved to have spent a little of his free time thinking about it, and together, we made real progress. By the time I called it quits, we had successfully partitioned a portion of my shop into a private space for consultations and measurements, replete with a three-way mirror, a carpeted platform, and several thick swatch books for sample fabric. I almost resented having to stop working so I could get ready for the encore film festival that night. I invited Giovanni to attend, but he declined.

Unlike my original vintage outfit, tonight I'd raided Uncle

Marius's side of the closet. He'd been a thin man, and his suit fit me easily. I went full Marlene Dietrich in a black cutaway tuxedo, white shirt, bowtie, and cummerbund. In lieu of a boutonniere, I pinned one of Aunt Millie's vintage brooches to my lapel and tucked my auburn hair behind my ears.

Vaughn picked me up with minutes to spare. "Not what I expected," he said.

"What can I say? I'm living and breathing suits these days."

The Villamere had arranged minimal staff for our private viewing. A full bin of popcorn had been popped, and large buckets were prefilled for us. Devontay greeted us at the door, dressed in Laurence's oversized magenta blazer. If he knew I had briefly suspected him of anything, he didn't show it.

"Welcome to the Villamere," he said. "Concessions and beverages are included in the rental, so order whatever you'd like. I can run the movies on the same schedule we did on Saturday, but if you'd prefer me to hold off until more people arrive, I can. Just give me ten minutes to get them going."

"Saturday's schedule is fine for us, right, Poly?" Vaughn asked.

"Fine by me." I headed toward the concession stand.

Devontay called after me. "Poly, wait."

I turned back.

"Can I talk to you for a minute? Alone?"

I glanced at Vaughn. "Large popcorn and a large bottle of water."

"Candy?"

"Goobers and Raisinettes."

Vaughn raised his eyebrows.

"I did my research. They're the only two candies offered here that were also sold in the thirties."

"Goobers and Raisinettes it is."

After Vaughn was a few feet away, Devontay asked me to follow him to a private spot in the hallway. "I talked to Laurence today. He said he told you about my past."

"I was trying to make sense of the situation."

"I don't blame you," he said. He looked at his feet, his head hung low, as if embarrassed by the situation he'd found himself in. "I'm not sorry that Ben Schaffley is dead, but he didn't deserve to die that way."

"Devontay, what's your connection to Ben Schaffley?"

"You don't know?"

"Laurence thought it was important to keep your confidence."

A couple of seconds passed. I heard my name and turned, spotting Genevieve by the popcorn stand. She waved, and I smiled but turned away, not wanting anything to interrupt my conversation with Devontay.

"I got into some trouble when I was younger," the thin Black man said. "I took a couple of years off after high school so I could save up for college. This one night, I was out with some friends. I was the designated driver. We went to a liquor store. I waited in the car while my friends went in to buy beer, or so I thought. They stuck the place up and made me an accessory to a felony after the fact. It's what the courts call a wobbler. It can go either way—felony or misdemeanor. The liquor store hired a hotshot lawyer, and my public defender had more interest in his daily crossword puzzle than my case."

Heat pricked the back of my eyes. Stories like this probably played out all over the country, but this was the first time I'd had a personal connection to one.

"The thing is, the hotshot lawyer for the liquor store was Ben Schaffley."

"What happened?"

"I didn't know what those guys were doing in the liquor store, and the public defender said it could go either way for me. But Ben, he made it sound like I needed money for school, and that we'd planned the whole thing, that the phrase 'designated driver' meant I was designated to drive the getaway car. He said we were using the phrase as code. When I found out what my friends did, I knew I was in trouble, but after the hearing, the charges got bumped up to felony, and I ended up serving six months."

"What happened to your friends?"

"I cut all ties with them. I got a job here and enrolled in business classes at night. Larry and Reggie looked out for me, and that meant something. I wanted to make them proud."

I didn't miss the fact that he'd referred to the theater manager and theater owner by more familiar names than most people used. It indicated the same thing Laurence had said, about believing in fresh starts and looking out for Devontay.

"When I first heard Mr. Schaffley's firm was handling Reggie's will here at the theater, I didn't want to be anywhere near him. I asked for the day off. But then he was murdered. And I got scared. There's a connection between me and him, and my fingerprints are all over this place. I didn't know what to do." He stopped, and for the first time since pulling me aside, he looked me in the eyes. "I broke into the records office and stole my file. That was stupid. I know that now. I already told Sheriff Clark. Breaking in violated my parole. I messed up. It might mean I'll go back to prison, but I'll take whatever punishment I get."

I liked Devontay. It was clear that Laurence liked him too. But there was a reason this was coming up now. Anyone would understand why Devontay might not like lawyers, but we weren't just talking about dislike anymore. We were talking about murder.

"Devontay, where were you when the will was being executed?"

"Speaking to a support group of recent parolees about fresh starts. My PO arranged it. We're on about half a dozen cameras in and around the civic center where it took place."

"Did you tell Sheriff Clark any of this?"

"Yes. I figured my connection to Ben Schaffley was going to come out, and if anybody placed me at the records office, I'd look guilty. I'm not proud of what I did, but I don't want to hide anything anymore."

"You did the right thing. You've got strong character witnesses on your side, and things like this have a way of working out."

Vaughn approached us. He had a large popcorn in one hand and two boxes of candy in the other. Bottles of water jutted out of his blazer pockets. A clump of napkins stuck out of his breast pocket like a pocket square.

"Are you ready to go in?"

"Ready when you are."

Devontay smiled at me. "Thanks for understanding, Poly. Enjoy the movies."

We headed toward the theater.

A few seconds later, he returned. "I almost forgot to give you this." He reached into his pocket and pulled out a shiny brass key. "This unlocks the storage room. You'll still need an employee to unlock the entrances, but once you're inside, you can come and go as you wish. I haven't used the key yet, so try it before you leave to make sure it works."

I closed my hand around the key and glanced at Vaughn.

He smiled. "Go. I'll get seats."

We went separate directions: Vaughn to the theater, Devontay to the projection booth, and me to the back hallway. I sidestepped the red velvet stanchion and entered the hallway. So much had happened since that first day when I learned about my inheritance. Lives changed, some for the good and some not so much. I reached my fingertips out and touched the wall, tracing them over the edge of the art deco mural that had been painted on the wall decades ago. The romantic in me hoped nothing about this place would change, but the realist in me knew the odds were not in my favor. I was so lost in my thoughts that I didn't hear the voice until I was right outside the storage room. The door was propped open by a cardboard core of a bolt of fabric. I peered inside and saw a pile of upholstery fabric pooled on the floor.

"What's done is done," the voice said.

I'd heard that voice before. It was Mike Bozer, one of the remaining named partners of Bozer and Schmidt. Formerly Schaffley, Bozer, and Schmidt. Possibly the one person who had benefited the most from Ben Schaffley's death.

I stood, rooted in place, for an indeterminate amount of time. Nobody should have been inside that room, especially the lawyer who wanted me to empty it out. Devontay had just told me I had all the time in the world. Which one was playing me?

"Somebody is going to find out," a female voice said. "You know how this works. Someone always finds out."

It didn't take much for me to put two and two together and come up with Taylor and Mike. Taylor, pregnant with Mike's baby. This wasn't a threatening rehash of a murder, it was a private interlude between consenting adults trying to figure out how to keep a secret that was destined to reveal itself. The lawyers must have had access to the Villamere too, and these two probably assumed the storage closet was a private place to talk. I was about to turn around and head back to the theater when my cell dinged with a text. It was Vaughn telling me the trailers were about to start.

While I texted a reply, the door to the storage closet opened and Mike stared at me. His bruises were faded, but the traces of them that remained lent a menacing cast to his features. I shoved my phone in my pocket and glanced past him. Taylor was in the back of the room, arms hugging herself. Her face was red and streaked with tears.

"How much have you heard?" he demanded.

But before I had a chance to answer, he grabbed my wrist and yanked me inside.

33

I TRIPPED OVER THE CARDBOARD THAT HELD THE door open and stumbled to regain my footing. Mike didn't release my wrist, which had the effect of keeping me from falling. Taylor watched me from her corner, a fresh wave of tears coating her face.

"What are you doing here?" Mike asked.

I could have told them I was excited about my fabric, or I wanted to try my new key. Or that I wanted to stand in the middle of the room and take it in without thinking of it as the place where I'd found Ben Schaffley's body. I could have said a lot of things, but none of them seemed relevant. Nothing except one question that had already been asked.

"What are *you* doing here?" I asked.

Mike and Taylor looked at each other. Aside from the rough manner in which Mike had jerked me inside the room, they didn't seem violent—yet they were here, in the room where I'd found a body, and now that I was face to face with Mike again, I couldn't help noticing how tall he was. Tall enough to hit someone over the back of the head without having to stand on a ladder.

"It was you," I said. My eyes shifted back and forth between him and Taylor. "That's why you wanted me to clear out this room. Something in here incriminates you." I looked to my left and right, and the heavy cardboard tube caught my eye. "Is that what you hit him with? The core from a bolt of fabric?"

Mike held his hands up in a nonthreatening manner. He stepped toward me, and I stepped back. He stepped toward me again, and Taylor called out, "He didn't do it."

Mike dropped his hands and turned back to her. "Taylor, don't try to save me. I have to pay the price for my actions."

She buckled over and buried her face in her hands, her body wracked with sobs. Mike forgot all about me and went to her. He put his hands on her arms and guided her to the shelves I'd emptied when I took the wool. She sat down, and he stooped in front of her. "It's going to be okay. I promise. Go home. Try to relax. You need to think of our baby."

Taylor stood, and I watched the two of them, the way they interacted with each other. There was a gentleness, not the boss-employee relationship I had witnessed at Material Girl a few days ago. She made no move to leave the room.

Mike touched her cheek tenderly. "It's okay. It's better if I own up to what I did."

Taylor kept her eyes on the floor and left. I watched, wondering if I should detain her in a citizens' arrest, but something about her and her boss felt nonthreatening. Unlike the bravado I'd experienced when Mike came to the fabric store, today he had a defeatist attitude.

"What happened in this room the day Ben Schaffley died?" I asked.

"Taylor said she told you about the bullying at the law firm."

"She did. She said one night, she and Ben were working late, and after she found the precedent to his case, they celebrated. She told him about the other law assistants, how they treated her. She said he handled it. She was promoted by the end of the week. She also said she never told anybody."

"She didn't—not when it happened. I don't think she ever would have. I didn't plan to fall in love with a paralegal. It violates a hundred different rules of the firm and can destroy both of our careers."

"What does this have to do with Ben Schaffley?"

Mike pulled his phone out and turned on the voice memo app. He held the phone between us. "Ben Schaffley was behind the bullying at the firm. He wanted to toughen Taylor up. He orchestrated it. He also tampered with my cases. He set me up for a malpractice suit because he wanted Taylor to look bad. I would never have known if I hadn't found the missing documentation from an old case in the Villamere file before the reading of the will. I confronted Ben about it. He told me it was for the benefit of the firm. We needed the best people, and if Taylor couldn't rebound from a mistake like that, she didn't deserve to keep her job."

"Ben set Taylor up to fail, and he used your case as the bait."

Mike nodded. "It was the most corrupt behavior I'd ever seen in a lawyer, and he was my partner. I didn't know if it was a one-time thing, or if he'd been doing things like this forever. I lost faith in our case record and in the firm's reputation."

"Is that why you killed him?"

"No." He looked from me to his phone. The timer was still running. "We were arguing in this room. The textiles absorbed the sound, so nobody heard us. I told Ben as soon as we received our payment from the Villamere estate, I was leaving the firm. I had no offers, but I knew I couldn't stay in that partnership."

"How did he react to that?"

"He said I might want to rethink my timing. He said there was a significant scandal connected to the Villamere estate that, once exposed, would net the firm millions."

"A scandal?"

"The woman who claims she's Josephine Barkley isn't Josephine Barkley. Schaffley uncovered paperwork to confirm that she legally changed her name. And then he said he used Taylor for the casework, so any blowback would land on her. The last thing he said was that taking the moral high ground wasn't the wisest move when I had a baby on the way."

"He knew about you and Taylor."

"He not only knew, he showed me an anonymous letter he'd drafted that suggested the relationship happened under duress. That her work had been shoddy, and I'd pressured her into a sexual relationship to cover it up. He had half a dozen case files that he manipulated like he had mine. Not only was he willing to tank my cases, but he was going to blackmail me into staying at the firm and destroy her reputation." His hand tightened around his phone. "That's when I slugged him."

"Slugged?" I repeated. Were we dancing around the specifics of the crime?

"I hauled off and punched him. Harder than I thought, because I knocked him backward. He hit one of the fixtures. He stumbled toward me, and instead of catching him, I backed away and left. I thought he would get up. It was a freak thing. It had to be. I didn't know he died until you found the body."

"That's not true," I said quietly. "You did know. You must

have. You went to the Broadside and picked a fight, didn't you?"

Mike looked up at me. "I was blowing off steam."

"I don't think you were. You were establishing an alibi."

The cell phone fell from Mike's hand and clattered against the floor. He'd been of sound mind when he first turned on his phone and confessed, but now, it seemed as if his mind had retreated to someplace else. He'd functioned for a week, hiding behind his competent legal alter ego, but as he talked through the events of that day, it appeared he was in a state of shock about how the punch he'd thrown had ended in murder. As the reality of his crime overtook him, he deflated in front of me like a cake when you slam the oven door mid-bake.

"Get the sheriff. I'm ready to make a statement."

I bent down and picked up his phone, careful not to erase the recording.

"Poly?" Vaughn called in the hallway. "The movie is starting. Are you coming?" He poked his head into the room and saw Mike and me. "What's going on in here?"

"Mike Bozer has something to tell Sheriff Clark about the death of Ben Schaffley," I said gently. "Tell Devontay we're going to need him to postpone the film festival."

* * *

Fortuitously, Giovanni showed up to work on Tuesday morning per our arrangements, allowing me a chance to pay a visit to Laurence. It was hard to believe that a mere twenty-four hours had passed since I'd been there last, but even in sleepy small towns, things changed overnight.

On my way, I stopped at Tea Totalers and picked up a basket of Genevieve's latest baked goods. There was a dearth of lawyers in the café, and her display cases were bursting with fresh muffins, cakes, and cookies. She stood behind the counter, a cute pout on her face.

"I still don't have the hang of this business plan thing. I understand supply and demand, but how do you predict either one? I was up all night perfecting a new financier recipe, but now there's no one to buy them."

"What's a financier?"

Genevieve perked right up at the opportunity to show off her latest creation. "They're delicious! They use beurre noisette —brown butter, but you know me and French—and almond flour and egg whites, here, taste one!"

She slid a tiny cake the diameter of a cookie out of her case and, before I could protest, popped it into my mouth. The sweet flavors melted against my tongue, rich and delicious.

I swallowed the pastry in one gulp and pointed at the case. "I'll take a dozen."

"Take two dozen. I have another seven cooling in the back."

"Seven dozen is a lot even for you."

"Once my staff gets in, I'm going to make deliveries around town, starting with City Hall. Wallis has been avoiding my calls, but I'm not going to give up! If I bribe her secretary, I might just talk my way into a meeting."

I laughed at Genevieve's new single-minded focus. "B-school has turned you into a monster." I popped another financier into my mouth while she filled a basket, then I left.

I drove to Grosvenor Arms Apartments and signed in. The security officer called to tell Laurence I was there. The call went unanswered.

"I'm sorry, Ms. Monroe," the building security officer said. "I can't let you up if he's not there."

"Can you try again? Maybe he was indisposed."

The elevator doors chimed, and Laurence stepped out. "Ms. Monroe. I was on my way to see you. I believe I have something you'll want."

I picked up my basket of goodies, but Laurence, sensing the offer, held out his hand in protest. "You are too kind, but my blood sugar levels force me to decline." He turned to the desk officer. "Please help yourself."

I handed the basket to the security officer then followed Laurence across the lobby to a red velvet bench bathed in golden sunlight. Outside the window was a view of blooming bougainvillea. I lowered myself onto the bench, but when Laurence remained standing, I stood back up. His expression was clouded in conflict. He held a rolled copy of the *San Ladrón Daily Ledger* in one hand, and he unrolled it and extracted a multi-page document that he handed to me. When I saw what it was, I sank back down onto the cushion.

It was the second will.

34

I FLIPPED THROUGH THE PAGES OF THE LEGAL document. It was the same one Vaughn and I had found, and it left Reginald Villamere's estate to Laurence Thibodeaux, save for the Villamere Theater, which he left to the historical society.

"Is that what you spotted in my dresser drawer?" he asked.

"Yes. Where did you find it?"

Laurence lowered himself onto the bench opposite me. His chest rose and fell with a tortured sigh.

Instinctively, I reached out and put my hand on his. "It's okay," I said. "You shouldn't feel guilty about the inheritance. It's what your partner wanted."

"No," he said. "We discussed this, of course. And he knew I was not looking for anything of this magnitude. Quite the opposite. We agreed that his estate could do far more if it went into the hands of the city, into the hands of the employees who dedicated their lives to keeping the Villamere alive. I have no children. I have more than enough to live out my life in a manner more comfortable than most people do. My art collection will be donated to museums. Reggie knew this was not only not necessary, it's wasteful."

"Where did you find this?" I repeated.

"It was where you said it was. I found it several days ago. It didn't make sense, not then, not now. The will that was executed last week, that is what Reggie wanted." Laurence tapped the paper in my lap. "Bringing this to the public's attention would only serve to complicate the matter unnecessarily and keep the rightful inheritors from receiving their due."

"Do you believe this is real?"

"Does it matter? Ben Schaffley's killer has confessed. Other secrets have been revealed. If this remains a secret, then the matter can die here."

As much as it troubled me, I folded the document and held it out to Laurence. "If you believe that, then why did you show me this? You could have shredded it and never had it come to light."

"If the document is real, then you are correct. But if it isn't, then someone else knows of it, and that means there's one more secret to be revealed in our small town."

I held the revised will in my lap and thought about so many things I'd learned in the past week. The people I'd met. The trouble they'd gone to to cover up or expose their secrets.

"Mr. Thibodeaux, you showed me a photo that you carry around in your wallet. It's you and Mr. Villamere and a young woman. Was that woman Josephine?"

Laurence stood and removed his wallet from his trousers, flipped it open and extracted the creased photo. He stared at it for several seconds. "Yes," he said. "That was the day we first met her. Reggie arranged for her to come to San Ladrón. It's the only photo we ever took with her. It was a special day."

This time he didn't hand me the photo. He kept it in his hands, and I sensed that even though he was a seventy-year-old man who had recently lost his life partner, in his mind, he was forty years younger.

I closed my eyes and turned to face the window. The golden rays of the sun warmed my face. A patch on my forearm grew hot, and I shifted away from the light.

"What would you have me do with this?" I asked, indicating the will.

"I don't know," he said. "Ms. Monroe, I am an old man whose life will not change based on those five pages of paper. I leave the matter in your hands. Do with them what you will."

He stood and nodded once. He pulled a pair of vintage Ray Bans out of his jacket pocket and placed them over his eyes. The green lenses were dark enough to shield him from the incoming light, but I suspected it was emotion, not sunshine, that he wanted to avoid.

I stood too. "Thank you for trusting me."

"I'm sorry not to be more social, Ms. Monroe, but I have a prior engagement and must be on my way."

I hugged Laurence goodbye. As happy as I was that Ben Schaffley's killer was behind bars, I couldn't shake the feeling that we were all missing something. I almost convinced myself that my imagination was overstimulated by Genevieve's baked goods.

Almost.

I picked up the pen to cross my name off the ledger. That was when it hit me. The day I'd been here with Vaughn, we had both Laurence's permission and his key, and he'd called ahead to tell the officer at the security desk that we were on our way. And still, we'd had to sign in. I remembered it clearly because of what the security officer said. Rules are rules.

I closed the logbook then opened it to the first page. The page was dated about two weeks ago. I flipped through until I reached Vaughn's and my names. The will had been in Laurence's dresser before we'd gotten there, so if someone had planted it, it would have been before that. I flipped backward, a page at a time, running my finger down each line, looking for something that fit.

Two pages before Vaughn's and my names, on a page dated the day after the will reading, was a name I knew: *Wallis Wilson.* The very same person who, according to Ben Schaffley's notes, had contested the will and suggested that there was a new one.

I slammed the sign-in log shut and pushed it toward the security officer. "I need to take this to Sheriff Clark. Can you start a new sign-in book?"

"Sure."

Considering we had Mike Bozer's confession, I didn't think Sheriff Clark was going to give anything I said now much credibility. I didn't even know if he'd take my call. I asked the security officer to call the sheriff's office directly to tell him I was on my way with new evidence, and I left with the sign-in book in hand.

Clark called me before I'd left the parking lot. "The Schaffley case is closed. Bozer confessed."

"Mike Bozer confessed to punching Ben Schaffley. He assumed his punch led to Schaffley's death, but what if it didn't?"

"What's this new evidence?"

"It needs context."

"That's not how this works."

"It's a logbook from the Grosvenor Arms that shows that Wallis Wilson signed in to the building two weeks ago. That's the day Vaughn and I found the revised will hidden in Laurence Thibodeaux's drawers."

"Is that a euphemism?"

"No. We found a new will sandwiched between his periwinkle and navy cashmere sweaters. That's the night we packed a bag for him to stay at the Waverly House." I misjudged a traffic light and punched the gas pedal to shoot through a yellow. "Can we go over the details when I'm there? I prefer not to get into an accident because I'm driving while distracted."

"Bring it to city hall. I'm scheduled to testify at a court appearance and won't be back at the mobile unit until this afternoon."

As luck would have it, City Hall was the opposite side of town from Grosvenor Arms, and I had to drive directly past my fabric shop to reach it. The distance was about two miles, but traffic lights and pedestrians out with their dogs kept me from zipping there quickly. My mind rubbed up against the information I'd just found like a party balloon against a bolt of cashmere, sticking on the questions about the alternate will and the fact that, with millions of dollars at stake, Wallis had both motive and opportunity.

I arrived at City Hall twenty minutes after I left Grosvenor Arms. The one-story building was a classic example of California mid-century modern architecture. The roofline was flat, designed with hot San Ladrón sunshine in mind and a need for insulation. Concrete columns set off the entrance, and a courtyard of variegated bricks in a herringbone pattern added to the majestic facade. In addition to the activities of the courts, the building housed several government offices and hosted monthly meetings of both the city council and the Senior Patrol.

It was also the home base for the historical society.

I waited impatiently at the back of the security line. The air was redolent with pastries and honeysuckle. I spied one of Genevieve's baskets of pastries on the check-in desk and texted her. The text went unanswered.

By the time I was through the security checkpoint, all manner of details had woven themselves together, revealing a quilt of suspicions and conclusions. I found Sheriff Clark in the hallway outside a courtroom and barreled toward him.

"You have to look at this," I said, thrusting the security log from the Grosvenor Arms at him. "It's the security log from Laurence Thibodeaux's apartment building."

"What does this have to do with Mr. Bozer?"

"Remember when Vaughn and I went to pack a bag for Laurence? We found a new will hidden between his sweaters. It wasn't signed, and Vaughn said nobody had claimed the possibility of there being a new will—him being the executor, he would know—so we pretended we didn't see it."

"Why tell me now?"

"When I spoke to Laurence yesterday, he didn't know anything about a second will. We looked for it, but it was gone. He knew it was there. He pretended it wasn't." I opened the back cover of the sign-in log and pulled out the now-folded pages. I thrust them at Clark. "Look."

Clark unfolded the pages and scanned them. When he got to the part about leaving the theater to the historical society, his eyebrows went up. "Mr. Thibodeaux didn't have a problem with you taking this?"

"He gave it to me."

"If that will is found to be authentic, then Mr. Thibodeaux stands to inherit a lot."

"He said that's a red flag. That Reginald Villamere knew he

—Laurence—didn't want or need an inheritance. Have you seen his apartment at the Grosvenor Arms?" Clark shook his head. "Laurence Thibodeaux is not hurting for money."

"Could be an act," Clark said. He closed the book and studied me. "Why didn't you tell me about a second will when you found it?"

"Nobody else mentioned a new will, except for the notes made on the legal pad I turned over to you. Notes about a second will, about the historical society contesting the original."

I pulled the sign-in book toward me and flipped through several pages until I reached the one with the telltale signature. I spun the book around and tapped the page. "See anybody we know?"

Clark studied the page. "Wallis Wilson. Adelaide's friend."

"Right. This new will leaves Reginald Villamere's house to Laurence, but it leaves the Villamere Theater to the historical society. That's what she wanted all along. How closely have you looked at her in connection to the case?"

Clark pulled out his phone and pressed a number from his recent calls. A moment later, he identified himself.

"This is Sheriff Clark. Do you have video surveillance from your lobby and elevator banks?" He glanced at me. "Good. I'll send someone to pick them up." He hung up and made a second call. "Sack, it's Clark. I need you to go to Grosvenor Arms and collect the surveillance tapes from the security officer. He'll have them ready for you. Yes. Tapes. There's a television with a VCR in the storage closet. Take the tapes to the mobile unit and review them. Make a note of anybody you recognize in conjunction with the Villamere Affair." He paused and glanced at me to see if I was listening. "I mean the Schaffley case."

Clark disconnected.

A young man in a navy suit and tie jogged over to us. "Sheriff, the lawyers settled the case, so you don't have to stay."

The sheriff nodded. "Thanks."

"Sheriff Clark," I said. I pointed toward the elevator wells. "Seeing as you have some free time on your hands, and you're already here, maybe you want to pay Wallis a visit?"

I looked around to see if anybody else had noticed, but the people outside seemed more interested in their own conversations.

"Where's her office?"

To my right, a directory hung on the wall. The Historical Society was listed in room 132.

Clark saw it at the same time I did and took off at a brisk pace. He didn't tell me to stay where I was. I doubted I would have listened if he had.

Unlike the rest of city hall, which bustled with lawyers and police and other employees of the judicial system, this wing was empty, like a ghost town within the building. We made it down the short hallway, counting off room numbers until we reached the one on the end. Clark rapped on the door, and when there was no answer, he tried the knob. The door was locked.

At the end of the hallway was an exit. I leaned into the heavy door and was temporarily blinded by the bright sunlight. After my eyes adjusted, I scanned the bustling parking lot. Professionals were clustered together, negotiations taking place or dinner plans being made. There was too much activity to make sense of any one person's actions. It was a perfect place to hide in plain sight.

While I stood outside, the exit door closed behind me. I turned at the sound of the latch clicking into place and realized there was no external knob. I slapped my hand on the door, hoping Clark wouldn't leave me hanging, and glanced around the gravel by my feet for a possible place one might hide a key. A small brick sat a few feet away from the door, and I imagined it being used to prop the door open.

And I remembered another brick that had been used to prop a door open.

I picked up the brick. It was old and whitewashed with sun and rain and looked like every other old brick I'd ever seen except for two things: the words VILLAMERE THEATER stenciled on one side, and what looked like traces of dried blood on the corner. I'd bet that fancy forensics lab funded by Vaughn's dad would determine it was a match for Ben Schaffley.

I set the brick where I'd found it and called Clark.

"I'm talking to a judge about a warrant to search Ms. Wilson's office. Can this wait?"

"This should help your case. Outside the exit next to her office is a brick taken from the Villamere. I think it's your murder weapon."

"I'll send Sack."

I didn't like the fact that Wallis's office had been locked, or that while Clark was in with a judge and Sack was on his way to me, no one was looking for Wallis. I tried the door again and, having no luck, turned and headed around the side of the building.

Ten feet in front of me was a peppy, titian-haired Francophile who had come to City Hall with the express purpose of securing a mentorship. Genevieve, once the most timid business owner in San Ladrón, had come a long way since she'd opened her café, and she was determined to go even further.

Genevieve was armed with a basket of baked goods and her

binder of business ideas. She blocked Wallis's path, her eyes alight.

"Wallis, I'd like five minutes of your time to discuss a mentorship. I've brought my business plan and samples of my tea and pastries, and I won't take no for an answer."

35

CLARK INTERRUPTED GENEVIEVE'S PITCH, WHICH earned him a nasty scowl from Genevieve and an array of emotions from Wallis—from gratitude for the interruption to panic as she realized why it was Clark, of all people, confronting her. She looked from Clark to me, and her expression hardened. Her jaw set in a firm line, but a telltale tear escaped from the corner of her eye and made a slow track down her cheek.

Clark reached out and snapped a handcuff on her left wrist then pulled her right arm down and snapped the other side on it. "Wallis Wilson, you're under arrest for the murder of Ben Schaffley."

She raised her chin and said, "I did it for the preservation of history."

It *had* been a crime of passion. Just not the kind of passion most people thought.

———

THE NEWS about Mike Bozer came and went. The lead story in the *San Ladrón Daily Ledger* was about a new tulip farm on the outskirts of town. The name Josephine Barkley had already been forgotten by all but the die-hard San Ladrón Trivia folks.

Thanks to Wallis's strong ties with the community, the judge set a reasonable bail. She declined. She said her money was earmarked for the Historical Society and she didn't want to tap it in exchange for her freedom. She really did believe in her mission statement.

The medical examiner returned conclusive findings that Ben Schaffley did not die as a result of the punch his law partner had thrown. There was a bruise where Ben had hit the fixtures of fabric, but it was not the fatal wound. That came from a second wound that matched the brick found outside Wallis's office. She'd replaced the one from the Villamere with a similar brick, never once thinking anyone would notice. She wouldn't say why she kept the murder weapon close instead of disposing of it where it would never be found, but a part of me wondered—did she just not have it in her to treat a relic from the historic theater as garbage? Or had she planned to return it to the theater one day when the Schaffley case had been closed?

When Mike had first heard the news about Ben Schaffley's death, he'd incorrectly assumed his assault on his partner had had fatal results. Once the truth came out, Mike provided a more detailed account of his activities in San Ladrón. He'd picked a fight at the Broadside Tavern, fired his gun into the bushes outside his office to make it look like he'd been assaulted, and filed a false police report to divert the focus of Sheriff Clark's investigation from the law firm and Taylor. Mike had tried to make his legal team look like victims, because he thought victims wouldn't be looked at too closely for their potential guilt. The charges against Mike Bozer were dropped before Taylor hit her second trimester.

Speaking of the law firm, Taylor used her skill for ferreting out information to locate Ben Schaffley's dossier on Josephine Barkley and the proof he'd claimed to have that she was a fraud. What Schaffley didn't know, and what Taylor had discovered, was that Josephine Barkley had legally changed her name because she'd gotten divorced. The name change had simply restored her given name, the one in the will. There was nothing fraudulent about that.

Taylor also gave the judge a statement about the bullying she'd experienced at Schaffley, Bozer, and Schmidt, and a couple of other paralegals came forward with similar claims. When Mike shared his own knowledge of Schaffley's corrupt behavior, everyone breathed a sigh of relief that it was over.

Sack reviewed the footage from the security camera at Grosvenor Arms and identified Wallis entering the apartment lobby with a briefcase. A little bit of help from Hutch at the records office showed that while the Grosvenor Arms apartment building was owned by a management company, they were under oversight by the historical society. The security officer confirmed that Wallis had used her position to come and go without signing the logbook. That was enough for a signed search warrant from the district attorney that granted Sack access to her office. He bagged the contents of her shredder and the hard drive of her computer.

The Villamere Theater was in a state of flux. I never did get to see the international festival, since the films and costumes had been returned to the studios and museums from which they'd been loaned. But that didn't deter the staff from proposing a new plan. In the days after Clark arrested Wallis, the ushers arranged to buy out Josephine Barkley's stake in the

Villamere Theater. By the end of the week, they'd scheduled a meeting with Vaughn to draft a business plan and operating budget for the next five years, including a full-scale renovation of the interior to restore its former glory.

In the meantime, they agreed to my pitch to host a launch event for my custom suit shop. I moved Tiki Tom's mannequins to the Villamere and searched Reggie Villamere's closet for his own vintage suits to display. Devontay and his staff brainstormed a list of classic movies featuring men in suits and called in favors to obtain the copies on short notice. Even Josephine chipped in, hiring the father-daughter team of a costume shop in her hometown of Proper City to round out the display with their own vintage costumes. Giovanni worked tirelessly to complete a sample suit that was suspiciously close to his own measurements.

By the time Vaughn picked me up to take me to the theater, he had a few more details about the outcome of the events of the last few weeks. "It doesn't look good for Wallis. Clark found the fake will on her hard drive among the recently deleted files. He turned her shredded documents over to the forensic lab to try to piece together, but even if they work all month, it's going to take some time to put those snippets of paper together. But she *was* at the will reading, and she *was* at the theater the next day. She's the only person who contested the original will and claimed there was a new one. Laurence had a dinner party last month, and she was on the guest list. She would have known the layout of his apartment, and she would have known where to hide the fake document.

"And by rewriting it so Laurence inherited Reggie Villamere's estate excluding the theater, it would look like Laurence had a motive, not Wallis. She was crafty enough to give away everything except the one thing she really wanted."

While we talked, Sheriff Clark approached us. He'd changed out of his khaki uniform and into a loose-fitting suit that looked to be several years old. He smelled faintly of mothballs. It struck me how rarely I saw Clark in civilian clothes.

"Sheriff," I said.

"Tonight it's Ryan." He glanced across the lobby toward the bar, where Charlie was fixing two scotch and sodas, probably heavy on the scotch. She glanced up and raised both glasses in our direction, took a pull from one, and then carried them our direction and handed the other to Clark.

"Anybody know what really went down here last week?" she asked.

Clark swallowed half of his drink, the first indication that the past two weeks had taken their toll on him. He glanced over each of his shoulders, which was a little funny since the four of us were the only people in the lobby.

"You didn't hear this from me," he said.

"Who else would we hear it from?" Charlie asked.

"Okay, you heard it from me, but if I find out you repeated it, you're spending the night at my place."

Charlie raised one eyebrow.

"I meant the holding cell."

I stifled a grin, as did Vaughn. A part of me wanted Clark to catch Charlie in the act of committing a crime just to see him arrest her. Living in San Ladrón was having an effect on me. I'd never once wanted one of my friends to get arrested when I lived in Los Angeles.

"From the statements we've taken from Mr. Bozer, the theater staff, and Ms. Wilson, it looks like Mr. Bozer and Mr. Schaffley got into an argument. Mr. Bozer struck Mr. Schaffley—"

"If we're going to use your first name, then you can use theirs," I said.

"Mike slugged Ben hard enough to knock him off balance. He stumbled backward into a fixture then fell. Mike left. Wallis found Ben in the storage room and confronted him about the will. He was in a bad mood from the fight with Mike, and he took it out on Wallis. She told him there was another will. Ben already had plans to undermine Josephine Barkley. There was a clause in the original will that gave Bozer, Schaffley, and Schmidt power of attorney, and after exposing Josephine as a fraud, he planned to use that loophole to divert the estate to the law firm, where he could take his thirty percent."

Vaughn whistled. "There's over half a dozen counts of fraud in there."

"Not to mention extortion," I said.

"Wallis says Ben threatened her, but there's no way of knowing if that's true or if she's setting up a possible self-defense plea."

"She would have had to leave the theater and get the brick from outside the back door, come back in and strike Ben in the back of the head, and then take the brick with her," I said. "Even a first-year law student could argue premeditation."

"Plus Reginald Villamere's will has been on file for three decades, and there's a paper trail of meetings with him and the law firm. If he wanted to change it, he had ample opportunity."

"What about Adelaide?" I asked Vaughn. "What does she have to say about all of this?"

"Mom's in disbelief. She and Wallis have been friends for a long time. She said she always knew Wallis had a greedy side to her, but Mom never believed Wallis was capable of murder."

While I stood in the theater lobby, I watched as new friends and old joined us for the night. Taylor and Mike walked casually through the display of suits, pausing every so often to touch a lapel or inspect a pocket. Other lawyers from the firm were there too, drinking, laughing, and relaxing now that the drama was over. I thought about what Taylor had said, about Ben Schaffley's bullying at the law firm, and I wondered how many of these people had experienced it.

In addition to the lawyers, I spotted Tiki Tom talking to Earl from Earl of Sandwich. Duke and Genevieve had already claimed their seats in the theater. Giovanni and Jun Wong stood off to the side, Giovanni with one foot on a chair and the leg of his pants turned up while Jun inspected his seams. The theater staff was busy: popcorn popping, drinks being poured, candy being sold, tickets being torn. All the money raised from the night was going to go back into the theater's operating budget, and from the looks of it, all of San Ladrón was down with that decision.

I thought back to the day I'd arrived at the Villamere with my invitation in hand. How I'd sat in the back of a room of inheritors, privy to the reading of Reginald Villamere's will. How it had felt to learn that I'd inherited a piece of history.

When you don't expect anything, you're always surprised. You're surprised by generosity of spirit and mind. You're open to opportunity. Since that day, learning that I'd inherited hundreds of yards of wool I never knew existed had led me to a new idea. It had inspired my suit shop concept. It had led me to ask for Giovanni's help, which had led to a more permanent solution to my staffing problem. From Reginald Villamere's generosity, dispersing his estate to people in San Ladrón he believed would benefit from what he'd built, many lives had changed for the better.

I wondered what would have happened if Wallis had

accepted the terms of the original will. Would Josephine Barkley have been interested in Wallis's plans for the future of the theater if it became part of the historical society's portfolio? What might the Las Vegas resident, no expert in the business of running a historic theater, have said to the idea of a partnership?

And what might have happened if Ben Schaffley had simply done his job instead of seeing the Villamere Affair as a money grab? While that question was moot now, thanks to Wallis, I couldn't help seeing the pattern of destruction, fraud, and abuse Ben Schaffley had exhibited before he'd died. If the system had worked, somewhere along the way his actions would have caught up with him. But now, the system had no chance of righting that ship.

"At least it's over now," Vaughn said. He put his hand on mine. "Tonight's a break from all of this."

"You're right." I kissed him on the cheek. "Thank you for the reminder."

Invitations had been spread amongst our circle of friends, but the Lopezes were busy with the donut shop. Duke was busy at the bar, and Genevieve was busy looking for a new mentor.

I followed Vaughn into the theater, where we had our choice of seats. I thought about the people our community had lost and the people we'd gained. I thought about the rules that had been upheld and broken and how both had played a part in what went down. I thought again about the event of the season, the reading of Reggie Villamere's will, and how I'd shown up thinking my invitation had been a mistake. And I thought about how sometimes you don't need an invitation to know you're exactly where you're meant to be.

AFTERWORD

If you've been a long-time reader of Poly's Material Witness mysteries, then I hope you enjoyed this latest installment!

If you are new to Poly's world and find yourself interested in some of the things mentioned in this book, here's a quick and dirty guide:

Want to know about Vaughn finding those kittens in the dumpster? You'll want to start with SUEDE TO REST.

Interested Genevieve's story? You'll want to read CRUSHED VELVET.

Curious about Charlie's past? Go with SILK STALKINGS.

I don't think there are any references to TULLE DEATH DO US PART in this book, but it has all the usual suspects and a wedding.

...and if you want to find out exactly how Poly broke her ankle, check out the Hitchcockian novella SHEER WINDOW.

Enjoy!
　　Diane

ACKNOWLEDGMENTS

I thought I had a handle on what the next Material Witness mystery would be. Cotton, I believed. A Cotton Club. Jazz. Jazz at the Villamere Theater. The only problem was I couldn't figure out how to start, where to start, what the plot would be. It was a rare case (for me) of staring at a blank screen uninspired.

While the laundry stacked up and the grass grew, I remembered the original title for the first Material Witness mystery: Last Wool and Testament. We didn't use that title for competitive reasons, but I'd always loved it and heck, a decade had passed and surely that meant I could use it, right? Fully inspired, I immediately pictured the plot of the book: Wool. Suits. A will. Lawyers. But what will? The will from the owner of the Villamere Theater!

The book practically wrote itself after that. The only problem was, somewhere in the home stretch, I discovered a fellow cozy author with a new book on preorder. The title? Last Wool and Testament.

My first and biggest shout out goes to my writing group: Lisa Q. Mathews, Ellen Byron, and Gigi Pandian, for talking me out of keeping my title and helping me brainstorm a new one. Dodged a bullet there!

Thanks to Lynne, Irene, and Caroline from Red Adept

Editing for your work on this project, and to the Polyester Posse for your ongoing support.

Thank you to Fabric Mart for getting me thinking about projects and small businesses.

Thank you to my readers who read my books, Poly and the rest of the gang. I appreciate that you've given them a home! An extra-special big thank you to the Weekly DiVa club members for coming along with me on this journey.

Xo,

Diane

ABOUT THE AUTHOR

National bestselling author Diane Vallere writes funny, and fashionable character-based mysteries. After two decades working for a top luxury retailer, she traded fashion accessories for accessories to murder. A past president of Sisters in Crime, Diane started her own detective agency at age ten and has maintained a passion for shoes, clues, and clothes ever since. Find out more at dianevallere.com.

ALSO BY

<u>Killer Fashion Mysteries</u>

Designer Dirty Laundry

Buyer, Beware

The Brim Reaper

Some Like It Haute

Grand Theft Retro

Pearls Gone Wild

Cement Stilettos

Panty Raid

Union Jacked

Slay Ride

Tough Luxe

Fahrenheit 501

Stark Raving Mod

Gilt Trip

Ranch Dressing

Murder Italian Style

<u>Madison Night Mad for Mod Mysteries</u>

"Midnight Ice" (prequel novella)

Pillow Stalk

That Touch of Ink

With Vics You Get Eggroll

The Decorator Who Knew Too Much

The Pajama Frame

Lover Come Hack

Apprehend Me No Flowers

Teacher's Threat

The Kill of It All

Love Me or Grieve Me

Please Don't Push Up the Daisies

The Glass Bottom Hoax

<u>Sylvia Stryker Outer Space Mysteries</u>

Murder on a Moon Trek

Scandal on a Moon Trek

Hijacked on a Moon Trek

Framed on a Moon Trek

Warped on a Moon Trek

<u>Material Witness Mysteries</u>

Suede to Rest

Crushed Velvet

Silk Stalkings

Tulle Death Do Us Part

Sheer Window

Contesting the Wool

<u>Costume Shop Mystery Series</u>

A Disguise to Die For

Masking for Trouble

Dressed to Confess

<u>Mermaid Mysteries</u>

Dead in the Water

<u>Non-Fiction</u>

Bonbons for your Brain

DIANE VALLERE

where style meets sleuthing

or visit
dianevallere.com/books